"I hope you don't take this the wrong way, Lara," she began slowly, "but . . . well, I've been wanting to talk to you. You really have a very pretty face, you know? And I know it must be hard for you. I mean, some people in this school can be really cruel."

I stood there, rooted to the spot, mute.

"In junior high," she continued, "I weighed, like, fifteen pounds more than I do now, and I found this great diet to take the weight off, and it worked."

My face burned with rage and humiliation. "You want to give me your *diet*?"

"I don't want to offend you," she said quickly. "I just know what it's like to want to lose weight, and—"

"You don't know anything," I said in carefully measured tones. "You look at me and think you know, but you don't."

"Listen, just forget I said anything—"

"No," I replied, "you listen. A year ago, at my old school, I was homecoming queen. *Queen!* I was thinner than you are. Then I got this disease called Axell-Crowne Syndrome, and it made me gain all this weight. You think I'm just this fat girl that you pity—"

"I didn't mean it like that—"

"Yes, yes, you did," I said earnestly. "I know you did, because I was once exactly like you."

Life in the Fat Lane

Cherie Bennett

LAUREL-LEAF BOOKS

Published by
Bantam Doubleday Dell Books for Young Readers
a division of
Random House, Inc.
1540 Broadway
New York, New York 10036

The trademark Laurel-Leaf Library® is registered in the U.S. Patent and Trademark Office.
The trademark Dell® is registered in the U.S. Patent and Trademark Office.

Visit us on the Web! www.randomhouse.com

Educators and librarians, for a variety of teaching tools, visit us at www.randomhouse.com/teachers

---

ISBN 0-440-22029-7

RL: 5.2

Reprinted by arrangement with Delacorte Press

Printed in the United States of America

August 1999

10   9   8   7   6

OPM

For my grandmother Jessica Berman, who was so much more beautiful than I ever understood, and for my father, Dr. Bennett H. Berman, who always knew it.

And for my husband, Jeff Gottesfeld, who reads every word of every draft of every manuscript, including this one. His talent, brilliance, insight, and inspiration contributed to this book at least as much as the words I wrote.

Acknowledgments

Grateful acknowledgment is made to the following writers, media outlets, and publications: Fiona Soltes, staff writer, "Hard to Swallow," *The Tennessean* (Sunday, June 9, 1996, Living Section, p. F-1); John Stossel, reporter, "Growing Up Fat," ABC News, *20/20* segment aired July 28, 1995 (transcript courtesy of Journal Graphics); Karen S. Schneider, with Shelley Levitt, Danelle Morton, Paula Yoo (in Los Angeles), Sarah Skolnik, Alicia Brooks, Rochelle Jones (in Washington), Ron Arias, Liz McNeil, Jane Sugden (in New York City), Don Sider, Marisa Salcines (in Miami), Barbara Sandler (in Chicago), and Margaret Nelson (in Minneapolis), "Mission Impossible: Deluged by Images from TV, Movies and Magazines, Teenage Girls Do Battle with an Increasingly Unrealistic Standard of Beauty—and Pay a Price," *People* (June 3, 1996, pp. 65–74); Zibby Schwarzman, "My Weight, Myself: Do Ten Extra Pounds Make Me a Less Worthy Person?" *Seventeen* (August 1993, pp. 102,

216); Corina Hughes, age fifteen, as told to Alison Bell, "I Was Fat," *'Teen* (January 1996, p. 42 ff.); Dianne Neumark-Sztainer, Ph.D., "Excessive Weight Preoccupation: Normative but Not Harmless," *Nutrition Today* (March/April 1995, pp. 68-74); Janet Greeson, Ph.D., *Food for Love: Healing the Food, Sex, Love and Intimacy Relationship* (Pocket Books, 1993, 1994); Ken Mayer, *Real Women Don't Diet!: One Man's Praise of Large Women & His Outrage at the Society That Rejects Them* (Bartleby Press, 1993); Mary Bray Pipher, Ph.D., *Reviving Ophelia: Saving the Selves of Adolescent Girls* (Putnam, 1994; Ballantine, 1995); Naomi Wolf, *The Beauty Myth: How Images of Beauty Are Used Against Women* (Morrow, 1991; Anchor, 1992).

For medical information, special thanks to Kathleen Childers of the mobile unit of the Mental Health Coop of Nashville, Tennessee. Grateful thanks as well to Jeff Gottesfeld, my love, husband, sometimes collaborator, first reader, producer, and so much more than that; to Olga Silverstein, M.S.W., of the Ackerman Institute for Family Therapy (New York) for inspiration; to my teen readers around the world who have written me so many heartfelt letters on the subject of this novel; to Wendy Loggia, Beverly Horowitz, and my team at BDD; to the Charlotte Sheedy Agency and to Regula Noetzli; to the William Morris Agency; to the terrific teens and adults who critiqued early drafts of this novel—Amy, Claire, and Zoë Jarman, Gina Lodge, Carol Ponder, and Lisa Hurley. While actual people may be referred to in this novel, all situations (except for the *20/20* segment acknowledged above) and Axell-Crowne Syndrome are fictitious.

Life in the Fat Lane

MISS TEEN PRIDE
OF THE SOUTH

Entrant: Lara Lynn Ardeche

Age: 16

Hometown: Nashville

D.O.B.: May 9

Parents: Mr. and Mrs. James "Jimbo" Ardeche.

Education: Ensworth School; Forest Hills Middle School; currently a junior at Forest Hills High School, Nashville.

Special training: piano—8 years; dance (ballet, jazz)—6 years.

Scholastic ambition: to study music at Juilliard, in New York, and after college, to teach music to handicapped children.

Hobbies: piano, dance, working with kids, working out, musical theater, going to Vanderbilt football games.

Sports: dance, swimming, biking, tennis, field hockey, aerobic training.

Statistics: Height—5'7" Hair—Blond
Weight—118 Eyes—Blue

Scholastic honors: National Honor Society, Who's Who Among High School Sophomores, Tenth Grade French Honors Award, Superior rating for piano at Tennessee State Music Festival, Advisory board for Nashville Teen Peer Counseling Program.

Other accomplishments: selected as Most Beautiful, Most Popular, and Best Smile in tenth grade; school orchestra soloist; voted Most Charming at Miss Willa's School of Charm and Manners, age 12.

Employment: summer job as junior music counselor at Bosley Camp for Children with Special Needs. Voted Best Junior Counselor.

Family: Father James is an advertising executive; mother Carol owns an upscale catering business; and 13-year-old brother Scott is a skateboard champion.

Other facts: Lara learned her winning, can-do attitude from her wonderful, supportive parents. She believes that she has been given many gifts and that it is her responsibility to share those gifts with others.

Personal motto: "If you can dream it, you can achieve it."

Chapter 118

"Which would you rather be, fat or dead?"

"Fat. Pass me the chips."

"See, this is why I totally hate you," my best friend, Molly Sheridan, said as she heaved the jumbo-sized bag of chips at me. "You can eat anything you want and not get fat. Frankly, Lara, you deserve to die painfully, squeezed to death in size-eighteen jeans."

"Never happen," I said as I stuck a handful of chips into my mouth. "I am metabolically blessed."

"You're blessed, period," Molly said as she leaned back on the abs-crunch mat, balancing the Living section of *The Tennessean*, Nashville's morning newspaper, on her bent knees. She read the headline aloud: "*HARD TO SWALLOW: Younger and Younger Children Receive Society's Thin Message—and Find They Suffer from Eating Disorders.*"

"Bo-ring," I sang out, reaching for another handful of chips. I scrambled to my feet so that I could look at my reflection in the floor-to-ceiling mirrors that line the home gym my mega-rich grandfather had installed two years earlier as a Christmas present.

I used the gym religiously, every other day. You can't be a pageant queen and let yourself go.

Molly and I had just finished working out—well, I had worked out, she had kept me company—and I was feeling on top of the world. I was sixteen, madly in love with the most fantastic guy in the entire universe, and about to get ready for my school's homecoming dance.

The only thing that could possibly be any better would be to win homecoming queen. I didn't really believe I had a chance, but other people seemed to think I did. After all, I was only a junior, and there were at least two senior girls who I knew would get it before I would.

But that would be okay. I could win next year. This year I would just be named to the court and have fun with my boyfriend, Jett, and all my friends.

"You think Jett would like my hair up?" I asked Molly, holding my long, blond hair up off my neck. "Does this look sophisticated or stupid?"

" 'According to the National Institute of Compulsive Eating'—now *there's* a depressing place to work—'eighty percent of ten-year-old girls have worried about their weight enough to diet,' " Molly read, her head still buried in the newspaper. She reached for the chips. "It says here that there are, like, zillions of anorexics, or something."

Molly gave me a wistful look. "Hey, maybe I could get a mild case of anorexia. You know, just until I lost thirty pounds or something, and then I'd, like, snap out of it."

I snatched the paper out of her hands. "Mol! Tonight is *homecoming*. Amber and Lisa are coming over any minute. We need to plan." I pulled her to her feet.

"No, *you* need to plan," Molly corrected me. "*You're* the one who has an actual shot at homecoming queen. *You're* the one who bagged Jett Anston, world's hottest guy, and—"

"Cut it out," I interrupted, nudging her with my hip. We stared at our reflections. "I say we put your hair up, too. What do you think?"

"I hate standing next to you."

"Why?"

"Why?" Molly repeated. "Look in the mirror!"

"I'm looking." I peered more closely at my chin. "Am I getting a pimple?"

"Ignore your zit for a moment," Molly urged me. "Just tell me what you see."

"Me and you."

"Want to know what I see? One perfect blond goddess and one short, fat girl with a Lifetime Bad Hair Day."

"You're not fat, Mol—"

"Ha. I slide ever so gracefully into a size twelve—"

"Don't put yourself down like—"

"Okay, a tight size fourteen in jeans but if you tell anyone, I'll personally make sure you meet an untimely—"

"Mol—"

"In short," Molly concluded, "you are a future Miss America, the hopes and the dreams of—sob—an entire

3

generation, whereas I am a walking Chia Pet. And this pet has to pee." She took off for the bathroom.

I had to laugh. Molly could always make me laugh.

We had met in third grade. I was very popular, and my mother had, as always, sent me to the first day of school looking like the little pageant winner I already was (Miss Tiny Tennessee, among others)—frilly dress, hair curled and held back with a perfect bow. When our teacher, Mrs. Pissitelli, called on me, I addressed her as "ma'am."

Molly had sat next to me. She was the new girl, and she wore overalls and high-tops. She called Mrs. Pissitelli "The Pisser" behind her back and made fart noises when Mrs. Pissitelli bent over to get the chalk she had dropped. Molly leaned toward me and whispered that The Pisser probably had armpit hair so long she could braid it.

We had been best friends ever since that day. Most of my other friends didn't like Molly. They called her "The Mouth." But I thought she was funny, nervy, brave—all the things I wasn't. And I loved her for it.

From the first day I met Molly, she was plump and I was slender. It was just the way we were, and it didn't matter to us at all. Until, I remembered, gazing in the gym mirror, a certain day when we were both thirteen.

Molly had worn a babydoll dress to school, and Tommy Baigley had yelled out in the lunchroom in front of dozens of kids, "Hey, Sheridan, are you pregnant?"

"Yeah," Molly had shot back, "with Michael Jackson's love child."

Everyone had laughed, and Tommy had used his spoon as a catapult to shoot his peas at Molly, which got him kicked out of the cafeteria. After that, Tonika Ramone got one of her nosebleeds, which grossed everyone out, and everyone forgot all about what Tommy had said to Molly.

Everyone except Molly, that is. That night she'd slept over at my house. And as she lay there on my other twin bed I heard her voice in the darkness.

"You know what's really weird, Lar?" she'd asked me. "How you put on a certain outfit and you think it looks really good, so you go around feeling kind of cute. And then someone says something, like that you look pregnant, and you realize you don't look good. You never looked good. You look like a big fat slob and you were the only one stupid enough to think you looked good—"

"You *did* look good, Mol—"

"I'm never wearing that stupid babydoll dress again."

I had gotten up on one elbow and searched out her face in the moonlight that was streaming in through my window. "Listen, Molly, the dress is cute. Tommy is just an idiot—"

"He never would have said that to you," Molly had said, her voice low. "No one ever says anything mean to you."

"That's not true," I'd said, even as my mind scrambled for something. "In fifth grade Teresa Baker said I was stuck-up."

That's when I saw one tear curl down Molly's cheek. It was the first time I had ever seen her cry. I was amazed.

"You don't even know what I'm talking about," she'd said, her voice flat. She fisted the tear off her cheek. "It must be so great to be you. And it sucks being me."

I sighed at the thought. Molly was still chubby, still funny, and still brave. And she was still my best friend in the entire world. So what if my cool and popular friends didn't really appreciate her? So what if they only put up with her because of me? They just didn't understand. Molly didn't love me because I was popular or a pageant winner any more than I had stopped loving her because she wasn't.

With Molly, I could be myself.

"You know that icky little inspirational plaque in the bathroom about positive thinking?" Molly asked, walking out of the bathroom and over to me. "I've decided to take it to heart. I *positively* want to be as thin as you are."

"All you have to do is—" I began.

"God, can you imagine if I end up as fat as my *mother*?" Molly asked, making a face at her reflection in the mirror. "She's so fat I don't think my parents even *do* it anymore. My father has all these *Playboys* he hides in his bathroom."

I held my hair up a different way, trying to decide if I liked it. "Yeah, you told me."

"But here's what I didn't tell you," Molly said. "This morning—you're not even going to believe this—taped to our refrigerator was Miss September herself. Only Dad had drawn this little bikini on her with Magic Marker. And he stuck a Post-it note on it, for my mother: 'Margie: This is to inspire you to lose weight. I love you, Alan.' "

I made a face at our reflections. "That's so—"

"Lara, you are totally not gonna believe this!" Amber Bevin cried as she and Lisa James, both good friends of mine, ran into the gym, dropped their backpacks off their arms, and laid their plastic-covered homecoming dresses carefully over the handles of the StairMaster.

Amber is a petite brunette and Lisa is slender, with

gorgeous, straight red hair and a darling face. They're both really popular.

"Guess who has chicken pox and can't go to homecoming tonight?" Amber asked.

"Elvis?" Molly guessed.

"Denise Reiser!" Lisa squealed, ignoring Molly and grabbing my fingers between hers.

"Denise Reiser?" I echoed, my jaw hanging open.

"She called Angela Morgan and Angela called me," Amber reported. "Denise is totally covered in ugly scabs—"

Lisa squeezed my fingers. "Denise was, like, a shoo-in—"

"—but no way they're crowning a queen who isn't there—" Amber continued.

"Not to mention a human scab," Molly put in.

"—so half your comp is gone," Lisa crowed.

"Wow," I breathed, leaning against the mirror. "Are you . . . are you sure?"

"I'm totally sure," Lisa said, checking out her reflection in the mirror. "God, my hair looks like dog meat. I called her and acted like I felt really terrible for her, just to make sure it wasn't all a rumor. But it's true."

"Isn't that fantastic?" Amber asked me.

"I just *love* to profit from others' misfortune, don't you?" Molly chirped sarcastically.

Lisa gave Molly a pointed look. "Are you sure you and Andy wouldn't really rather go to homecoming alone? The limo's going to be awfully crowded with four couples."

"Oh no," Molly said cheerfully. "But thanks for looking out for me. You're a peach."

Was it really possible? Did I really have a chance at being crowned queen? "There's still Amy Caprice," I pointed out. "She is so gorgeous—"

"Yeah, but she's not that popular," Lisa argued. "She wasn't even at Forest Hills until last year and she's dating some college guy no one even knows."

"We have to go tell my mother," I said.

The four of us ran downstairs to my mom's office, where she was inputting something on her laptop.

My mother was incredibly gorgeous, young looking, and infinitely cooler than any of my friends' mothers. At the moment she was wearing size-six faded jeans, a white T-shirt, and sneakers. Her straight blond hair was held off her beautiful face with a slender ribbon. She easily looked ten years younger than the forty I knew her to be.

"Denise Reiser has chicken pox," I said momentously.

My mother knew exactly who Denise Reiser was and what her having chicken pox meant for me. She was very involved in my life as a pageant queen, just as her mother had been very involved in *her* life as a pageant queen.

"No," my mother breathed.

"Yes!" Lisa insisted.

My mother jumped up and hugged me hard. "Oh, sweetie, that means now there's just Amy Caprice."

"But, Mom, Amy is a senior, and gorgeous—"

"But she's not as popular as you are," my mother pointed out. "And she's never done pageants."

"And she's dating some guy no one knows," Lisa added.

My mother frowned slightly. "It's too bad you're not still with Danny. Danny is so popular—"

"Mom, I'm in love with Jett," I reminded her.

"I know that, honey, but—"

"Jett could hurt your chance of getting queen," Amber said bluntly. "He's just so . . . alternative."

"Yeah," Molly agreed, "an intelligent alternative to the brain-dead guys *you* date."

"Would you kindly shut up?" Lisa asked Molly.

I shot Lisa a look.

"I was only kidding," Lisa added hastily. She didn't want me to be mad at her for ragging on Molly.

Something was nagging at me. "I ought to call her—"

"And make sure it's true," my mother said, nodding.

"No, to see if I can do anything for her. I'd feel terrible if it were me—"

"That is so sweet, Lara," my mother said. "It's important to be sweet. Amy Caprice would never call."

I smiled at my mother. I knew everyone envied me for my perfect mom. Molly's mom was the same age as my mom, but she bought her clothes at this fat ladies' store, Lane Bryant, and she couldn't even cross one leg over the other. It was hard for me to understand how she could let herself go like that. I mean, Molly's mom was a *psychotherapist*! Amber's mom had lines on her face and gray hair, and she wore Doc Martens on her feet, which were always dirty from all the gardening she did. Lisa's mom, a high-powered lawyer with an ugly, short haircut, was never even home.

"So why aren't y'all upstairs getting beautiful?" Mom asked as she reached for the pack of cigarettes next to her computer. She pulled one out, lit it, and inhaled deeply. "I spent all day getting ready the day I won queen."

"Can I bum one?" Lisa asked.

"Oh, Lis, I thought you quit," my mom said.

"I did, but I started again after I gained two pounds," Lisa said, taking one out and lighting up.

"Not two pounds!" Molly shrieked in mock horror.

"I've got to quit, too," my mom agreed. "Jimbo just hates it. But like I told him: 'Honey, you'd hate it a whole lot more if I got fat.'" She took another drag and smiled at me. "We are just so proud of you, Lara. We'll put the photo of you in your crown right up on the mantel, next to mine—"

"But, Mom, Amy Caprice is going to win," I said, fear clutching my stomach.

She held me by my shoulders. "Honey, Amy Caprice is not Miss America material."

I tried to smile. "I just don't want to let you down."

"That could never happen," my mom assured me.

Amber tugged on the sleeve of my sweatshirt. "Come on, let's go upstairs and get gorgeous."

We ran up to my room, and I tried not to feel nervous. I had been so sure that Denise Reiser would get homecoming queen that there hadn't been any pressure. But now . . . what if I really did have a chance?

In my room, we were greeted by the rows of beauty pageant trophies that lined my dresser. The last one was from Miss Teen Pride of the South, four weeks earlier. Right after I had been announced as a finalist I'd broken out in angry-looking hives. I had barely managed to come in third, and that was only because my mother had covered the hives with thick, goopy makeup base. My pageant coordinator, Mrs. Armstrong, who had been grooming me for years, had been very distressed. She was sure that this year I had a real chance to win Miss Teen

10

Tennessee, which could one day lead to the big one: Miss America.

Third place didn't fit into the plan at all.

I checked my arms for hives. So far, so good.

"I'm going to jump in the shower," Molly said, kicking off her gym shoes.

"Why didn't you just shower at home?" Lisa asked her.

"Because I live to annoy you," Molly replied as she padded into my bathroom and shut the door.

I heard the shower go on. "Honestly, Lara, I mean no offense or anything but I truly do not see why you hang out with The Mouth," Amber said, flipping open a copy of *Glamour* that was on my nightstand.

"Molly's great," I said lightly. I'd had various versions of this conversation with my friends many times.

"Can't she go on a diet or something?" Lisa asked, sucking hard on her cigarette.

"And do something about that hair?" Amber added.

"Y'all, please," I said quietly. I hated it when they ragged on Molly, but I didn't want to really yell at them or anything. Beauty queens are friendly, controlled, sweet, and soft-spoken at all times.

"Hey, I'm gonna call Denise," I said, changing the subject. I pulled my address book out of my nightstand, looked up Denise's number, and punched it into my phone.

It rang three times. Then a recording of Denise's voice came on, telling me to leave a message. *Beep.*

"Denise, hi, it's Lara. Listen, I'm so sorry you're sick, and if there's anything I can do for you, just call me, okay? Bye."

"You are disgustingly nice, Lar," Amber said, study-

11

ing a "before" photo of a girl with a huge nose. "The bitch gene just passed you by." She held up the magazine for me. "Would you even be seen in public with this nose?"

"Smile, princess!"

It was my dad at the door of my room, aiming a video camera at me. Mom stood next to him. I put my hands over my face. "Daddy! You aren't supposed to film us until after we get dressed. I'm all gross from my workout."

"You look perfect, sweetheart," he told me, grinning from behind the camera.

My father was, if anything, even more fantastic than my mother. He was tall and muscular, with thick brown hair and beautiful blue eyes. Even after hours spent sitting on a plane from Los Angeles, he looked perfect.

"So, how does it feel to know you're about to be crowned homecoming queen of Forest Hills High?" he asked, the camera still pointed at me. "Your mom told me about Denise Reiser."

"Daddy!" I protested. "I'm not even a senior, I'm not going to win."

"Yeah, Patty Asher might win instead," Lisa said, puffing her cheeks full of air at the video camera.

This cracked everyone up. Patty Asher was by far the fattest girl in our class.

"Hey, that would be like getting two queens in one," Amber added gleefully.

"Y'all stop!" I pleaded, smiling to soften my words.

"It's okay if you don't win, princess," he assured me. "As long as you do your best."

"I know, Daddy," I told him. That was what he and

Mom always said—just do your best. I couldn't stand to disappoint them.

"So, Mr. Ardeche," Amber said, smiling flirtatiously at the camera, "are you going to dance with me tonight?"

It was a school tradition that while the juniors and seniors celebrated homecoming in the gym, the alumni would party in giant tents out by the football field. Then, right before the queen and her court were announced, all the adults would pile into the gym with us for the coronation. Then the court would be presented at halftime during the football game the next afternoon.

"Hey, he's my date," Mom said playfully. "Get your own!" She hooked her arm through Dad's and leaned her head on his shoulder. "Doesn't it seem like just yesterday that I was queen, honey? It was so perfect, remember?"

"Sure do," my father said. He smiled at me.

"It was the happiest night of my life," my mother recalled softly. "They called my name . . ."

"And you cried and cried," Amber said, taking over for my mother, since we had all heard this story so many times. "You had new silver high heels. Mr. Ardeche drank champagne out of one of them, and he swore he'd love you forever and that you'd get married as soon as you both graduated . . ."

"And we did," my mother said. "Which just shows that sometimes you really can live happily ever after." She gave my father a kiss. "Come on, honey, let's let the girls get dressed. I want you all to myself." She looked over at me and my friends as if we were her audience.

"Hey, come on," my dad said jovially. "I just got off an airplane! Let me get a shower, at least!"

13

"We'll take a shower together!" my mother suggested sexily, her eyes half closed. "Just remember, girls, these are perks you don't get to enjoy until *after* you're married." She hugged my father close.

"Lara, you have the greatest shower," Molly began as she came out of my bathroom, "but your towel won't even wrap around my—"

Molly stopped midsentence when she saw my dad.

"Omigod!" she yelped.

For some reason she panicked and spun around, as if her not seeing us would mean that we couldn't see her, either. We were treated to the sight of a sopping wet Molly, half wrapped in my pink towel, one fat thigh and one butt cheek half peeking out from the place where the towel didn't quite come together.

"My eyes were shut, Mol," my dad called to her as she banged the bathroom door closed. Then he winked at me.

"Now, how gross was *that*?" Lisa asked under her breath.

I gave her another look.

"I was only kidding," she repeated as always.

"Hey, what's for dinner?" my brother, Scott, age thirteen, asked from the doorway.

"You haven't seen your dad in three days and all you can say is 'what's for dinner'?" Mom shook her head at him.

"Hi," Scott mumbled. He carried his skateboard under his arm. Even in dirty, oversized clothes, he was unbelievably cute. All Scott cared about was skateboarding and listening to the Grateful Dead. Everything about him drove my father crazy.

"Hey, buddy," Dad said, hugging Scott, who suffered

through the embrace. "You take care of your mom and your sister while I was gone, big guy?"

Scott rolled his eyes and stepped out of Dad's embrace.

"I asked you a question, son."

"Yeah, well, it was a stupid question—"

"Don't start, you two—" Mom began.

"I'm not the one who starts—"

"That's enough," Dad told him sharply. He smiled at us so that we'd know he wasn't mad at anyone except my slacker baby brother. "It's Lara's big night and nothing is going to spoil it, right, son?"

"Whatever," Scott mumbled.

"Well, all I have to say is: the Ardeche men are really proud of our beauty queen," Dad said heartily.

"Beauty *queens*," my mother added gaily.

"God, gag me," Scott muttered.

Dad turned on him. "What was that, son?"

"Nothing. Forget it." Scott turned around and disappeared down the hallway.

"What is his problem?" Dad asked Mom, running his hand through his hair in exasperation.

"He's thirteen, that's all," Mom said.

"And he's turning into a total fox," Lisa added.

Mom laughed. "I guess he takes after his father."

"I'll say." Lisa gave my dad another flirtatious look.

Mom gripped Dad's arm more tightly and checked her watch. "The guys are arriving with the limo in two hours, so we'll meet you downstairs then to take videos. And meanwhile, don't disturb us, because I haven't seen my handsome husband in three days, and we'll be busy." She began to pull him comically from the room.

"Save a dance for your old man tonight, princess!"

"I will!" I called after him.

"I will, too!" Lisa added. She sighed and lay back on my bed. "Lara, your father is to die for."

"Hey, Mol," I said, tapping on the bathroom door. "You can come out now."

"Oh, I don't think so," she called back. "I'm thinking about spending the rest of my life in here. It's cozy."

"Can you even imagine being married to a guy that fine?" Lisa asked dreamily.

"He's *old*, Lis!" Amber exclaimed.

Molly opened the door, wearing the same sweats she'd had on before. "Tell me the truth. How much could he see?"

"Brad Pitt is old, too, but I wouldn't kick either of 'em out of bed," Lisa said.

"My butt?" Molly asked. "Just tell me if he could actually see my butt."

"He didn't see anything, Mol, I promise," I told her.

I lifted my sweatshirt over my head and dropped it into the clothes hamper. "Y'all, do you really, truly think I have a chance? Tell me the truth."

Lisa sat up. She and Amber traded glances. "Look," Amber began, "everyone knows you're the most popular girl in the entire school. If you were still with Danny, everyone would vote for you and you'd beat Amy, but— I'm just being honest because I love you—without Danny, it's a total long shot."

Lisa nodded her agreement. Molly shrugged.

"Well, that's okay," I said lightly, ignoring the bubble of disappointment that welled up in my stomach. Pageant queens never show their disappointment. They are gracious losers, always.

"Maybe I'll win next year," I added. "Anyway, let's

just have a blast tonight, okay?" I went into the bathroom.

As I turned on the shower I refused to let disappointment about homecoming queen get the best of me. After
all, everything in my life was utterly, totally wonderful.

The only thing that could possibly make it any better
would be if, by some incredible miracle, my friends were
wrong and I somehow actually won homecoming queen.

Then it would be perfect.

Chapter 118

(continued)

"Did I tell you how great you look?" Jett asked me. I was in his arms, swaying to the music of a hot local alternative band, the Sex Puppets. The skinny, flat-chested lead singer had sexy, kohl-rimmed eyes, purple lipstick, and multicolored hair with two-inch black roots. Her cheeks, nose, and eyebrow were pierced. She wore a stretchy top that read ANARCHY, a tiny polyester miniskirt, and combat boots.

In contrast, I had on a pale peach satin dress that bared my shoulders and dipped low in the back. Diamond studs sparkled in my ears. My hair was twisted off my face with a slender peach-colored ribbon.

"Hey, did you see Amy?" Amber asked, dancing near us with her boyfriend, Blake Poole. "She keeps looking over at you. You've really got her nervous!"

"She doesn't have anything to be nervous *about*," I replied.

"Let's hope she does," Molly said loyally. She was standing near us, swaying by herself to the music. Her boyfriend, Andy, had gone off somewhere with some of his wrestling teammates awhile earlier.

"Love ain't nothin' but a hormone scream,
Love ain't nothin' but a hot, wet dream . . ."

The girl with the pierced cheek screamed and moaned into the microphone.

"I'm definitely getting my nose pierced," Molly said, watching the girl onstage sing.

"You would," Amber said, rolling her eyes.

Jett deliberately danced me away from my friends, his arms tightening around my waist. "Much better," he murmured, gazing down at me. "God, you're beautiful."

"Love ain't nothin' unless it's obscene . . ."

Jett laughed. "Interesting lyrics for a love ballad."

I smiled and leaned my head on his shoulder. *Love ain't nothin' but a hot, wet dream.* That sounded so sexy. And dangerous. Kind of like Jett. I moved closer to him.

"Hi, Lara."

I opened my eyes. It was Danny Fairway.

He might have been my ex, but he was still so handsome that he took my breath away. He looked like a younger, blonder, better-looking Andre Agassi. And like Andre, Danny was a tennis player—the number one singles on the school tennis team. He was also Mr. Everything: junior-class president, great grades, church youth-group leader. Everyone loved Danny. Even my parents. I would look at him and I would think: Our life together will be perfect, just like Mom and Dad's.

I never, ever thought we would break up. But at the beginning of the summer Danny had started really pressuring me to have sex. I had always known I wanted to be madly in love the first time I made love, and one day I looked at Danny and I thought: No. You're not the one.

How can you explain something like that?

But still, I didn't break up with him. I liked him a lot, I didn't want to hurt him, and I didn't want him to be mad at me.

So we just went on. And maybe we would have gone on forever if it hadn't been for Jett.

Jett and I had discovered each other in July, when three generations of my family had gone on vacation, compliments of my rich grandfather, to Sea Pines, this ritzy resort on Hilton Head Island, off the coast of South Carolina. I had a sexy new white bikini, and right after we'd checked in, I put it on and went to the beach.

By pure chance Jett Anston, who was a year ahead of me at Forest Hills High, was a summer lifeguard there.

We had seen each other around school, but we didn't know each other, exactly. I knew *about* him, though. Jett's move to Nashville the year before had been reported in *The Tennessean*. Not because of him. Because of his mother, Anastasia Anston, the sculptor. Her famous piece, *Embrace,* a huge marble abstract of a mother, father, and baby, was in the permanent collection at the Museum of Modern Art in New York City. Now she was artist-in-residence at Vanderbilt University.

Jett was an artist, too. I had seen his watercolor that

had won the Metro schools art contest—a homeless man playing a battered guitar as a plain little girl looked up at a huge billboard of gorgeous Shania Twain.

I'd never met anyone like Jett before. He wore his self-confidence like an old shirt: comfortable, a perfect fit, no need to impress anyone. He had a ponytail—all the other guys I knew had cut theirs short. He wore cowboy boots—every other guy wore sneakers or work boots.

His parents had named Jett after the character James Dean had played in the movie *Giant,* and Jett seemed like a character out of a movie: quiet, mysterious, deep. Tall and very thin, dark-haired and dark-eyed, he wasn't nearly as gorgeous as Danny. But he had this . . . thing. This intensity, this heat. Like he was looking right through you, seeing you naked, finding out all your secrets.

And you liked it.

Jett had already been at Hilton Head for three weeks when I got there. He'd lifeguard by day, and at night he'd draw. I was told this by another lifeguard, Heather Something-or-other, who also told me that she and Jett were a couple.

As in "hands off."

But that night it was me, not Heather, Jett invited to walk with him on the beach. We built a driftwood fire and Jett drew my portrait by the light of the flames, his beautiful, slender hands flying over his sketchpad while I wondered what those hands would feel like on me.

Then Jett talked me into playing piano for him in the resort center. After that, we went back to the beach and talked. I lost all track of time; I didn't care.

We were still there when the sun came up.

Nothing mattered but me and Jett and the total perfection of being in his arms.

The first time he kissed me that night, I knew. Danny was over. Jett was the one I had been waiting for.

By the time school started, we were madly in love. All my friends thought I was crazy, giving up Danny for Jett. Even Mrs. Armstrong felt that Jett was not helpful to what she called "a winning pageant image." I loved Jett too much to care.

The only really bad part had been breaking up with Danny. He cried, which made me cry. I hated myself for hurting him, but not enough not to do it. So, when Danny told everyone *he* had broken up with *me*—to save his own rep, I suppose—I was glad. No one would hate me for us ending.

As Danny smiled at me, Jett's arms were still securely wrapped around my slender waist. "Hi, Danny," I said.

"So, you look great," Danny said.

"Thanks. Where's Candy?" I knew he was dating a cheerleader, Candy Bingham.

"Around here somewhere," he said vaguely. He thrust his hands in the pockets of his dinner jacket. "It looks great in here, huh? And how about the band?"

Jett snorted back a laugh. Well, the whole homecoming thing was pretty funny, I had to admit.

Through the magic of aluminum foil and thousands of tiny white Christmas-tree lights, the high-school gym had been transformed into Moonlight on the River. Danny and the other class officers had picked the theme for the homecoming dance. But the band had been picked by a vote of the entire student body—including that large percentage who thought that homecoming was

22

the stupidest idea in human history and would not be caught dead there on a bet.

By the time the class officers had figured out that voting should have been restricted to homecoming-dance ticket holders only, it was too late.

It was Moonlight on the River, with the Sex Puppets.

Jett thought the whole thing was hilarious. But then, he was only at homecoming because I'd wanted to go.

"The band is great," I told Danny.

The Sex Puppets finished one song and began a new ballad. "So, mind if I dance with Lara?" Danny asked Jett.

Jett held his hands up to Danny. "Hey, man, she can answer for herself."

I didn't know what to say. It felt as if everyone's eyes were on us, watching to see what I would do.

I turned to Jett. "Would you mind?"

He smiled. "I think I can risk it." He kissed me on the temple and walked away.

I moved into Danny's arms. Some people around us started buzzing. Lara and Danny again. What did it mean?

"This reminds me of old times," Danny murmured.

"But you're with Candy now."

"Yeah. And you're with the brooding *artiste*."

"He doesn't brood."

"Yeah, right," Danny muttered. We danced silently for a minute or so. "I still can't believe you fell for that."

"Danny, let's not have this conversa—"

"What, you think he's so cool, so much better than me?"

"I don't think that," I assured him. "I . . . I can't explain it. And I never meant to hurt you."

23

Danny sighed. "Yeah," he said. "I know."

"You look really pretty, Lara," Amy Caprice said, dancing by with her boyfriend.

"I love your dress," I told her. "Good luck tonight."

She smiled at me, and Danny pulled me closer. "You really meant that, didn't you?"

"Sure," I said as I tried to mean it. "Maybe I'll win next year."

"You're the most beautiful, nicest, sweetest girl in this school, and everyone knows it," Danny said, his voice low. "Hey, I voted for you."

I smiled up at him, and he pulled me closer. I closed my eyes and for just a moment enjoyed the comfortable, safe feeling of being in Danny's arms again. But then the music ended and there was Jett, next to me.

"So, see you," Danny said.

"See you."

He walked away into the crowd.

Jett took me into his arms. "You miss him?"

"No."

"He's not a bad guy," Jett said.

"I know that. But he's not you."

As we swayed to the music I felt Jett's arms tighten around me. They didn't feel safe like Danny's did. They felt like something else I couldn't name.

Someone bumped into my back so hard that we stumbled.

"Sorry," the girl mumbled.

It was Patty Asher, the fattest girl in our class. She wore a red velvet dress that fell tentlike over her massive form. She was hurrying toward the gym door.

"Geez, take up some space, why don't you!" Lisa yelled after Patty's retreating form.

"What a pig!" Blake said.

"God, did you *see* her?" Lisa asked. "That *dress*! I didn't know velvet could stretch that far!"

Some people around us laughed as the Sex Puppets finished their song and took an intermission.

"Give the girl a break, huh?" Jett said.

"*Girl?*" Blake echoed. "You mean *tub*! Tub-o'-love, baby!"

More laughter.

"Y'all, come on," I chided them softly.

Jett turned to Blake. "That make you feel special, putting her down like that?"

Blake scowled at him. "What's your problem?"

"Y'all, just forget about it," I said quickly. "Patty must have a lot of problems, the poor thing."

"Who's she here with, anyway?" Amber asked, her arms around Blake's waist.

"Probably one of the faggot geeks from the drama club she hangs out with," Blake said with disgust.

I had gotten to know some of those "faggot geeks" when I'd played the piano for the school musical, *Bye Bye Birdie*. I kind of liked them, and I hated to hear anyone make fun of them, or of anyone else, for that matter. Pageants had taught me to appreciate all kinds of people.

"Oh, look, there's Patty's boy-toy, Mr. Studly!" Blake said gleefully.

I turned around. Blake was pointing to Chris Zeeman, a tall, thin, effeminate guy who hung out with Patty. He'd been the stage manager for *Bye Bye Birdie*.

"Oh, *Chrissy*!" Blake called to Chris in a falsetto, his wrist limp. "Having fun, sweetie?" He made kissing noises in Chris's direction.

Chris pretended he didn't hear Blake, but his face turned bright red, so I knew that he had.

"Blake, you really—" I began to protest.

"He was only *joking,* Lara," Lisa insisted.

"Let's take a walk," Jett suggested, his jaw set hard.

I said good-bye to my friends and we walked away, hand in hand.

"They're only fooling around," I told Jett. "Blake is wasted, or he wouldn't say those things."

He gave me a cool look. "Yeah, right."

"They don't really mean anything by it," I insisted. "I mean, I'm not saying it's right, because it isn't—"

"They're jerks," Jett said.

"Yo, Jett, lighten up, dude!" Blake said, walking unsteadily over to us, his arm around Amber.

"Hey, have you guys seen Andy?" Molly asked, pushing through the crowd to get to us. I noticed how cute she looked in the black chiffon A-line dress I had helped her pick out. It hid her big hips, and the rhinestones around the neckline drew attention to her face.

"Last time I saw him, he went out the fire exit with a bunch of guys and a bottle of Jack Daniel's," Amber said. "They rigged it so the alarm wouldn't go off."

"Gee, no wonder I love him so," Molly said sarcastically. "Lara, come with me to the bathroom?"

"Sure." I turned to Amber. "Want to come?"

"Can't," Amber said. "If I let Tiger here out of his cage he'll fall in love with someone else."

"In lust, maybe, babe, not in love," Blake slurred.

"Come on, big guy, it's black coffee for you," Amber told him, leading him in the direction of the buffet table.

"That guy is a major-league butthole," Jett said.

"Nah, he's a pretty typical butthole," Jett sighed.

"You don't realize it because you're some kind of highly evolved guy-mutant. You want to know what most guys dream about? Miss February."

She made kissy lips with her mouth and batted her eyelashes. "Hello. I'm Bambi," she said in a breathy voice. "I weigh nothing, and I'm built like a bud vase with two basketballs balanced on top. I'm a Scorpio, and my hobbies are nuclear fusion and oral sex." She linked her arm through mine. "Ta-ta!" she called, waving over her shoulder at Jett as she pulled me toward the girls' bathroom.

"You crack me up, Mol," I told her, laughing.

"You realize that Jett is, like, light-years beyond any other guy in the entire school," Molly said as we pushed open the girls' room door. "I mean, I actually believe that he'd love you even if you were *slightly* less perfect looking than you are."

"Looks have nothing to do with real love," I told her.

She gave me a look. "I know you don't believe that."

"Yeah, I do," I said.

We checked our reflections in the mirror. Someone had scrawled *BLAKE POOLE WANTS FATTY PATTY BAD!* on the mirror in red lipstick, and some of the letters covered Molly's reflected right cheek.

Molly puffed out her cheeks. "I look like a cow."

"You don't. You look cute, honest."

Molly kept staring at her reflection. "Too bad Fatty Patty isn't in here. Next to her, even *I* look thin."

"I thought you had to pee," I reminded her.

"Nope."

"Then why are we in here?"

"What am I supposed to do, stand around like an idiot while my so-called boyfriend is outside getting

27

wrecked?" She sucked in the skin below her cheeks. "Maybe I need that cheekbone surgery," she continued, "where they suck the fat out and it gives you high cheekbones like Kate Moss."

"Mol, you don't need surgery." I pulled a tiny perfume vial out of my satin purse. "If you come over three afternoons a week, and we work out together, you'll see a huge difference in no time." I spritzed her wrists with perfume, then mine. "But you have to really work out, not just watch me do it."

"I hate working out," she said. "It's so much *work*."

"Molly," I said, "you make your own reality."

"Every time you say that, I want to hurl," Molly said. "Because you know it's true."

The bathroom door opened, and Jennie Smith, a willowy girl with long, shiny brown hair, sailed in. She had on a white dress with the middle cut out. I knew for a fact it cost over six hundred dollars because I had seen the price tag on it at the Paris Shoppe.

"Lara, honey, I heard about Denise Reiser and I am just so *thrilled* for you!" she cried, her voice dripping honey. She threw her arms around me and hugged me tight, then air-kissed me in the vicinity of my left cheek. She ignored Molly completely.

Jennie Smith was the richest, thinnest girl in our class. We were supposed to be friends, but the truth was, I didn't really like her much. Still, the pageant motto had been drummed into my head: be sweet to everyone. Besides, Jennie had a lot of power. And she was one of those girls who could turn on you at any moment.

"I don't think I'll win, Jennie, but thanks," I told her. "Amy Caprice is—"

"I heard Amy Caprice has herpes." Jennie checked out her narrow reflection in the mirror.

"Really?" I asked. "That's terrible!"

"Well, maybe it's just a nasty rumor." She grinned maliciously. "I mean, who would be wicked enough to start a rumor like that?"

"Could it be . . . you?" Molly asked brightly.

Jennie gave her a cool look, then turned back to the mirror. "I just *hate* myself. I was so *bad*. I ate, like, *four* of those little fruit tarts on the dessert table!"

"Oh my God, you—you *farm animal*!" Molly cried in mock horror. "You're going to go up to a size three, for sure!"

Jennie looked Molly up and down. "Did you know our beloved principal just busted your boyfriend?"

"For what?"

"He and some of his friends came in staggering around, and a pint of Jack fell out of his pocket."

"Oh, great, just great," Molly said. "I gotta go save him, Lara. Come find me." She dashed out the door.

Jennie smoothed her hair and shook it back off her shoulders. "I don't want to toot my own horn, Lara, but I did manage to talk a bunch of people into voting for you."

"By starting a rumor about Amy?" I asked her.

"Would I do a thing like that?"

I didn't answer. I smiled instead. "It was so sweet of you to get people to vote for me, and—"

"It wasn't easy," Jennie said, "what with you and Danny breaking up, and you and The Mouth—"

"Molly's great."

"Please." Jennie fixed her lipstick and checked for

mascara flecks under her hazel eyes. "I don't mean she's a total loser like Fatty Patty or something. But she's not exactly in your league, and she could be what keeps you from getting queen, no matter how hard I worked to help you."

"Molly's my best friend," I said quietly.

Jennie shrugged. "Whatever. I'm only telling you because I love you to death, Lara. Hey, whatever you do, don't let me eat anything out there, okay?"

"I'll watch you like a hawk," I promised.

"You're a sweetheart," Jennie said, air-kissing me again and sailing out the door.

Behind me, a toilet flushed. I was surprised. I didn't think anyone else was in the bathroom.

But someone came out of one of the stalls.

It was Patty Asher.

Chapter 118

(The End)

I just stood there, trying to think of something to say to Patty.

I'm sorry?

My friends didn't know you were in here?

If you'd just go on a diet no one would be able to humiliate you like that?

Patty walked over to the sink and turned the water on. But something was wrong with the faucet and water shot out in every direction, spraying the entire front of her dress.

"Damn!" she swore. She looked like she was going to cry.

I reached into the wall dispenser for some paper towels, but it was empty. A few used ones swam in dirty water on the floor, under the row of sinks.

Patty plucked a Kleenex from her purse and was about to dab at her dress when I stopped her.

"Don't do that!"

She stopped, the tissue an inch from her sopping dress.

"Tissues on wet velvet are a disaster," I explained. "They leave little balls of gunky white fuzz that sort of *fuse* to the velvet."

"Great," she groaned.

I looked around, trying to think of a solution. My eyes lit on a hot-air dryer on the wall, which was supposed to be used to dry your hands. "Stand under this."

I pressed the On button and Patty stood under it, awkwardly aiming her massive stomach toward the warm airflow.

"It's working, I think," she said, looking down at her dress.

As she stood there under the hot-air nozzle, I couldn't help noticing just how overweight she was. Although she had beautiful long brown hair, her brown eyes, which might have been pretty, were sunken under twin cushions of fat. She had two extra chins quivering under the first, and no neck to speak of. Her shoulders, which weren't all that broad, blossomed into a huge bosom. Below that, her waist exploded into an inner tube of fat, which sat on top of an even huger roll of flesh.

All I could think was, how in this world could anyone allow themselves to look like that? Then I felt awful at having such an ugly thought.

I smiled at Patty. "I don't even think it's going to leave a spot at all."

"Uh-huh," she agreed.

"Good thing they have that dryer in here, isn't it?"

"Uh-huh."

I decided to try being extra nice to her. After all, it

must be so horrible to be the butt of everyone's jokes. Butt jokes. I was making jokes about her in my own mind in spite of myself!

"So, are you having fun?" I asked her brightly, clicking and unclicking the clasp on my little satin purse. I really wanted to go, but it seemed too rude to leave her in there alone.

"It's okay."

Patty's eyes slid toward the mirror and landed on the lipsticked graffiti: *BLAKE POOLE WANTS FATTY PATTY BAD!*

How terrible. How humiliating. My heart went out to her. I took her Kleenex and leaned over to wipe the letters away, but all I did was smear the lipstick around. At least you couldn't read it anymore.

"I'm really sorry," I said, throwing the tissue into the overflowing trash bin.

"Why, did you do it?"

"No! God, no!" I exclaimed, horrified.

"Then why are you apologizing?"

I couldn't think of a good answer. And I really wanted to go find Jett, but I just stood there. As if I knew Patty. As if we were friends.

We weren't, of course. But she had played a character role in *Bye Bye Birdie*—Albert's fat, smothering mother—and I had actually spoken to her a few times. It wasn't like we didn't know each other.

"So, I'm kind of nervous," I confided, still clicking and unclicking the clasp on my purse. "About homecoming queen. Not that I expect to win or anything . . ."

"You'll win," she said.

"You really think so?" I asked eagerly.

33

"No, *I'll* win," she said sarcastically.

I tried to smile. It must be so awful being her.

"Well, I think I'm dry," Patty said, moving away from the dryer. "Have fun." She started for the door.

Suddenly an idea occurred to me. A really good idea.

"Patty, wait a sec," I called to her.

She turned around.

I took a deep breath. "Look, I know that the things people say to you . . . well, I know it must really hurt your feelings."

She just stared at me.

"I mean, I know we aren't really friends," I rushed on. "But . . . but we could be. You know Molly Sheridan? We've been best friends forever. Well, she kind of has a weight problem, too. So, we're planning on exercising together. You know, on a regular basis? We have this home gym? And I was thinking that the three of us could work out together! You know. At my house. You have such a pretty face."

A muscle jumped in Patty's fat cheek. "So, you're going to save me, is that it?"

"Well, no, I just meant—"

Her face flushed with anger. "Where do you get off talking to me about personal things? You've never said more than two sentences to me before."

My cheeks burned with embarrassment. "We worked on the play," I said defensively. "We talked."

"Right. Once you told me it was amazing that I could play an old lady so convincingly without using makeup."

"I meant that as a compliment, that you're so talented—"

"I'm fat, not stupid," Patty spat at me.

"Look, I didn't mean to insult you—"

"No? So what did you *mean* to do?"

"I just want to help you—"

"What in the world makes you think I want help from you?" she asked me.

"Look, I know you're just reacting this way because you're embarrassed—"

"God, you're amazing!" Patty exclaimed. "Do you think I don't know that you and your little band of oh-so-cool friends think I'm this fat, pathetic loser? Well, guess what, Lara Ardeche? I think *you're* pathetic! If you get crowned queen, it'll be the highlight of your pathetic little life!" She turned and stormed out of the bathroom.

I just stood there, my mouth open, my hands shaking. I couldn't believe what had just happened. There I was, being nice, trying to *help* her, and she acted like I had done something terrible!

"Lara, what are you doing in here?" Amber demanded, running into the bathroom. "All the alums just came in and your parents are looking for you. They're about to announce the court. Are you sick or something?"

"No, I'm fine," I told her as the two of us hurried down the hall toward the gym. "Do I look okay?"

"Perfect," she assured me.

I saw my parents standing near the buffet table, waving to me. I waved back and started to make my way over to them. About two hundred adults had been at the alumni party, and now the gym was so crowded it was hard to move.

"Hey, Lara! Wow, you look great!"

It was Sarah Lodge, a really nice, smart girl who sat next to me in precalculus. She wasn't in the cool crowd, but I liked her a lot.

"So do you," I said as someone bumped into me from behind. "It's a zoo in here!"

"Primates in formal wear," she said, laughing and moving off with her date. "I hope you win queen!"

"Lara, honey, bless your heart, don't you look lovely!" a friend of my parents' said, kissing me as I went by. "We're pulling for you, honey."

Chris Zeeman waved to me. "I hope you win," he mouthed shyly.

"Thanks," I mouthed back.

"It's so crowded," I said when I finally reached my parents. They looked perfect in their formal wear.

"This is it, princess," my father said, putting his arm around my shoulders.

"Please, Daddy, I'm not going to win. I'm just a junior, and—"

"Oh, there's Danny!" my mom exclaimed as her eyes lit on him in the crowd. She waved. "He looks so handsome."

At that moment, to my horror, I started to feel that itchy feeling on my arms, just like when I had gotten the hives at the Miss Teen Pride of the South pageant.

Please. I couldn't get hives now. I just couldn't.

"Have you seen Jett?" I asked, looking around in vain, trying to ignore my itchy arms. The Sex Puppets started a new song, very loud. I really, really wanted to find Jett. I would be okay, if only—

And then, there he was. He wrapped his long arms around me.

Suddenly I had this urge to run away with Jett, somewhere where no one knew either one of us.

"Hope you get it, Lara!" a guy from my French class called.

I smiled and mouthed, "Thanks," again. I shifted myself into pageant autopilot. I had to keep smiling, especially if they called Amy Caprice's name instead of mine. No matter how I felt. No matter what.

I gently scratched my arms.

The Sex Puppets scowled to the end of their song, and Mrs. Conway, our principal, made her way to the microphone. The Sex Puppets stepped back. My father stood on one side of me, holding tightly to my right hand. Jett had one hand on the small of my back.

"I feel a little sick," I whispered to Jett.

He leaned over and kissed my cheek.

From across the room Molly caught my eye. She made a praying gesture with her hands.

Oh, God.

"Students of Forest Hills High, parents and guests, honored alumni," Mrs. Conway said into the microphone. "It's the moment we've all been waiting for, time to announce this year's homecoming court."

I could feel people's eyes on me. My arms itched like crazy. My stomach felt as if it had dropped to my knees. I smiled even harder.

"As you all know, there will be three princesses and their queen, all of whom will be accompanied up to the stage by their escorts, and will then be presented at halftime during the game tomorrow."

My father smiled at me and squeezed my hand even more tightly. Traditionally, each girl on the court was accompanied to the stage by her father.

"As I call each girl's name, please come forward,

along with your escort, to the stage. And please, let's all hold our applause until the entire court is announced."

I could feel sweat trickling down my spine. I smiled so hard my jaws ached.

Please, God, please, God, I prayed. *Please, just let me have this one thing.*

"Our princesses are . . . Carrie Anne Macey, Lisa James, and Whitney Summers," Mrs. Conway said into the microphone.

My parents looked at each other, slack-jawed with shock. Amy Caprice's name hadn't been called, and neither had mine. One of us had won, and one of us wasn't even on the court.

Oh, God.

"Lara, it has to be Lara," my mother breathed. Her eyes were shut tight, the fingers on both hands crossed.

My father squeezed my fingers more tightly still. Sweat beaded up on his forehead.

The smile was still plastered on my face.

But inside, now, I wanted to cry. It was one thing not to be queen, but I hadn't even made it onto the court.

"And our homecoming queen is . . ."

Time stood still. I couldn't think, couldn't breathe, couldn't—

"Lara Ardeche!" Mrs. Conway called triumphantly.

My mother screamed, my friends screamed, and my father whooped the loudest of all, pumping his fist into the air. I jumped into Jett's arms, and for the briefest moment, he held me. Everyone was applauding, yelling, whistling.

"May I?" my father asked me gallantly, holding out his elbow, so proud.

I took it, and then, like in some wonderful movie,

bodies parted, and my father and I walked up on the stage, where last year's homecoming queen put the crown on my head. Someone else handed me a dozen long-stemmed red roses.

"Ladies and gentlemen, I give you the Forest Hills High School homecoming court!" Mrs. Conway exclaimed.

Everyone cheered again, cameras flashed, and I could see my mom videotaping everything. Tears welled up in my eyes, and my father tenderly wiped them away with his handkerchief. I mouthed, "Thank you," at everyone and let the tears come again. Pageants teach you that it's okay to be swept away by big emotions, as long as you're the winner or busy congratulating the winner.

So few moments in life live up to your fantasies of how they'll be. But that moment, when I was crowned homecoming queen and my parents were so proud of me and Jett loved me, lived up to every fantasy I had ever had. I looked out at that sea of happy faces—even Danny was smiling up at me—and I thought how I had known most of them forever, and now they had picked me to be their queen. I felt surrounded by so much love, just waves of it coming up to me on that stage. I was a part of all of them, they were a part of me.

And then, out of the corner of my eye, I saw Patty Asher coming in the gym door. She stared up at me. She wasn't smiling.

If you get crowned queen, it'll be the highlight of your pathetic little life!

Poor Patty. She must be so miserable.

I sent up a little prayer of thanks. That I had won. That I had Jett.

That I wasn't anything like poor Patty Asher.

Chapter 128

"**H**oney, are you gaining weight?" my mother asked as she slid a blueberry pancake from the skillet onto my plate.

It was a month later, the Sunday morning before Halloween, and we were having our usual Sunday morning breakfast of blueberry pancakes and turkey bacon.

Not that Mom ate any kind of bacon at all. Ever. Every morning she had the same thing: one half of a whole-wheat English muffin with one teaspoon of all-fruit jam. Half a grapefruit. Two cups of coffee, black.

"She's a warthog," Scott said, reaching for the butter.

"That's enough from you," Mom told him. She sat down and cut into her grapefruit.

"Do I look fat?" I asked anxiously.

"Of course not," Mom said, spooning up some grapefruit. "But your jeans look a little tight, sweetie."

She was right. They *were* a little tight. A *lot* tight.

Right after homecoming I had started getting hives almost every day. Sometimes my lips and my eyelids swelled. My parents took me right to the doctor. Stress, he said. But I didn't feel stressed. I felt fantastic. It didn't make any sense.

When my hives wouldn't go away, my mom took me to an allergist, who put me on a drug called prednisone, which seemed to work. But the prednisone made me retain water. So I'd stop taking the prednisone, and get the hives back, and then I'd go back on the prednisone.

According to my scale, I had gained ten pounds. *Ten pounds!* In a month! I now weighed 128. It was more than I had ever weighed in my life.

I could hardly zip up my jeans. My stomach pressed against the zipper. The tiniest roll of skin poufed above the waistband. I looked over at my mother. She had on white leggings and a cropped white T-shirt. Perfectly slim and perfectly aerobicized.

"That's it, I'm on a diet," I said, pushing my plate away. Scott grabbed it and dumped the pancake on top of his own plate, then drenched it with maple syrup.

Mom frowned at him. "You don't need all that sugar."

"Oh yeah, I do," he said, his mouth full.

I poured myself a cup of coffee and resisted the urge to add cream and sugar. I took a sip. It was so bitter. I eyed the package of English muffins and decided to toast the other half of my mom's.

"Your very first diet," Mom said, sipping her coffee. "Now *this* is something we can definitely bond over."

"All it takes is willpower," I said coolly. "I'll up my workouts. It's not a big deal."

"Try skateboarding," Scott suggested, his mouth full of pancake. "It'll take the lard off you real fast."

"Your sister doesn't have any lard, it's from the prednisone," Mom told him. She lit a cigarette.

"It was a joke," Scott explained. "You know. Humor?"

"Well, it wasn't funny," Mom said. "Gaining weight is no joke." She turned to me. "I can write out a great diet for you, if you want."

"Mom, I know how to diet."

"I just meant that you never had to do it before, and I could help you," she explained. "Believe me, I know every trick in the book."

"Yeah, like cancer sticks," Scott said, taking another bite of pancake. "Better thin and dead than fat and kickin', right, Mom?"

"Very funny. I'm going to quit," Mom added, taking a deep drag on her cigarette.

"Sure," Scott said sarcastically.

I could hear my dad coming down the stairs. Mom quickly put out her cigarette and waved at the air.

"Oh yeah, like *that's* gonna fool him," Scott said with disgust.

Dad came into the kitchen, his hair still wet from the shower. He looked as fit as my mom. I felt like a blimp. I decided to skip the muffin and just go with black coffee.

"Morning, all," Dad said. He sat down and poured himself some coffee. "It smells like smoke in here, Carol."

"Mmmm, you smell good," my mom said, hugging him from behind. "Want pancakes? Turkey bacon?"

"One pancake, no bacon," Dad said, patting his

stomach. He took a sip of orange juice. "So, what's up with you today, princess?"

"I have to practice piano for two hours, for my recital," I said. "Then I'm working out with Molly, and after that Jett's coming over to help me with precalculus."

"Good girl," Dad approved. Precalculus was the only class where I didn't have an A average. He looked at Scott, taking in his baggy shorts and even baggier T-shirt. "Son?"

Scott just shoveled more pancake into his mouth.

"Would actual words be too much to hope for?" Dad asked him.

"You know, whatever," Scott mumbled. "Hanging."

"Hanging?"

"With my friends. You know."

Dad sighed. "What about homework?"

Scott shrugged again.

"A shrug is not an answer!" Dad exploded. "If I ask you a question, I expect an answer!"

"Yes, *sir*!" Scott replied, saluting as if he were in the military. "Whatever you say, *sir*!"

Dad pushed his chair back. "I give up. I really give up."

"Come on, guys," Mom pleaded, "let's have a nice Sunday—"

"Well, tell him to get off my back, then," Scott suggested icily.

"Scott, all Dad did was ask what you were doing today," Mom pointed out.

"And I *told* him. But what I said wasn't *good* enough!" Scott got up and stormed out of the room.

Dad turned to Mom. "Are you sure he's really our kid?"

"It's a phase, honey," Mom soothed. Her fingers, with no cigarette to hold, drummed nervously on the table.

Dad scowled into his coffee.

Mom began to knead his shoulders. "Come on, Jimbo," she coaxed, "don't get all tense over Scott."

Dad shook her off. "I don't need a backrub, I need to get through to my kid. He acts like he hates me."

"I love you, Daddy," I told him.

He grinned at me and cut into his pancake. "Yeah, I know you do, princess. Thank God for you, that's all I have to say." He looked at the empty place in front of me. "Aren't you eating?"

"I'm not hungry."

"Lara's been putting on a little weight," Mom explained.

"Mom!" I exclaimed. "It's because of the prednisone."

Dad frowned. "How much?"

"Just a little," I said nervously, sipping my coffee.

"You have to nip these things in the bud, princess," he said sternly. "Otherwise, forget it. One day you're perfect, and the next day you wake up looking like Molly."

"It's just water retention from the allergy medicine. I only gained four pounds, and I'm going to lose it."

"It looks like more than four," Mom said.

"Well, it isn't," I lied.

"Okay," Dad said. "Let's drop this subject. I know my princess, and she accomplishes anything she sets her mind to, right?"

44

"Right," I said firmly.

"That's my girl."

Mom leaned over and put her hand on Dad's. "Hey, how would you like a date with your wife tonight?"

"Can't," Dad said. "I've got to catch a plane at six for Philly."

"Tonight?" Mom sounded surprised.

"I told you last week. I guess you forgot," Dad said. "This could be a big client for us, all the agencies are after him."

"Can't you leave in the morning?" Mom asked.

"I'm playing golf with their CEO in the morning, Carol," he said. "I can't be on a plane and on the golf course at the same time, now, can I?"

"No, of course not," she agreed.

Dad got up and kissed me on the forehead; then he kissed Mom. "I'm going over to the club to play a few sets. Why don't you meet me there for lunch? Say, twelve?"

"I'd love—" Mom began.

But Dad was looking at me. "I hardly ever see you, princess. Between school, piano, your friends, and Jett, you're one busy girl."

Mom's face reddened with embarrassment, but Dad's back was to her so he didn't see.

"You're always working, Dad," I said. "You and Mom should have lunch together."

Dad picked up an apple from the fruit bowl and bit into it. "How about it, Carol? Can't have both my girls shoot me down!"

"Lunch is fine," Mom said.

"Great." Dad took another bite of his apple and

winked at me. Then he strode out of the kitchen, picked up his tennis bag, and went out the front door.

As soon as she heard the front door close, Mom pulled out a cigarette and lit it. She inhaled hungrily.

"Is he mad at you or something?"

"Of course not, honey," she said, her voice as bright as overexposed film. "He's just preoccupied with work." She paused. "If you didn't know me, Lara, how old would you say I was?"

My stomach rumbled. Maybe I would eat just half a grapefruit. I eyed the other half of Mom's, sitting wetly on the kitchen counter.

"I don't know. Thirty."

"Thirty," Mom repeated with satisfaction.

She inhaled from her cigarette and blew the smoke out slowly. Then her eyes focused on me. "Which of my features do you like best?"

"I don't know."

Half a grapefruit couldn't be that bad.

"Come on, which?"

"Your eyes, I guess."

Mom nodded. "Your eyes are nice, too."

I really wanted that grapefruit.

Suddenly my arms started to itch. And I had already taken my prednisone.

"Your nose is a little short and upturned, a little too cute," Mom mused, studying me. "Mine is more classic." She pulled on her cigarette. "You know, if you have a small, upturned nose and you gain weight in your face, it can look kind of piggish."

"I'm on a diet," I said lamely.

"I know you are, sweetie." She patted my hand, got up, and kissed me on the top of my head. "And I have the most wonderful, perfect daughter in the whole world."

"Thanks, Mom."

I went upstairs and tried to ignore my grumbling stomach. Willpower was the key.

"Hey, did he leave?" Scott asked, sticking his head out the door of his room.

"He went to the club."

"Great, I can breathe again," my brother said. "Man, he's so suffocating that he, like, sucks all the air out of the room." He sucked air through pursed lips. "The Amazing Vacuum Man!"

I followed Scott into his totally trashed room.

"What is it about Dad that bugs you so much?" I asked Scott, leaning against his wall.

He plopped down on his unmade bed and reached for a Hacky Sack that lay on his pillow. He threw it in the air and caught it, over and over. "He's a pain in the ass."

"No, he isn't."

"Sure, you don't think so, *princess*," Scott jeered.

"So what if he calls me princess? I think it's sweet."

"Did Vacuum Man send you in here?" Scott asked warily.

"Of course not! I just can't stand to see the two of you fight."

"Yeah, it's bad enough that *they* fight all the time."

"They do not!"

"They do so. He hates her. He treats her like cold crap." Scott tossed the Hacky Sack into the air again. I leaned over and caught it before he could.

"Scott, come on . . ."

" 'The Ardeche men are really proud of our beauty queen,' " Scott said, imitating Dad, his voice deep and

mocking. Then he switched to a falsetto. "Uh-uh!
'Beauty *queens*!' " he said, imitating Mom. "Gimme a
major break!"

"What's wrong with being a beauty—"

"I'll tell you what's wrong!" Scott exploded. "Everyone in this family cares more about how things look than
how they really are!"

"That is totally not true," I said vehemently.

"It is true," Scott said bitterly.

"That is so stupid—"

"Just leave me alone. Leave me alone and get out of
my room!"

"Fine," I replied, "just fine." I tossed his Hacky Sack
at him and walked out. He slammed his door behind me.

What a brat. No wonder my parents fought.

It was *his* fault.

" 'I've lost seventy-five pounds and have a new life,' "
Molly read to me from a magazine.

It was after lunch; we were back in my home gym. I
had just finished forty-five minutes on the StairMaster,
up from my usual thirty. It was weird—I was hardly
sweating, though my face felt flushed from the exertion.
Maybe I was just raising my fitness level. Molly, who had
been on the treadmill at the slowest possible setting, had
long since gotten off and plopped down on the floor.

I stepped onto the treadmill and reprogrammed the
setting to five miles per hour.

"Who lost seventy-five pounds?" My legs moved
steadily over the treadmill, and I leaned into the front
handles.

"Ms. F. P. Stevens," Molly read. "F.P. must stand for

Former Pig, huh? She says here that the Skinny Strip changed her life."

I upped the speed controls. "What's a Skinny Strip?" I asked, breathing harder.

" 'You will see how the Skinny Strip makes you lose that weight, really lose that weight,' " Molly read. " 'With no dangerous medication and no tough exercise.' "

I laughed. "Anything that eliminates exercise is for you, right, Mol?"

She ignored me. " 'Skinny Strips are sold all over Europe, but now with this risk-free trial offer, you can try it right here in America.' "

"It's a scam," I said, wiping a single bead of sweat from my forehead. "If it were for real, it would be on the front page of every newspaper in the country."

"How can it be a scam if it has a guarantee?"

"I don't know, but it is."

"But what if it isn't?"

"Mol-ly," I groaned.

"What? I'm a desperate woman!" She stood up and shoved the magazine in my face. "It says that some doctor saw weight loss of as much as thirty-eight pounds in a month. Do you realize that means I could be thin in a month?"

"While you're reading that, you could be working out."

I raised the speed setting again. I could feel my heart pounding. I felt strong, in control. After having nothing but black coffee for breakfast, I had eaten just half a bagel with the insides scooped out, and a dollop of fat-free cottage cheese for lunch. Molly couldn't believe it.

"I'm on a diet," I'd told her primly.

"Get out of here," she'd guffawed.

"I'm completely serious. I've gained ten pounds from the medicine I'm taking. So now I have to lose ten pounds."

"Well, color me shocked, boys and girls," Molly had said. "I never thought I'd live to see the day."

"Dieting is just a matter of willpower."

"Uh-huh." There was a smirk on her face.

Well, let her smirk. I always accomplished everything I set my mind to. Losing ten pounds was nothing. I loved Molly to death, but frankly, she was lazy.

I bumped up the speed setting on the treadmill yet again.

"I'm sending for this strip thing," Molly decided. She leaned on the handlebars of the treadmill. "I have one eensy little problem, though. I can't have it delivered to my house."

"Why not? Your parents don't read your mail."

"True," Molly said. "But what if it says Skinny Strip on the return address and my mother picks up the mail? She'll give birth. So can I have it sent here?"

"Mol . . ."

"Pretty please and I'll be your best friend forever?"

I laughed. "You are a pain in the butt."

"No, I'm immensely charming. It's to compensate for my immense thighs. And thank you for your love and support."

"Hey, you two, what's up?"

It was Jett, an hour early.

"You're not supposed to be here yet," I scolded him. "Don't look at me, I'm a mess."

"Nah, you look cute like that." He looked over at

Molly, lolling on the floor. "Gee, Mol, strenuous workout?"

"The Skinny Strip is about to change my life," she told him solemnly.

I jumped off the treadmill and wrapped the towel around my neck. "You are seeing me at my total worst."

He grabbed both ends of the towel and pulled me to him. "You really think I care?" He kissed me tenderly.

"How come you're early, anyway?"

"I was sketching at Radnor Lake and it started to rain. So I thought I'd see if you wanted to grab a pizza before we study. You too, Mol."

"Gotta get home, but thanks," Molly said.

"Oh, I already ate," I told him.

"So?" Jett asked.

"I'm just not hungry," I lied.

"Ha!" Molly barked. I ignored her.

"Hey, you're not going to turn into one of those girls who pretends to eat like a bird, are you?" he asked me. "You love to eat."

"As long as it doesn't show on her hips," Molly added.

"That is totally unimportant," Jett told her.

"You don't by any chance have a twin brother who's been visiting distant relatives, do you?" Molly asked hopefully.

Jett laughed and turned to me. "Come and watch me eat, okay? I can't face math with a growling stomach."

"Don't worry. Her stomach is growling, too," Molly said wickedly.

"Kindly shut up," I told her.

She pretended to zip her mouth shut, her eyes dancing with mirth.

Okay. I could see the humor. If I was fat and my best friend was thin and had to diet for the very first time, I suppose I'd enjoy it, too. So I decided to forgive her. In fact, I said she could use my address for her Skinny Strip.

After I showered, we drove Molly home. Then Jett and I headed for Pizza Doctor, the best pizza place in Nashville.

The fantastic smell of baking pizza assaulted me before we even got out of the car. My stomach felt concave with emptiness.

"Want to split a medium?" Jett asked as we stood in front of the counter.

"No, I told you, I already ate." I salivated. I was *so* hungry.

"That's never stopped you from eating pizza."

He ordered a medium with everything and got us both drinks, and we settled into a booth. Over the blaring jukebox, we talked about everything—Jett was so easy to talk to. He showed me the new sketches he had done that day, I told him about piano practice, and for a while I actually forgot how hungry I was.

Until the waitress brought the pizza to our table.

"Help yourself," Jett told me as he lifted a fragrant, steaming slice to his lips.

"I'm really not hungry," I lied.

He wiped his mouth. "Listen, you're not doing anything stupid like dieting, are you?"

"Why would it be stupid to diet?" I asked, swallowing the extra saliva in my mouth.

"Because you don't need to. Because it's stupid to think you have to conform to some arbitrary standard of how other people *think* you should look." He took a large bite out of his slice. "I mean, it's pointless. Like, take that girl, the one that sings with the Sex Puppets—the one with the pierced cheek? Didn't you find her beautiful?"

"I take it you did," I said, making sure there was a sweet smile on my face as I said it.

"I'm just trying to say that there are all different kinds of beauty, that's all," Jett said. He reached for another slice.

"I don't think there's anything wrong with wanting to look your best," I argued.

Jett shrugged. "Whatever that means."

"What? Are you saying you could be attracted to a girl like, say, Molly?"

"Sure," Jett said.

I folded my arms. "I don't believe you."

He took a sip of his drink. "I guess you don't know me as well as you thought you did, then."

I was so hungry I didn't think I could stand it. And I had only been dieting for two meals. How was I supposed to last for an entire week? Or an entire *month*? How long did it take to lose ten pounds, anyway?

"You're staring at the pizza," Jett pointed out.

"What? Oh, I was just . . . thinking. So, tell me more about your sketches."

He talked, but I didn't really hear him. I could actually *feel* a slice in my hand, taste it in my mouth. All I had to do was reach out, and—

No. I was not going to eat that pizza. I was going to stay on my diet. I knew I could. It couldn't be that big a deal to lose ten pounds. My friends did it all the time, and I was definitely more disciplined than they were.

All it would take was willpower. I was sure of it.

Chapter 136

It was three days before Thanksgiving, but I was not filled with the holiday spirit. I had gained eight more pounds in four weeks from the prednisone, and I now weighed 136 pounds.

I was fat.

Me. Fat. All because of a stupid drug for some stupid allergies. I stopped taking it and my lips and eyes swelled up. So I took it again, vowing to eat even less. Prednisone was not going to get the best of me.

It was no use. I got fatter.

Everyone knew I had gained weight, they just didn't know how much. Except my mother, who could peg my weight gain to the pound. She was appalled at how I looked and found it impossible to believe that it was just because of prednisone. So she watched every bite I put into my mouth.

She also called the allergist and demanded an appointment, which was set for the next day, two days before Thanksgiving.

Dad, away on a long business trip, called often and asked how my weight was. He talked about willpower and positive thinking. I told him I'd try harder to lose.

And I did try. Only it wasn't working. I was turning into this fat *thing*.

It was a nightmare. Most of my clothes no longer fit. Just today after school I had made a desperate, secret trip to the mall, where I'd used the credit card my grandfather had given me on my last birthday to buy exact copies of many of my clothes, in a larger size. I hoped against hope that no one would realize they were a size nine/ten instead of a five/six.

And now, as I lay at home in my bed after an hour on the treadmill, two hours of piano, and two more of homework, my stomach growled with emptiness. Breakfast and lunch had both been diet Coke and lettuce. For dinner I had eaten a small, skinless chicken breast, three tomato slices, and half a plain baked potato.

Here it was midnight, and I was *so* hungry.

But no. I wouldn't eat. Would not. Eat.

I padded to my door and opened it. Mom wasn't home yet from the after-theater dessert party she had catered that evening. Scott's room was quiet.

I could picture the inside of our refrigerator: fried chicken left over from Scott's dinner. Half of a coconut cream pie a neighbor had made. And in the freezer, ice cream. Chocolate Häagen-Dazs, with nuts. Behind it, two jumbo-sized frozen Snickers bars.

Before I knew it, my feet were carrying me downstairs, into the kitchen. My hand was in the refrigerator. I brought a fried chicken drumstick to my lips, and—

No. I wouldn't eat it. Would not. Willpower.

I put it back and turned to walk out of the kitchen.

And then someone who was not me went back to the freezer and took out both frozen Snickers bars. That someone ran with them up to her room.

Whoever she was, she didn't even turn on her light to eat. She just sat there in the dark, like some fat, feral creature of the night, cracking the frozen chocolate off with her teeth, loving the sensation of rich, sweet, comforting chocolate in her mouth, mixing with her saliva, sliding down her throat.

The candy wrappers got stuffed behind her bed.

It wasn't me.

"One hundred and thirty-six pounds," the allergist's nurse, Mrs. Rankin, said as I stood on the scale in the examining room. She wrote it on my chart. "And you're five feet, seven inches, right?"

"I know I'm too fat," I said quickly, my face burning with embarrassment. "I'm on a diet, but—"

"Honey, you're not fat," the nurse said, chuckling. "All you young girls are so obsessive about your weight. The doctor will be in to see you in a few minutes." She bustled out the door, her tree-trunk legs rubbing together as she walked.

I sat there staring at my enemy: the scale.

The only two people who didn't seem to care about my weight were Molly and Jett. When dieting didn't make me lose weight, Molly enjoyed seeing that I was, as she put it, "human after all."

As for Jett, he didn't seem to mind, either. I did, though. I felt so ugly—certain that he felt the roll of fat at my waist every time he held me, disgusted that my thighs were probably bigger than his.

I glanced over at a wall calendar from some pharmaceutical company and counted the days until New Year's Eve. In a little over a month Jett and I were going to Amber's New Year's Eve party. But I refused to shop for a new dress in a size ten.

I had to lose weight. I *had* to.

"Hello there, young lady," Dr. Fabrio said, coming into the examining room. He was tall and thin, with a long nose and bloodless lips.

"Hello."

He scanned my chart. "How's that prednisone doing for you?" he asked, sitting in the chair opposite me.

"I think I should stop taking it," I said.

"Have the rashes recurred?" he asked.

"Not really. But look at my weight."

He looked at the chart again. "You've gained . . ."

"Eighteen pounds," I filled in for him.

"Eighteen pounds," he repeated, nodding, still looking at the chart, "that's over, what . . ."

"Almost two months. You said I could retain water . . ."

"Exactly," he agreed. "But also, some people report that prednisone affects their appetite and they feel hungry all the time. That can lead to weight gain."

My hands clenched the sides of my chair, my knuckles white. *That* explained why I was starving all the time. *That* explained why I couldn't stay on a diet!

I put on my best beauty-pageant smile. "You didn't mention that to me before."

He smiled benignly at me. "Why put the idea into your pretty little head? You'd be amazed how often patients just happen to develop whatever negative side effect of a drug we tell them is a possibility."

"But the scale doesn't lie," I said timidly.

He sighed and rubbed his chin. "No, it doesn't. And I have to say this is a fairly large weight gain in a short period of time, even for someone on prednisone. But your allergies are under control now, and it should taper off."

I forced my clenched fists under my legs so he wouldn't see them. I was careful to keep my voice sweet. "Excuse me, Doctor, but I'm kind of concerned that I'm getting fat."

"Ms. Ardeche, I would not call one hundred thirty-six pounds on a healthy, five-foot-seven-inch teenager fat."

"You don't understand," I said slowly. "None of my clothes fit. Everyone in my family is thin."

"Did a parent come with you today?" Dr. Fabrio asked.

"My mother. She's very upset about this."

What I didn't add was that it had been everything I could do to keep her out of the examining room.

Dr. Fabrio tapped his finger against his lips. "How are things at home for you, Lara?"

"Fine," I replied.

"No problems?"

"None."

"Getting along okay at school?"

"I was homecoming queen."

59

He tapped my chart against his knee again. "Family pressure, urticaria, origin unknown, weight gain, and you seem very tense."

I lifted my hand to smooth my hair and then put both my hands back in my lap, one on top of the other, in perfect, ladylike pageant form.

"Doctor, I appreciate your concern." I smiled at him. "But you see, I'm supposed to compete in the Miss Teen Tennessee pageant early next year. At this weight, I might as well not even enter."

"See if you can follow me here, Lara," Dr. Fabrio said. "I think what is happening is that you are blaming the reaction to the problem on your stress, rather than blaming the problem itself."

I looked at him blankly.

"In other words, the rashes, the weight gain, are symptoms of something that is bothering you."

Smile. "You're saying this is all in my head?"

"Look, Lara, it's nothing to be ashamed of. The teen years are very, very tough." He rubbed his chin again. "I'd like to put you on Doxepin—it's an antidepressant with strong antihistamine effects. You'll take two at night before you go to sleep."

"And I can stop the prednisone?" I asked eagerly.

"Slowly," Dr. Fabrio cautioned. "Take half a pill less every two days until you stop, is that clear?"

"The Doxepin won't make me gain weight?"

"That is not a known side effect of this drug."

"Thank you, thank you, that's wonderful," I said happily. "I'm so relieved."

He patted my hand. "I hope Doxepin is helpful. But you might want to consider some kind of counseling to help you with whatever is stressing you out." He stood up. "There's no shame in it. It can be very beneficial."

He scribbled out a prescription for the new drug, and I clutched it in my hands like a lifeline as I rushed into the waiting room. Now it all made sense. I wasn't crazy. It was the *prednisone* that was making me so hungry. But now that I could stop taking it, I would lose the eighteen pounds quickly and I could pretend this whole, awful experience had never happened to me.

"What did he say?" my mother demanded, standing up.

"No more prednisone!" I cried happily, hugging her.

"Oh, honey, that's great," my mother said, hugging me back. "What a nightmare this has been, huh?" She went to the front desk and gave them her medical insurance card.

"Mom, do you think I'm stressed out?"

"Now, that's ridiculous," my mother said.

"Do you think I need counseling?"

"You?" She laughed.

"That's what I thought." I smiled. "Let's just go fill this prescription."

We bundled into our coats—the weather had turned chilly—and, our arms around each other's waists, headed out of the doctor's office.

"Is it my imagination, or was that the worst movie I ever saw?" I asked Jett as we left the movie theater that evening.

"Worse than that, even," Jett joked as he held the door open for me.

"Snow!" I sang out. While we had been suffering through a terrible movie, it had started to flurry. I lifted my face to it and stuck out my tongue.

"Let's go get ice cream," Jett suggested, pulling me toward the Baskin-Robbins at the end of the strip mall.

"I don't need ice cream," I told him.

"Hey, everyone needs ice cream." He kissed my cheek.

Baskin-Robbins was already crowded with other loud moviegoers. "What do you want?" Jett asked, getting in line.

I smiled at him. "Nothing, and don't try to talk me out of it."

He turned and put his arms around my waist. At first I flinched, sure he felt the circle of fat at my midriff. But now that I knew I could throw out the prednisone and what he felt was truly temporary, I relaxed in his embrace.

"So, is it my imagination, or are you happier tonight than you've been in a while?"

He was so amazing, so sensitive to my moods. Yes, I wanted to tell him, I am happy! I don't have to take prednisone anymore. I'm going to lose all the weight I gained. The nightmare is over!

But I didn't say any of that. I just smiled, said, "You're right," in what I hoped was a provocative, mysterious way, and kissed him lightly on the lips.

"Well, good, whatever it is." He gently pushed a lock of hair off my face. "You look really beautiful tonight."

"I do?"

"Yeah. Incandescent. Lit from within."

"Hey, Lara," Jennie Smith called, entering the store. She had on a short wrap coat, and even under tights, her legs looked bony. She was so skinny. Her date, a tall, nice-looking guy I'd never seen before, hung back by the door talking to another guy.

"Oh, hi," I said. "Did you just go to the movies?"

"We saw the new Brad Pitt thing," she said. She turned and waved to her date, then turned back to us. "He goes to Father Ryan," she explained, mentioning a private school not far from our high school. "Do you think he's cute?"

"Sure," I said.

"He's okay." She shrugged. "I'm trying to decide if I should bring him to Amber's party." She put her hands on her stomach. "I don't know what I'm doing in Baskin-Robbins. I am so *fat*. Besides, this stuff is poison. Dairy and fat—ugh."

"Ugh," Jett echoed, trying to keep a straight face.

Jennie looked me over with X-ray vision. "*You're* not eating *ice cream,* are you, Lara?"

"No, of course not," I assured her.

"I *never* eat ice cream. I guess I'll get a diet Coke and watch Taylor eat. Well, see y'all."

"That girl is a piece of work," Jett said ruefully.

"I don't blame her for wanting to stay thin," I said.

Jett turned and put his arms around me again. "Hey, how about if we blow this off and go back to my house? My parents are in New York, meeting with my mom's agent."

Alone with Jett. It sounded blissful. Exciting. And dangerous. What if he wanted to . . . and was I ready to . . . ?

"Okay," I said, "but not . . . I mean . . ."

He cupped my chin in his hand, his eyes searching mine. "Lara, there's plenty of time for that."

63

"There is?"

"When we're ready, we're ready. It doesn't have to be now. What I meant was that I want to draw you."

Draw me. He wanted to be alone with me to *draw* me.

"I'd love that," I whispered, nuzzling against his chest. I felt all these different things: relief, excitement, disappointment.

He hadn't asked to draw me since that very first night on the beach. But now I looked "incandescent." Beautiful. All because my anxiety about my weight was gone.

We slowly drove back to Jett's house, careful on the slippery roads as the snow changed over to sleet. It was a ranch house, set far back on a wooded lot. It was nice, though it wasn't nearly as large as my house.

We went into the family room. In the corner was a beautiful old upright piano. On the wall above it were framed photos of sculptures Jett's mom had done for various corporate art collections.

"Hey, play something," Jett said, cocking his head toward the piano. "I love to listen to you play."

Jett sat on the couch and I went over to the piano and got comfortable. I began to play the piece I'd be playing for my upcoming recital, Chopin's Sonata in C minor. I closed my eyes and the music washed over me, transporting me to some timeless place of perfect grace, beauty, love.

"I know how you feel," Jett said quietly.

I opened my eyes. He was sitting next to me on the piano bench.

"I feel that way when I'm painting sometimes." His hand gently touched my cheek. "Come on, there's something I want you to see."

Although I had been to Jett's house before, I'd only been in the kitchen, dining room, and family room. Now Jett led me by the hand into the living room.

It didn't have the sterile perfection of our white-on-white living room—instead it had more color and emotion. The couch, deep midnight-blue velvet with stripes of blue satin, was set on a jewel-toned Oriental carpet. Incredible art hung on the walls.

"The art," I said in an awe-filled voice, looking around at the walls.

"By my mom's friends," Jett said. "But this is what I really wanted you to see."

He led me to the far corner, where a sculpture sat on a black marble pedestal, illuminated by a floodlight recessed into the ceiling. It was a nude young woman on her knees, head thrown back, hands raised to the sky. The engraved copper plate on the pedestal read THINGS I CANNOT CHANGE.

"This is so beautiful," I told Jett, barely touching the cool marble with one finger.

"It's my favorite piece of Mom's," Jett said. "It's just . . . it's all feeling. Like when you play the piano."

He understood. I reached up and kissed him. He kissed me back.

"What's it like, having your mom be so famous?"

He shrugged. "She had a piece in the Museum of Modern Art by the time I was two, so I have no basis of comparison." He sat on the sofa.

"What do you think it means, 'Things I Cannot Change'?"

He thought a moment. "That everything isn't in our control, even though we want it to be."

I was still standing by the sculpture. "You think she's happy or angry or what?"

"I say both," he decided. "Happy to believe in a power greater than she is, and angry that she has to surrender to it."

I sat down next to Jett. "I believe we create our own destiny."

"Yeah, but there's a lot we just don't control."

"A lot of times that's just an excuse," I said firmly.

"But a lot of times it isn't." Jett sipped his Coke and lifted a lock of my hair. "Sometimes . . ."

"What?"

"Sometimes I wish I were a musician," he mused. "Or—I don't know—a photographer. Anything but an artist."

"Because you think people will compare you to your mom?"

"No, because I *know* people will compare me to my mom." He sighed. "Hey, how about if I build a fire?"

"That'd be great. I can never get a fire started."

"Don't be impressed—my parents bought these fake cheater logs," he explained as he knelt in front of the fireplace and held a match to the synthetic log. The flame took. He got up and turned out the light, then came back to me on the couch.

"Nice," I said. I leaned my head against his shoulder, his arm around me. Slowly he turned toward me, holding my hair away from my face. He looked so beautiful in the firelight.

"I think about going to Europe, you know?" he confessed. "To art school? And changing my name, just so no one will know I'm her son."

I didn't say a word.

"Sometimes I think that's all I'll ever be—famous artist Anastasia Anston's son."

"No," I said firmly. "Someday she'll be famous artist Jett Anston's mother."

And then he kissed me, softly at first, and then more passionately.

"Jett, I—I . . . ," I said breathlessly.

"What?"

I didn't know what to say. I want us to make love? I *don't* want us to make love?

"The light on your skin is so beautiful," Jett said. He got up from the couch. "I'll be right back."

I sat there, panicked. Please, God, I thought, don't let him come back in here naked. No, he would never do that. He could never—

His *sketchpad*. He came back in with his *sketchpad*.

I had totally forgotten that was why we were supposed to be there.

Without a word he stretched one hand out to me, and I took it. He lifted me off the couch. And that's when he said it.

"Take off your clothes," he whispered.

"What?"

"So I can draw you."

"Not *naked*!"

"But, Lara, you're so beautiful—"

Not anymore! Not with eighteen pounds of hideous fat on my body! Why, oh why, couldn't this moment have come just a few weeks later, when I would be thin again?

"I am *not* taking off my clothes," I said firmly, crossing my arms over my breasts.

He reached out for me. "Look, if you think this is some sophomoric bid to get your clothes off—"

"Forget it." I moved away from him.

"Okay, okay," he said, holding his hands up.

"Just forget it," I repeated, my arms still wrapped around my body.

"Look, I said okay." His voice had an edge to it.

I sat back down on the couch. He sat next to me.

"I'll draw your portrait. Neck up."

The mood was completely broken.

"Fine," I said.

I sat there and he drew me, and the drawing was good and we pretended everything was fine, only it wasn't.

I had ruined everything.

As he drove me home I started to open my mouth a dozen times, to tell him that I felt self-conscious because my medication had made me gain so much weight. To tell him that I was about to change medications, and that soon all the extra weight would be gone and everything would be normal again, and that one day I would want him to see me naked and beautiful, and that this was just temporary.

But I couldn't. I just couldn't. So I didn't say anything at all.

I just sat there like an idiot, clutching my purse, which had my Doxepin in it. Soon that same Doxepin would change everything and I'd be restored to the real me, and then Jett would understand.

And maybe, after I was thin again, I'd even create a classical piece on the piano, kind of an answer song to Jett's mom's sculpture, and I'd tell Jett the truth in the only way I could. The song would have no words, only feelings that I knew to be true.

I would call it "Things I Can Change."

*T*wo weeks later I was off prednisone, and the Doxepin was completely controlling my allergies. Best of all, I'd lost five pounds. The beginning strains of my answer melody rang in my head. I really *could* change things.

I was on my way back to being me.

chapter 158

I stared at my dinner plate.

One half piece of plain bread. One half cup of fat-free cottage cheese. A colorful medley of raw vegetables. One small orange.

This was my Thursday night dinner on the eight-hundred-calories-a-day diet, handwritten by my mother, now posted on the refrigerator. I'd been on it for a week.

The reason I was limited to eight hundred calories was simple. It was two days before Valentine's Day now. Since Thanksgiving I had gained another twenty-two pounds. If you included the five pounds I'd temporarily lost when I switched from prednisone to Doxepin, I had actually gained twenty-*seven* pounds.

I weighed 158 pounds. God, I could hardly bring myself to *think* the number.

I looked over at Scott's dinner. Meatloaf. Mashed potatoes swimming in gravy. Buttered biscuits.

The nightmare of the past ten weeks washed over me again, and I closed my eyes. I had been so hopeful, so full of resolve when I'd weaned myself off prednisone and had success with Doxepin.

Then I'd started gaining again.

We called Dr. Fabrio in a panic. He said the prednisone would take some time to leave my system, and I needed to be patient.

My mother didn't want us to be patient. She took me to the top diet guru in Nashville, who put me on a twelve-hundred-calorie-a-day diet, and I stuck to it, too. Okay, I cheated now and then when I got so hungry I couldn't stand it, but that wasn't enough to make me actually gain weight, was it? When I was working out five days a week?

And yet I got fatter. And fatter. After three weeks we called Dr. Fabrio again. He said that at this point my allergy drugs had nothing to do with my weight, and he urged me to seek counseling for my emotional problems. My mother told him that was absurd. So with great reluctance, he referred us to an endocrinologist—a specialist who could see if my weight gain had a metabolic cause.

My mother called the endocrinologist, Dr. Laverly, immediately, but she had absolutely no openings available until mid-February. We took the first appointment we could.

I continued to gain. My mother cried and took me back to the diet guru. She begged him to put me on some new wonder drug. He refused. He said I was too young and not overweight enough for him to even consider prescribing drugs for me. Then he lectured me about feeding emotional hunger with food, while Mom nodded in agreement.

I gained more weight. Photos of the thin me mocked me. I mourned for my old self the way you mourn for a lost loved one. And sometimes, when I got really sad, I ate. And then I'd hate myself. Which made me want to eat even more, just to numb the pain.

With every pound I gained, I was filled with an ever growing, impotent rage. Some monster was swelling up inside me, making me get fatter and fatter. I had to force myself to be nice, sweet, good Lara, when actually I felt like this ugly, angry, hideous monster-Lara.

I didn't even know who I was anymore.

At the beginning of February I'd gotten in to see the endocrinologist. Someone had canceled, and I was moved up. Mom came along, though it was clear she didn't believe there was anything wrong with me.

Dr. Laverly examined me and asked a million questions while her nurse took gallons of my blood. Yes, she was concerned that I'd gained forty pounds but said that the odds of its having a biological cause were very small. In any case, she promised I would have the test results the following Friday.

I called Dr. Laverly that Friday, my heart pounding, but her nurse said that someone in her family had died, and she'd had to go out of town, and that it might be the following Saturday before we would hear from her.

The following Saturday. More than a week more to wait. The days themselves felt fat and heavy—time crawled by. The worst thing was, I didn't know what I'd do if Dr. Laverly couldn't help me. Not only was I getting fatter—I was also losing my mind.

I opened my eyes and the tasteless, meager dinner still confronted me. I pushed the food—the enemy—away and stood up.

"I'm not really hungry," I lied. "I think I'll just go work out."

"That's the spirit, honey," my mother encouraged. "Eating when you're not hungry is a trap."

I went into our gym and tried to avoid my reflection in the floor-length mirror. I got on the treadmill and walked quickly, then raised the speed until I was running. I ran until I felt like throwing up.

I had done that instead of eating dinner for the past three days. In school I felt faint. I couldn't concentrate. I got a C+ on a history test. But as long as I didn't eat, I didn't care.

I walked over to the scale in the gym and stepped on it. 159. I had gained another pound.

I stood there, shaking with impotent rage.

"Honey?"

It was my mother. She stood in the doorway of the gym, looking impossibly thin.

"Did you lose?" she asked anxiously.

I didn't answer her. I just stepped off the scale.

"Would you like some raw vegetables for a snack?"

I couldn't speak. I felt like putting my fist through the raw vegetables, the wall, my mother.

That night I lay in bed in the dark and promised myself I would not give in. But the other me, the crazy, out-of-control me, whispered seductively in my ear. *What's the use? You starve yourself and gain weight anyway. Just go eat. Just go do it.*

I did it. I snuck downstairs and, standing in front of the refrigerator, stuffed my face with every leftover I could find, all the while keeping my ears open for any sound. If someone came, I would throw the food into the sink and pretend I'd been getting a glass of skim milk.

No one came.

I went back to bed, my stomach now distended, groaning.

I was disgusted with myself. Action. I needed to take action. I rolled off the bed, ran into my bathroom, and knelt in front of the toilet. I put two fingers down my throat and tried my best to make myself throw up. I tried and tried. But I couldn't do it.

So I laid my head down on the toilet seat and silently cried.

"Which one?" My mother held two dresses up to herself, one in each of her arms.

One was long, slinky, and silver, with sheer chiffon inserts from the neck to the cleavage. The other was short, strapless, and black.

It was Valentine's Day, and my family was throwing its annual Valentine's Day party. My friends and I would get dressed to the max. It was always a blast, and this year would be no different.

Except for the fact that I didn't plan to attend.

Not that I had mentioned this yet to anybody. But there was no way I was going to be there, with everyone looking at me, whispering behind their hands, their eyes full of pity.

It was bad enough that everyone at school had watched me blimp up to 159 pounds. Now I was supposed to greet my parents' friends, many of whom had not seen me since last year, and stand there while their faces went from shock, to pity, and then to some mask of false gaiety while they tried to cover up what they really felt: disgust.

And who could blame them? I *was* disgusting.

I stared at the row of pageant trophies on my dresser, and at the photo of me and Jett from homecoming, which I had stuck into the edge of my mirror. I felt tears coming to my eyes again. I was getting used to them.

"Honey?" Mom asked. "Maybe I should wear silver, and you can wear black. Black is very slimming."

I wanted to kill her. But of course she hadn't done anything. It wasn't her fault if I was an out-of-control disgusting fat pig.

"Okay, fine, I'll wear black," I told her.

She sat down next to me. "I want you to know I'm with you a thousand percent, honey," she said quietly. "It's the new year, and a new start, right?"

I nodded dully.

"First, we have got to acknowledge that there's a problem, which we do, right?"

Not we, I wanted to scream. *Me. You still wear a size six. You still have a twenty-five-inch waist.*

"Maybe Dr. Laverly will find something," I said.

Mom sighed. "Maybe."

I rubbed my temples. "Mom, I'm really not feeling well. I might just stay upstairs tonight—"

"Lara, you can't run away from your problems," my mother said. She snapped her fingers. "I know! Tomorrow we'll go register you for Jenny Craig. And we'll simply find a doctor who will put you on diet drugs. That—"

"Please, Mom," I said, trying to steady my voice. "I'm not going to Jenny Craig. And I'm not taking drugs, either. Those things are for fat failures with no willpower."

Mom's silence said it all.

I was the fat failure.

She put her arm around me. "Come on, honey. We can lick this together. Where's the girl who accomplishes anything she puts her mind to, huh?"

Mom went to my closet, took out my new black dress, a forgiving size twelve, and laid it on the bed.

"What did Dad say to you?" I asked, my voice tight.

My father had just returned that morning from a weeklong trip to New York. He had walked into the house, his usual perfect-looking self, and come into the kitchen to see me there, pouring coffee. I had on my long, oversized sleeping T-shirt. I saw the look of disgust in his eyes as he scanned my porky body.

"Hi," he'd said. He didn't rush over to hug me.

"Hi."

"Just having coffee?" he had asked.

"Yeah."

"Well, good. How's the diet going?"

I felt like throwing up.

"I'm working really hard at it, Daddy."

"Sweetheart? Is that you?" Mom had flown into the kitchen and wrapped her sinewy arms around his neck. She had on a pink leotard and black bike shorts. She was so thin. "Ooo, I missed you!" she'd squealed.

He'd given her a perfunctory kiss. "I'm beat. I'm just going to run upstairs and shower."

That was the last I'd seen of him all day. I'd stayed in my room. He never came to see me. But I knew that behind closed doors my parents had to be talking about their fat failure of a daughter.

"All he said was that he's concerned," Mom said. She hesitated, her nervous fingers plucking at my quilt. "Is this about me, Lara? Something I did?"

I felt such rage. And I felt so guilty that I felt it.

"No, Mom. You're wonderful. Don't blame yourself."

"Something I didn't do, then? You have so much going for you. I just don't understand! You have parents who love you; we've never deprived you of anything, have we?"

I didn't reply. The monster was choking me.

"I just can't stand to see you ruining your life like this!" she exclaimed. "You're lucky that Jett has stuck by you. Do you think your father would still be with me if I had let myself go like you have?"

Red-hot fury filled me, blowing me up with a burning acid. I stuffed the feeling down, down, until I could breathe again without breathing fire. Then I turned away from her.

I heard her stride out of my room.

I lay on my bed and stared at the ceiling.

"Hi," Scott said from the doorway.

My eyes were still on the ceiling, my arm over my forehead. "Go away."

He came in instead. "So, this party thing tonight is pretty lame, huh?"

"Scott, I'm really not in the mood, okay?"

I felt the bed sag from his weight as he sat next to me. He threw his Hacky Sack in the air and caught it.

"Scott, please."

"I kinda wanted to talk to you," he mumbled.

I rolled over onto my hip so I could see him. "What?"

The Hacky Sack went into the air again. "Well, I guess you're kinda, like, basically miserable."

"Good guess," I replied.

"Me too, a lot of the time," he said. He threw the Hacky Sack again. "Well, see, I know you've, like, gained weight . . ."

"The whole world knows I've gained weight, okay?"

He shrugged. "But what I wanted to say is, well, it's not important."

I got up on one elbow. "It's not *important*?"

Scott pulled at his T-shirt hem, stretching the shirt out even bigger. "Everyone in this family is, like, so into looks all the time. I always thought those pageant things you did were so stupid, you know? It's just . . . it's lame."

"Well, lucky you, you won't be bothered by pageants for a long time," I said bitterly.

Mrs. Armstrong had called me a few weeks earlier, because I hadn't gotten my application in for Miss Teen Tennessee. I told her I had decided not to enter. She refused to take no for an answer—after all, she had already invested years in grooming me—and asked if she could come over so that we could discuss it. I told her I had infectious mononucleosis. And that I was giving up pageants. And dedicating my life to piano.

Ha. I had stopped taking piano lessons in December and dropped out of the winter recital.

Scott stood up. "Look, it's not like you're some big fat freak, you know. I mean, you don't look *that* bad. That's all I wanted to say." He headed for the door and practically collided with Molly.

"Whoa, traffic cop needed at this intersection," she

said, dodging around him. She bounded in and plopped down next to me, dropping her overnight case on the rug. "So, what did the doctor say?"

Molly knew all about Dr. Laverly. What she didn't know was how much I really weighed. I couldn't bring myself to tell her. Because now I weighed more than she did.

"She hasn't called me yet."

"She's gonna have the answer, I know it," Molly said.

"You think?" I rolled onto my stomach.

"Absolutely." She got up off the bed and stripped off her T-shirt. "I'm taking a shower, okay? Our water heater broke again."

"Whatever," I said, too depressed to move.

She dropped her jeans and padded into my bathroom in her underwear, closing the door behind her. I scooched over to the end of the bed and looked at her jeans, lying there in a heap.

I got up, pulled the extra-long T-shirt I had been wearing over my head, and tried on Molly's size thirteen/fourteen jeans from The Gap. She'd made me promise never to tell anyone she wore such a huge size.

They fit.

I had been living in stretch leggings and baggy sweats. I hadn't worn my jeans in weeks—in fact, I had pushed them all to the back of my closet. I didn't want to know.

Now I knew. And I wanted to die.

The phone on my nightstand jangled and I snatched it up.

"Hello?"

"Lara? This is Dr. Laverly."

"Yes." I sat on the edge of my bed.

"Are your parents there?"

"No," I lied.

"Well, have one of them call me on Monday. In any case, I've got the results back from the tests we did on you, and it's good news."

Hope surged through me. "You found something?"

"I mean your tests were all negative. You check out fine."

"But . . . But that can't be right," I sputtered.

"Well, there is always a possibility of lab error," the doctor said, "and we could repeat them. But I suggest you try a controlled eating plan and see how you do."

I clutched the phone so hard that my knuckles turned white. Had she forgotten everything I had told her in her office? "But I've been dieting for months," I reminded her, trying not to cry. "I still keep gaining."

"Often people eat a lot more than they realize," the doctor said. "Now, a food diary would—"

"I already *did* that," I told her. "I'm seeing a diet specialist. I've done *everything*."

"Well, it's possible there's something that just didn't show up on the tests. I'm afraid nothing is one hundred percent accurate."

"So you'll do them again?"

"We could," the doctor said. "But my best advice right now is that you continue with your diet specialist. And perhaps look into some counseling. Some teenagers find that—"

I hung up on her.

Right after I did it, I stared at the phone, aghast. I had never hung up on anyone in my life. No pageant winner would ever, *ever* do such a thing. But monster-Lara would. I could taste the triumph of it, like bittersweet chocolate.

I took off Molly's jeans before she came out of the bathroom. I pretended Dr. Laverly hadn't called. I forced my heart to play dead. I got dressed for the party, and I vowed to myself that no one was going to see me cry.

"Pretty out there, huh?" Jett said, coming up behind me.

I was standing at the picture window in the living room, looking out at the snow, which had been falling for the last two hours.

"Very," I agreed.

It was near ten o'clock, and the party was in full swing. About twenty of my friends were there, dancing, eating, having fun. I had told all my girlfriends that my weight gain was some kind of thyroid thing and they all pretended to believe me, but I knew they really didn't. I could feel things changing. A homecoming queen does not wear a tight size twelve.

Over in the corner I saw Amber whispering with Lisa, and then they both looked over at me. I just looked away.

"Want to dance?" Jett slid his arms around me.

"I don't really feel like it."

"Want me to get you something to eat?" he asked.

"Eating is the last thing I need to do, Jett."

"Drink, then?"

"I've had about six diet Cokes already, but thanks."

"Wow, some bash," Molly said, walking over to us, eating a petit four. "I love the decorations!"

The living room was lit with tiny pink lights. Red and pink Cupids were suspended from the ceiling by wires so thin that the Cupids appeared to be flying.

"Where's Andy?" I asked her.

"Upstairs playing Nintendo and listening to Jerry Garcia with your little brother and the Junior Deadhead Society. Would you please tell me why I go out with him?"

" 'Cuz you love him," Jett pointed out.

"Nah, I think he's just a habit—like brushing my teeth."

Jennie Smith waved from across the living room and came over to us. She had on a tiny tangerine-colored satin minidress that would have looked like a washcloth on me.

"Jett, you're going to dance with me, aren't you?" she asked prettily, putting her arm through his.

"Not right now," he replied.

"I'll get you yet," she said playfully; then she air-kissed my cheek. "Did I tell you how much I love your dress, Lara? Where did you get it?"

"The Paris Shoppe."

"Really? Well, it's just so cute. It's really flattering, you know, cut full in the hips like that."

My hands clenched into fists. "Thanks," I said.

"I swear, I am so *stuffed*! I ate *three* of those tiny seafood tarts. They were so good I couldn't help myself!"

I smiled at her.

"You really have to try them, Lara. In fact, be a sweetheart and eat them all so I won't be tempted." She threw her head back and laughed. "Great party, honey!" She drifted back to her date, the guy from Father Ryan.

"Let's beat her up," Molly suggested. "Wait, better yet, let's tie her down and force-feed her."

Jett laughed. I managed a grin.

Molly hugged me and waltzed away.

"What a bitch, gloating over the fact that you've gained weight," Jett said.

"Everyone gloats about it," I said. "The only difference is that Jennie gloats to my face."

Jett shook his head. "That isn't true. Some people don't care. Like Molly. Like me. Like—"

"How's my big, beautiful doll?" my grandfather asked, his voice booming. He came over and gave me a bear hug. My mother's father was a big man, tall and barrel-chested. Everything about him was outsized—shoulders, feet, belly, cigars. Even his generosity. Although we never talked about it, it was his money that allowed our family to live in the style to which we had become accustomed.

"I'm fine, Grandpa."

"Helluva party, huh, sweetheart?"

"It always is," I said, trying to sound cheerful.

"Better be, cost me a bundle!" Grandpa said. "Hey, did you try that smoked salmon? It's damned good!"

"I'm on a diet, Grandpa."

"Coulda fooled me, from the looks of ya!" he boomed. Then he hugged me. "Aw, I'm just kiddin', kitten. Now there's just more of you to love!" He hugged me again, winked at Jett, and went off to dance with Grandma, a tiny woman who lived in my grandfather's oversized shadow.

How could he say that in front of Jett? I fought back tears of embarrassment. But I would not cry. I would not.

"Lara?" Someone tapped me on the shoulder. It was Mrs. Armstrong, my beauty pageant coordinator.

"What are you doing here?" I blurted out.

83

Her eyes took in the horror that was me. "Your mother was kind enough to invite me." She reached out and gently touched my arm. "Sweetheart, what happened to you?"

I stumbled away from her, from Jett, from everyone. I ran upstairs to my bedroom. I could hide in my bathroom and cry where no one could see.

A lot of coats were piled on my bed, and someone's fur had fallen to the floor. As I went to pick it up, I heard voices in my bathroom. The door was open a crack and I could see the edge of a silver dress I recognized, and one slender leg. I knelt behind the pile of coats and peeked out.

"I just couldn't believe it when I saw her!" exclaimed the woman in the bathroom with my mother. "How could you let it happen, Carol?"

I knew the voice. It was my mom's friend Elaine Hirschbaum, who had moved to Nashville from Los Angeles with her doctor husband three years before.

"What am I supposed to do, lock up all the food in the house?" my mother's voice replied.

"You know it can't be easy for her, having you as a mother," Elaine said.

"I happen to be a very good mother—"

"Oh, I know that," Elaine said. "I just meant I think she feels competitive with you, that's all."

"Look, this is not my fault—"

"No need to get so defensive, Carol," Elaine said.

"I just don't know what to do with her anymore!" my mother moaned.

I saw the silver skirt and the leg move, and now I could see my mother's cheek resting on Elaine's shoulder. They were hugging.

"Hey, now, don't get so down about it. At least it's not you who got fat, huh?" Elaine said.

My mother laughed through her tears. "God, Jimbo would kill me."

"How are things with you two?"

"Great!"

"Well, thank God for that, anyway," Elaine said. Her head turned so that she was facing the mirror. "This lighting makes me look like death. I look like I'm carrying my luggage under my eyes. Getting old is the pits, Carol. But at least I'm not fat."

"Maybe I need to get Lara some counseling," my mother said nervously.

"Maybe?" Elaine echoed dryly.

"Jimbo doesn't believe in it," my mother explained.

"Well, honey, he told you he doesn't believe in having affairs, either, but that didn't stop him from having one, did it?"

"That's just a vicious rumor, Elaine."

They started out of the bathroom, and I fled. It was all just too horrible. I ran down the back stairs, away from everyone and everything. I wanted to run into the snow and disappear. I wanted to go to sleep and never wake up.

I stood in the backyard, the snow swirling around me, and I didn't feel a thing. How could I? Everyone was shocked at how I looked. My mother had invited Mrs. Armstrong to the party to try to shame me into losing weight. People were spreading lies about my father. I hated myself and I hated my life.

"Hey."

It was Jett. He put his leather motorcycle jacket around my shoulders and turned me to face him.

"I saw you come outside," he told me. I began to

shiver and he slipped my arms into his jacket, then cupped my freezing hands in his.

"I just heard . . . something terrible," I managed to get out, my teeth chattering.

"What?"

I couldn't tell him. It seemed so disloyal. Besides, it couldn't possibly be true.

And then something flashed in my brain. Me, at about age eight, lying in my bed, late at night. Mom and Dad fighting in their room—loud, scary voices, vicious words, something about Grandpa's money. *Bitch,* he had called her. *Bitch.* Then she yelled that he would never be half the man her father was, and then there was the sound of a slap. And Mom was crying. *Stop,* I'd wanted to scream at them. *Stop.* But I didn't scream. I just put my hands over my ears and I sang to myself and pretended I was winning Miss America and my parents were in the audience and they were so happy.

The next morning, at breakfast, no one had said anything. Mom and Dad had smiled at each other. Everyone had just pretended it had never happened. Including me.

"Lara?" Jett asked.

I blinked. There was snow on my eyelashes. "I can't tell you." I gulped hard as he held me. "You can hardly get your arms around me anymore."

"I can get my arms around you fine," he assured me. He lifted my chin and kissed me softly. "You're so hard on yourself, Lara. You need to quit beating yourself up."

"I just want my life back," I said tearfully.

"Some things change," Jett said, looking into my eyes. "And some things don't. Like how I feel about you. That hasn't changed."

"But—"

"It hasn't changed," he said firmly, kissing me again.

The snow fell on us, and I clung to him. Hanging on to Jett was the only thing that seemed to make any sense. Thank God he still loved me.

Thank God.

Chapter 180

ara?"

I put down the magazine I'd been pretending to read and stood up, all 180 pounds of me. "Yes."

"I'm Karen DeBarge. Come on in."

I didn't want to "come on in." I wanted to scream or spew obscenities or slap her skinny, patronizing face. I wanted to act like the horrible monster that I felt everyone saw when they looked at me.

But that would be crazy. Lara Ardeche was sweet and polite, a pageant winner everyone admired. And she did not weigh, dear God, 180 pounds.

So, clearly I really had turned into someone else, morphed into some hideous, fat monster-creature, full of sizzling rage.

I held the monster at bay and followed Karen DeBarge into her office.

She was in her forties, very thin, wearing a bright red suit with a conservative skirt that fell just below her knees. The ugly blouse she wore under her suit jacket had little cherries parading all over it. Her hair was sort of no-colored, and short. So were her nails. She was a bone-thin total stranger with no taste in clothing, and I was supposed to bare my soul to her, tell her the most intimate details of my fat, messed-up life.

It was April first. It had to be an April Fools' joke.

"Please, make yourself comfortable," she said, waving me toward a tweed couch. She sat opposite me in a hard-backed chair. On the wall above her was a framed photo of her, some thin guy with an overbite, and their two thin, horsey-looking children already in need of ortho-dontia. Next to that was a framed diploma from Trevecca Nazarene College's graduate school of counseling, and a certificate from the State of Tennessee.

"Are you comfortable?" she asked.

No.

I nodded.

"Good. And please, call me Karen. I can call you Lara?"

I nodded again.

"This will just be a brief get-acquainted meeting, and then you can decide if you'd like to pursue this or not, okay?"

I gave my patented nod again.

"Your mother mentioned that you've been having some problems you might want to discuss. But I'd like to hear from you why you're here."

I felt strangled by the rapid pounding of my heart.

"I've . . . gained a lot of weight," I managed to choke out.

She nodded.

"I used to weigh one hundred eighteen pounds. I'd win beauty pageants. I was homecoming queen."

She nodded again, waiting.

"Well, look at me!" I blurted out. "I'm some kind of fat freak now!"

"Is that how you think of yourself?"

No, I think I'm walking perfection.

I took a deep breath, folded my hands prettily in my lap, and smiled at Karen's skinny face. "I work out every single day," I explained. "My mother found a doctor who put me on a diet drug. Even though I hardly ate, I gained weight, plus it made my heart race. Then he tried a different drug. It made me sick, but I would have stayed on it anyway if I had lost even a little weight. I didn't. I just gained more. I've tried everything and I've had all these tests. Nothing works."

"How are you doing in school?" she asked, changing subjects.

"I get practically straight A's."

She nodded. "Homecoming queen and straight A's. You must be a very hard worker."

"I like to do my best," I replied.

She nodded again. "Sometimes it's a lot of pressure to do your best all the time. How are things for you at home?"

They suck. My parents are ashamed of me.

"Just fine," I said.

"Tell me about your family," she suggested.

I ran through the basic family unit quickly. "And my parents are really wonderful. Perfect."

"Perfect?" Karen echoed.

"And my mom is gorgeous. And thin."

"How do you feel about that?"

I swallowed the monster feelings of rage and tried to answer her question. "I used to always think it was great. Everyone said I looked just like her."

"And now?"

"And now . . . I don't look like her anymore."

"How do you feel about that?" she asked again.

"How do you *think* I feel?" I replied, my voice rising. "That is a *stupid* question!"

"I sense you're feeling some anger," Karen said.

Well, aren't you a rocket scientist.

I took a deep breath. I smiled. Control. "Excuse me. What I meant was that the answer to that is obvious."

Karen leaned toward me. "Sometimes our own motivations are hard for us to see." She slid one thin leg over the other. My legs didn't do that anymore. My thighs rubbed when I walked. I hated her and her thin thighs.

"Let's talk about your dad a little. How do you feel about him?"

He's so disappointed in me.

"He's great."

"What is his reaction to your gaining weight?"

He hates me. He doesn't even call me princess anymore.

"He encourages me to lose," I recited dutifully.

"He'd like to see you thinner?"

No, you bony twit, he'd like to see me fatter.

"Yes," I said sweetly. "Of course. He loves me."

"And how do your parents get along with each other?"

None of your business.

"Perfectly."

"Perfectly?"

"That's what I just said. Perfectly."

Karen nodded. I could tell she didn't believe me. She was so sure she knew better.

"Perfect parents, perfect life," Karen mused. "It's not uncommon for perfectionistic, overachieving young women who feel great pressure to succeed, to develop eating disorders."

"But I don't think I have an eating disorder. I mean, I don't eat that much," I mumbled guiltily. "I think there's something wrong with me—physically, I mean."

"Your mom mentioned that you'd seen a number of doctors, and you had a battery of tests done to see if there was any metabolic cause for your weight gain," Karen said. "What were the results?"

Yeah, like you don't know.

"They were negative," I admitted. "But . . . the doctors could have been wrong. Couldn't they?"

"It's possible," Karen said.

You don't believe me. Humor the fat girl.

"You're feeling . . . ?"

I stared at her blankly.

"Angry with me for asking you these questions?" Karen prompted me.

"No," I said. My smile didn't crack.

"You're not angry?"

"No."

"Really? Even though you've gained so much weight?"

I wanted to smack that supercilious look off her skinny face. I couldn't take it one more minute. I stood up. The monster had finally gotten loose.

"Okay, I'm angry!" I yelled, looming over her. "Now that's a big duh, huh? You sit there, all smug and superior, and you don't even know me! You've decided I have an eating disorder because you think my family is messed up. Well, my family is *not* messed up. They're fine. I'm the one who has a problem. I'm not eating, and I *keep gaining weight.* That's why I'm here and they're not, get it? Now, do you believe me, or not?"

"What I believe isn't important," Karen said.

"Then what the hell am I doing here?" I screamed.

She looked at me mildly. "Would you care to sit down again?"

I sat. My whole body was vibrating.

"It's hard to live up to perfection, Lara. You've set extremely high standards for yourself—straight A's, pageants. It's a lot of pressure."

She glanced at her watch. "I hope you'll think about this, Lara. Sometimes it can be more difficult to be from a family with high expectations than from a family that expects nothing at all."

She stood up. "The weight is just a symptom, a release valve, if you will, for the pressure within. If you'd like to work with me, I think we can go on quite a journey together. Just call my secretary if you would like to set up regular appointments." She reached for my hand.

Not on your life, bitch.

I stood up, too, pointedly ignoring her outstretched hand, which hung in the air between me and her, at the end of her skinny arm. I knew I should take it. The old pageant me would definitely have taken it, no matter how much I disliked her. The new me looked at it with disdain.

So I won't win Miss Congeniality. So fucking what?

Karen left her hand there, but turned it palm up when she spoke. "Lara," she said. "One last thing. You're not alone."

I got into the Saturn my grandfather had bought me and pulled out of Karen DeBarge's parking lot, turning up the radio as loud as it would go. I never, ever, *ever* planned to go back there. I hated everything about her. The monster-creature me wanted to strangle her and watch her skinny arms plead for mercy.

But it was over, behind me. I told myself not to think about her anymore. Instead I'd think about all the good things that were still in my life.

Molly was still my best friend. And miracle of miracles, Jett still loved me.

Impossible to believe, but it was true. He still seemed to find me beautiful. I just couldn't figure that out. He joked around, and tried to tell me that there had been different standards of beauty in different eras and that, by today's standards, Marilyn Monroe was overweight.

In public, now, I found myself touching him, hanging on him in the same annoying way Mom hung on Dad. I kissed him a lot, held his hand, leaned my head on his shoulder, as if to say: Look, I might be fat, but I can still get a cute guy.

The fatter I got, the more Jennie Smith flirted with Jett. In fact, she'd invited him to her indoor pool party the week before, and she hadn't invited me. I knew all about the party. Everyone at school was talking about it. They all just assumed I had been invited. I didn't tell them different.

Then, in study hall, Amber had told me that Jennie

had told her that she hadn't invited me. But that Jennie had invited Jett. "I'm telling you this as a friend," Amber had said. "I don't think it's right."

I didn't ask Jett about it, because I knew he wasn't going to the party. We had a date that night. He was going to hide the invitation from me, to spare my feelings.

Then, the day before her party, Jennie had stopped over at my house. And she had explained why she hadn't invited me.

"I didn't want you to be embarrassed, Lara," she had told me, all sweetness and light. "I mean, *you*? In a *bathing suit*? I wouldn't put you through the *humiliation*!"

My hands tightened on my steering wheel as if it were Jennie Smith's throat. Murder colored my most vivid fantasies.

Lunch. I wanted to eat lunch. I vowed to stay on my diet. Wendy's had a salad bar. I pulled into the parking lot of the Wendy's on White Bridge Road, grabbed my purse, and went in.

"Welcome to Wendy's, can I take your order?" asked a short guy with a blond crew cut and bad skin. I recognized him, but clearly he didn't recognize me. Jimmy Porter. I had sat next to him the year before in history. He'd had a hard time keeping up, and some of the kids used to goof on him. I'd heard he'd transferred to a private school.

"Just the salad bar," I mumbled, trying not to make eye contact.

He cocked his head at me. "You look kinda familiar."

I shrugged and tried to duck my face down into the neckline of my sweater. It was warm out, but it was still too early in the year for the restaurant to use its air-conditioning. I felt flushed, and even though I wasn't sweating, I knew my fat face was candy-apple red.

"That'll be four dollars and twenty-nine cents," Jimmy said. I handed him the money, and he looked at me again. "I know you from somewhere," he said, handing me my change.

I was about to escape with my plastic salad plate when his face lit up with recognition. "Hey, I know! You're Lara Ardeche!"

A sickly little smile came to my lips.

"God, what happened to you?" he blurted out. "I mean, no offense or nothing, but, jeez-o-Pete!"

I dropped the plastic plate and ran out the door, practically colliding with two young guys wearing matching Nine Inch Nails T-shirts. "Thar she blows!" one of them yelled after me, and the two of them cracked up.

I sat in my car, shaking, wanting to die. I put my head down on the steering wheel and sobbed.

"Excuse me, ma'am, are you pulling out of that space?"

I looked out my window. In the car next to me were two very cute college-age guys.

"This spot is handicapped parking," the guy in the passenger seat explained to me. "So if you're pulling out, we can take your spot."

"Sure," I managed, choking back my tears.

"Thanks, ma'am."

And as I pulled out of the parking space, I realized he had called *ma'am*. He thought I was *old*! Because I was fat.

I had become a sexless, ageless, faceless blob.

I wasn't a pretty girl anymore.

I was the same person inside, the same girl that those two guys would once have flirted with. Only now I was a different girl on the outside, a girl who lived in the land of the fat girls. Teased. Shunned. Pitied. Overlooked.

The only guy who still thought I was beautiful was Jett, whose love I wore like a shield against my exile into fat land.

But without Jett by my side, I was just this disgusting blob. I was nothing. Less than nothing.

I pulled out of Wendy's parking lot and drove. I wanted to go home, crawl into bed, and pull the covers over my head. I wanted to hide forever, someplace where no one could call me names, laugh at me, pity me.

Lara Ardeche, a voice in my head said to me, *you are not a quitter. You can change this. And you don't need anyone's help. All you have to do is stop eating. Totally. No matter how hungry you get, or how bad that is, it can't be as bad as this is.*

Yes. That was what I would do. I'd just stop eating.

One of two things would happen.

I would get thin again. Or I would die.

Either way, I would win.

"**L**ara, you can't not eat at all," my mother said, sucking on her cigarette nervously.

"Yes I can."

It was that evening, and my mother and I were in the kitchen after dinner. Her dinner. I had consumed only water. Dad was out of town. Scott was at a friend's house.

"You'll get sick," she said. "Don't you think that therapist could help you?"

"I hate her," I said, "and I don't need her help. I've made a decision. I am not going to eat anything."

"We'll go to a different diet doctor—"

"No. I've made up my mind."

She inhaled on her cigarette and let the smoke out slowly. "I can't let you do that, honey."

"It's not up to you," I snapped. "It's up to me. You can't force me to eat."

"What if we don't keep any fattening foods in the house anymore?" she asked brightly. "I'm sure Scott would be willing to—"

"Mom, when is the last time you saw me eat anything except diet food?" I interrupted.

"I know you try, Lara, but—"

"I mean it, Mom. When?"

"You don't eat in front of me," my mother said, her eyes full of pity. "But Tammie told me she found candy-bar wrappers behind your bed."

"Our housekeeper's *reporting* to you now? You're *spying* on me?"

Mom got up and went to the drawer in the kitchen counter. She opened it and pulled out a small package. SKINNY STRIP was the return address. The package was addressed to me.

"This came in the mail last month," Mom said. "I can't believe you fell for such a—"

"It isn't mine," I protested. "It's Molly's! I only agreed to let her send it here because—"

"Lara, this lying has got to stop."

"I'm not lying!"

My mother rested one palm on her forehead, her elbow on the table. Her eyes peered at me from beneath her shaggy blond bangs. "Honey, I'm just worried about you. You sneak food, you keep gaining. The other day when Jennie Smith stopped over I looked at her and I realized: 'God, my daughter is twice as big as that girl.'"

"Listen to me," I said, my voice low. "Sometimes I eat candy. Maybe once a week, after I've spent days starving—"

"And you lose your self-control, I know."

I stood up. "You love me, right?"

She stood up, too. "Lara! What a thing to ask!"

"You love me, but you don't believe me. Okay. I'll prove it to you. I want you to spend every minute with me for the next five days. I won't go to school and you won't do any parties. I'm going to fast. If I lose weight, I'll do whatever you tell me to do—go see that obnoxious therapist, join Jenny Craig, anything. But if I gain weight or stay the same, you have to believe me: something is wrong with me physically."

She stubbed her cigarette out. "Lara, we've been back and forth to the doctors over and over. It isn't healthy for you to—"

"Five days," I said, my voice shaking.

"Your father would—"

"Daddy is out of town. He'll never know."

I could feel her wavering. "You'd do it if I was sick," I said, my voice rising. "Really sick. Dying. . . . That's how I feel, Mom. I feel like I'm dying."

She was silent for a long moment. "*Three* days," she finally said. "And you have to eat something."

"Slim-Shake," I countered, naming a popular over-the-counter milk shake used for weight loss.

"And vitamins," Mom added. "You'll take vitamins."

"Deal," I agreed.

We shook on it, her slender, lovely hand in my fat, bloated one.

Deal.

Chapter 190

"**A**nton, you asked Marielle to come on the show with you today because you had something to tell her, right?"

"Uh-huh."

Anton, who wore an oversized Dr. Dre sweatshirt and a red bandanna around his hair, turned to his overweight fiancée, a vision in leopard-print polyester. "Baby, you too fat."

"Don't even go there, uh-uh," she warned him, waving her long, blood-red nails at him.

"I gots to, baby. I mean, I still love you an' like that, but the fat be a real turn-off in the romance department, baby, you know what I'm sayin'? So if you don't be takin' the weight *off* by the wedding, you gonna be waitin' *on* the wedding!"

"Oooooo!" the audience exclaimed.

The camera came in on Marielle's pretty, round face,

which burned with embarrassment. Her head shook back and forth on her neck, all bravado. "You the one with the problem, Anton. I can kick you to the curb, it won't make no difference to me," she lied, trying not to cry.

She pried her engagement ring off her finger. "If that's how you feel, Anton, the wedding's off." She flung the ring at him. The crowd roared its approval.

Ricki Lake waded into the audience. "Yes, sir," she said, putting the microphone in a young guy's face.

"Well, I don't get it, Marielle," the guy said. "If you really love your man, lose the weight for him!"

Click. Next channel.

Sally Jessy Raphaël. "Our next guest says she knows what it's like to be the brunt of every joke at her grade school. She says kids have stuck pictures of pigs in her desk and put dog feces in her lunchbox. Please welcome ten-year-old Emily to our show."

Click. Next channel.

Richard Simmons, clad in tiny shorts and a sleeveless T-shirt, tears in his eyes, rested his hand on the stirrup pants of a thin, middle-aged woman with a bad bleach job.

"Mom, I know you want what's best for your child, but your daughter can't lose the weight because you want her to. You can't ridicule her into getting thin. Name-calling doesn't work—"

"But I'm just trying to help!" thin Mom said. "I've tried everything else, and *look* at her!"

"B-But if you would just leave me alone . . . ," her fat daughter blubbered, "then I could—"

Click. Next channel.

A commercial. A fat, sour-faced middle-aged woman sat with her husband in a restaurant. They had nothing to say to each other. They spread their muffins with a generic margarine spread. The husband's gaze wandered to another table, where a gorgeous, thin young woman spread cream cheese on her muffin.

"I want . . . cream cheese," the husband sighed wistfully.

"Half the calories, half the fat of margarine," the voice-over said, and the camera panned back to the fat woman, the margarine eater.

"How lame is that commercial?" Jett asked me. "It insults your intelligence!"

I clicked the TV off and dropped the remote control onto the nightstand.

"Dr. Towne, line three, please. Dr. Towne, please pick up line three," an amplified voice rang in the hospital corridor.

Jett turned to stare out the window. I lay heavily against the raised back of my hospital bed.

Why don't you ever really kiss me anymore? I wanted to ask him. But I didn't. I knew the answer.

The fat be a real turn-off in the romance department, baby.

"I can't wait to get out of here," I told him.

Jett turned back to me. "Yeah, I can imagine. But the whole thing will have been worth it if they figure out what's wrong with you."

It had been three weeks since my deal with Mom, where I had lived on Slim-Shake for three days. She'd kept her part of the bargain and stayed glued to me at all times. She'd even slept in the other twin bed, which we pulled in front of my door at night so I couldn't leave the room.

At the end of the three days, I got on the scale in front of her.

I had gained two pounds.

She finally believed me.

She called Dr. Laverly and demanded that I be admitted to St. Thomas Hospital for a controlled study, just like the one we had done at home. Dr. Laverly had agreed. But since I wasn't an urgent case, it would be two weeks before I could be admitted.

While I waited, I stayed home from school. I just stopped going. At first Mom tried to make me go, but I refused. She tried to get me to play the piano, too, but I wouldn't do that either. I just did nothing. Molly brought me my homework. I only talked to Jett on the phone.

Dad came home between business trips for one night. He sat by my bedside and gave a speech about the positive attitude of a winner. I wouldn't even look at him.

That night as I lay in bed, not quite asleep and not quite awake, I heard my parents, in their room.

"You'd better be goddamn glad my father will pay the hospital bills she's about to rack up," my mother seethed, "because your HMO isn't going to cover a thing."

"Daddy to the rescue again, huh?" my father jeered. "Did he make the house payment this month, by the way?"

"He better have," my mother snapped. "*You* can't afford to pay it."

"You're a real bitch, Carol."

"You're never here. You don't care. At least my father—"

"Why would I *want* to be here?" My father cut her off.

My fault, my fault. I pulled the covers over my head.

And I tried to imagine myself winning Miss America, with my parents in the audience, so proud . . .

It didn't work.

He was gone before breakfast the next morning. My mom pretended their fight had never happened.

Now I had been in St. Thomas Hospital for five days, living on some kind of supercharged, very-low-calorie liquid a nutritionist prepared. I drank it every six hours while someone monitored me. They also monitored me while I downed ten glasses of water a day. Twice a day, I got wheeled downstairs to spend thirty monitored minutes on a treadmill. They even monitored me in the bathroom, by measuring everything that came out of my body. I had to tell them every time I wanted to use the bathroom so they could unlock it for me: someone would go in afterward and collect a plastic measuring contraption that hung inside the toilet bowl.

In between all this, they did tests. My blood had been taken so many times I didn't think I could have very much left.

Today the nurses had weighed me for the first time since I'd been admitted.

I'd gained two more pounds.

They couldn't believe it. They made me get on and off the scale three times. Then they put me on another scale.

It read the same: 190 pounds.

"Uh-uh!" one oversized black nurse named Shawanda exclaimed, writing the number on my chart. She was one of the nicest nurses in the hospital. "Well, honey, all I have to say is, if I lived on what you're living on and I gained weight, I would just give *up*."

The other nurse gave her a warning look.

"I'm just sayin', is all," Shawanda said, shaking her head.

"Dr. Laverly will be in to see you and your parents this afternoon," the other nurse said.

So, at 190 pounds, I had finally proved that I wasn't crazy and that I didn't have an eating disorder. Something really was medically wrong with me.

I thought I would feel vindicated. But instead I felt nothing. Because no one looking at me cared *why* I was fat. I just *was*.

Jett came over to the bed and took my hand. "You're nervous, huh?"

He meant about seeing Dr. Laverly. He knew she'd have my new test results. I nodded.

"You know I'm with you, no matter what, right?"

I nodded again.

He reached over and tipped my head back. I waited for him to kiss my lips. He kissed my cheek. "I gotta run. Call me as soon as you can and tell me what the doctor tells you?"

"Sure."

He kissed my cheek again. "Hang in there." And then he was gone.

I reached for the remote and clicked the TV on again.

MTV. A drop-dead-gorgeous girl in a leather bikini was swishing her hair over a long-haired guitar player, who lay on his back and played a long, wailing riff. Now the girl and the musician were standing in front of a window, and the girl was wearing white lingerie and the guy was kissing her beautiful, slender neck—

"Can I come in?"

Patty Asher, of all people, was standing in the doorway of my room.

I turned off the TV. "What are you doing here?"

She didn't answer me, just came into the room and plopped her massive butt into the chair next to my bed.

"It's nice of you to visit, Patty," I said politely, the old Lara kicking in, "but I really didn't want any—"

"Do you believe in witchcraft?" she interrupted me. I just looked at her.

"Yeah, sounds loony, right? I always put it right up there with, like, the Psychic Friends Network—so stupid, you know?"

She looked me over. "You're really fat now," she noted objectively. "Not just chubby or anything."

"Look, Patty—"

"Everyone at school is talking about you," she continued. "Everyone knows you're here at St. Thomas. Someone said you have cancer. Someone else said you have AIDS." She rested her intertwined fingers on top of her head.

"I don't have AIDS," I said, my voice low.

"Oh, yeah, I knew that was ridiculous," Patty said. "I mean, look at you. You don't get fat if you have AIDS. They're trying to figure out why you got so fat so fast, right?"

"Look, I don't want to be rude, but would you just please get out of here? I don't want any visitors. And as you pointed out to me at homecoming, we aren't friends."

She got up and looked out the window. "Yeah, homecoming. I'll bet you had a lot of fun that night, huh? Winning and everything?"

I didn't answer her.

"I have a confession to make, Lara," she continued, still looking out the window. "When I went home the night of homecoming, I lay in bed and had these really awful thoughts about you. First, I wished that you'd die. But then I thought of something even better. I thought: No, I don't want Lara Ardeche to die. I want her to get really, really fat, so she'll know just what it's like."

She turned back to me. "And now, you are. You're as fat as I am. Why, you might even be fatter—isn't that a hoot? So that's why I was wondering about the witchcraft thing. I mean, maybe I wished so hard that I put a spell on you, and it worked."

Tears stung my eyes. "I never did anything to you."

She walked back over to my bed and looked down at me. "Well, see, that's just the whole point. That's how you see it. It's funny, really. I mean, you never said mean things to me, like Blake or Jennie. You thought you were being nice, with your I-feel-sooo-sorry-for-a-fat-blob-like-Fatty-Patty. I guess I'll take pity on her and try and help her lose weight. You were sooo superior, weren't you? And I was supposed to be sooo grateful. And for that, I hated you most of all."

"Get out! Just get the hell out of here!"

"Okay," Patty said cheerfully. "I want you to know that I don't think I'm a very nice person or anything for coming over here to enjoy your misery. But you know what? I don't give a shit." And then she walked out the door.

I picked up the TV clicker and threw it at her, but I missed. It hit the wall and broke apart, the pieces clattering to the floor.

Sobs tore from my throat. "It isn't fair," I hiccuped to myself as tears ran down my face. "It isn't fair."

I heard my parents' voices before I saw them. They were arguing, their voices harsh, escalating as they got closer to my room. Quickly I rubbed the tears off my cheeks and pushed my hair off my face. I couldn't let them see me like that. It was bad enough that Dad hardly ever made a special effort anymore to come home between his business trips to see me. I didn't want to make everything even worse.

They came silently into my room. Dad looked tired, Mom looked stressed out. Dad gave me a cold kiss on my cheek. A terrible thought hit me—they knew something I didn't. That I had some rare horrible kind of tumors that were going to kill me, and that's why I kept gaining weight.

"If I'm dying, I want you to tell me," I blurted out.

"What?" Mom asked, taken aback.

"I mean it," I insisted. "If it's cancer or something, don't pretend it's not."

"It's not cancer," Mom said. "And you're not dying."

"I'm sure it isn't anything terrible," Dad added.

"The nurses weighed me," I told them. "I've gained two more pounds."

"How is that possible?" Dad asked with distaste.

"We don't know, *Jim*," Mom told him with exaggerated calm. "That's the whole point of her being here, isn't it?"

"I know that, *Carol*," Dad said, his mouth tense.

"Then why did you ask such a stupid question, *Jim*?"

"I meant it rhetorically, *Carol*."

They spit out each other's names as if they were insults. I couldn't stand it.

"How was your business trip?" I asked Dad.

"Fine," he said tersely.

"So, did you get the client in New York?"

Mom and Dad traded looks.

"What does that mean?" I asked.

No one answered. Then Dr. Laverly bustled into the room.

"Hello," she said. "How are you today?"

"I'm waiting for you to tell me," I replied.

She smiled and closed the door. "Yes, I guess you are. Mr. and Mrs. Ardeche, why don't you have a seat?"

I had a terrible feeling of dread. My mom sat on the edge of my bed and took my hand. Dad sat on the chair.

"I have the results of all the tests we did on Lara," she said. "As you know, we repeated the same tests we did a few weeks ago, plus we did many more, including some very new genetic tests."

Both my parents nodded solemnly.

"The tests we repeated are, once again, negative," Dr. Laverly said. "In fact, all the tests are negative."

"But that's crazy," I said. "That can't be."

"According to your weigh-in today, Lara, you've gained two pounds while you've been here," Dr. Laverly continued. "It defies just about everything we know about nutrition and weight loss."

"That is just not acceptable," my father snapped.

Dr. Laverly nodded, then turned to me. "The other odd thing we noticed is that your urine output is a fraction of what it should be, given that you are drinking so much water and living, basically, on liquid food. You should be urinating easily five times as much as you are."

"So what does that mean?" I demanded.

"Have you also noticed that you don't seem to sweat as much as you used to, Lara?" Dr. Laverly asked me. "Say, when you exercise?"

"Yes, now that you mention it," I said.

Dr. Laverly nodded thoughtfully. "I can't tell you that

I know for sure what your problem is. But I read something awhile back about symptoms similar to yours, so I've been doing some research."

She opened a file and looked down at some notes she'd made on a yellow legal pad.

"The year before last, Dr. Bernard Axell, an endocrinologist at Beth Israel Hospital, in Boston, wrote a case-study paper about a teen patient of his who kept gaining weight, even on a very calorie-restricted diet. And last year, a British researcher, Dr. Maxwell Crowne, gave a speech at a symposium in London about two other young people—one in South Africa, one in Leeds, England—who were presenting the same symptoms. Crowne said that these teens ate next to nothing, under strictly controlled circumstances, yet continued to gain weight."

"Just like me," I said, nodding.

"Yes," the doctor agreed. "Axell and Crowne are working together now, and they theorize that these patients' bodies have somehow become superefficient, and just about all the food and water they take in is put to use. In fact, the less they eat, the more efficient their bodies are, so they actually gain *more* weight by ingesting *less* food.

"The other common denominator seems to be that the patient hardly sweats, urinates, or defecates," she continued. "They're preparing a paper now, which they hope to publish. They're calling it Axell-Crowne Syndrome."

"Is that what Lara has?" my father asked.

"I don't know," Dr. Laverly admitted. "There really isn't a test for it, per se. It's more an elimination of things, which is what we've done. Also, I should tell you, Axell and Crowne are catching a lot of heat. Many doctors don't think Axell-Crowne exists. They believe that in each case the young person has somehow been able to sneak food, that it's not a metabolic disorder at all."

"I've been watched twenty-four hours a day!" I protested. "How could I sneak food?"

"If that's what she has, how did she get it?" my father demanded. "And how do you cure it?"

"Axell and Crowne don't know yet what precipitates the syndrome," Dr. Laverly said. "The best theory they've got is that a virus or bacteria or an allergic reaction turns on something else genetic, and gives the body false signals that any and all nutrition should be stored."

"My allergies!" I exclaimed. "The rashes—"

"Possibly," Dr. Laverly said. "Also the fact that thus far all reported cases are adolescents leads Axell and Crowne to theorize that something in the growth process may be a catalyst to the onset of symptoms."

"Tell us more," Dad demanded, folding his arms.

"Frankly, we just don't know much more," Dr. Laverly admitted. "And as I said, much like Chronic Fatigue Syndrome, there is a whole school of thought out there that Axell-Crowne doesn't even exist."

"Okay, let's cut to the chase," my father said. "How do we get rid of it?"

"Unfortunately, Mr. Ardeche," Dr. Laverly said, "there is no known cure at this time, but—"

"No known cure?" I blurted out. "Wait, what do I do, just keep getting fatter and fatter until I *explode*? Until I *die*?"

"Axell and Crowne report an eventual leveling off of weight in all cases," Dr. Laverly said, "a halt in the syndrome, if you will. One girl leveled off at a gain of ninety pounds. Another gained one hundred and—"

"But I can't!" I wailed. "I can't! I have to stop it!" Tears coursed down my cheeks.

"Lara, this is not hopeless," Dr. Laverly said earnestly. "Of the six reported cases, two have begun to lose weight again. The boy in Leeds who had gained one hundred pounds is back to nearly his normal weight. No one knows why."

"So she could lose it all," my mother said, grasping at the possibility.

"Yes, it's possible," Dr. Laverly said. "And I want to add that Axell and Crowne are working right now to find out if, in fact, there are many more cases of Axell-Crowne that have just not been recorded. Duke University Medical Center is planning a pilot study—"

"That won't help me very much," I said bitterly, wiping the tears away.

"Hopefully, Lara, it will help you, eventually. I wish I had better news for you. And as I said, I can't be certain of a diagnosis of Axell-Crowne, either." She looked at my parents. "Do you have any questions?"

"Could she die?" my mother asked shakily.

"No," Dr. Laverly said. "If, in fact, this is Axell-Crowne, it doesn't seem to involve any other organic functioning." She turned to me. "I want you to make an appointment with the nutritionist, who will prescribe a diet for you that we can monitor closely. That will be coupled with a very specific exercise plan. Then you'll be weighed each week. We need to find the optimum program that will lead to the least weight gain."

"The lowest calories ingested and the highest degree of exercise, obviously," my father said.

Dr. Laverly turned to my father. "Perhaps you didn't hear what I said, Mr. Ardeche. In Lara's case, that simply isn't true. Her body could become more efficient and she could gain weight by eating less. Think of it like faulty chips in a computer. Her body gets sent the wrong signals."

The room was silent.

"That's it?" my father asked incredulously. "That's all you have to say?"

"I'm sorry." Dr. Laverly patted my hand. "Maybe if Duke does the study, you'll volunteer to join it. And there is hope that you'll go into full remission."

"When?" I asked bluntly.

She just patted my hand again.

"Well, I'll leave you alone now. I'm releasing you, Lara. Go home and go back to school. Full activities. Mr. and Mrs. Ardeche, if you'd just stop by the nurses' station and sign the release papers. If you have any questions, please call me." She walked out of the room.

"It can't be true," I whispered. "It just can't be."

"At least you don't have cancer," Mom said.

"I wish I did have cancer!" I yelled viciously. "I'd rather have cancer than this!"

My mother got up. "I'll go sign the papers."

"Look, this doctor could be completely wrong," my father said. "Here's what we're going to do. We'll find the best endocrinologist in the country. We'll fly to wherever he is. You can beat this thing. This . . . this isn't you, Lara," he said, waving his hand at my fat body.

Only this *was* me. The new me. A me he hated and loathed. A me *I* hated and loathed.

But it didn't make any difference.

It was still me.

chapter 208

" '**S**chool's out for summer!' " two seniors sang as they ran by me in the hallway. They were singing an old Alice Cooper song, recently covered by a new metal group, Scream. It was getting lots of radio play.

The last day of my junior year. Normally, I really looked forward to summer. I had planned to get a part-time job at the music store at the mall, hang out with my friends at our backyard pool, and spend time with Jett.

Well, now all that was one big fat joke.

The music store didn't hire fat girls, and I wouldn't be seen dead in a bathing suit at our pool.

I could hang with Molly, of course. She would stick by me through thin and, in my case, thick.

And there was Jett.

We had decided back at Thanksgiving that he'd spend

an extra year in Nashville working while I finished my senior year, and then we'd move to New York together. He'd go to Visual Arts. I'd go to Juilliard.

Of course, back at Thanksgiving, I'd only weighed 130-something pounds and I had thought I was *fat*! I would give *anything* to go back to 130-something pounds. Instead of the 208 that I now weighed.

I didn't go anywhere anymore. Where can a fat girl go without getting ridiculed or humiliated? I would have even refused to go to the prom with Jett, if he'd had any interest in going. Fortunately for me, Jett wasn't the prom type. I could just picture Blake Poole laughing at me like he had laughed at Patty Asher at homecoming.

The new me. Lara Ardeche, fat girl. I hated the new me. And I didn't understand why Jett didn't hate me, too.

"Aren't you hot in that?" Jennie Smith asked as she stopped to spin the combination lock on her locker.

I had on the same black stretch pants I had been wearing almost daily for months, with one of three oversized sweaters that still fit over my huge body. I used to love to shop for clothes. Now the idea seemed like the worst torture imaginable.

"I'm fine," I stated, taking the books out of my locker.

Jennie opened her own locker and took out her backpack. "Tonight's going to be a major blast, don't you think?"

She was referring to the junior-senior trip to Opryland amusement park. I had told Jett I didn't want to go. That wasn't really true. The truth was that I was afraid I wouldn't fit into the little seats they had on the rides.

Can you even imagine the humiliation of getting onto a ride and not being able to fit?

I could. Just the week before, my French class had gone to an old movie theater near Vanderbilt, to see a showing of Truffaut's *Small Change*. The theater's Doric architecture was beautiful, but the faded red velvet seats inside were from a bygone era—a bygone era where no one weighed what I weighed, evidently.

I was talking with Molly as I slid down into my seat. I wedged into the space, my fat bulging into the armrests. I couldn't put my arms down, either, because when I tried, the guy sitting on my left made a noise of disgust—I was spilling over into his space. I tried to cross my arms over my chest. That felt ridiculous. So I pushed my elbows into my body as much as I could, and locked my hands under my thighs.

"Wow, these are small seats," I said.

Molly sat down. Easily. Room to spare.

During the movie, the circulation was cut off in my legs from being wedged so tightly into the seat. And when I tried to get up at the end of the movie, I was basically stuck. I had to heave my body forward twice before I could stumble to my feet. Blake Poole, who was sitting a row behind me with Amber Bevin, saw me trying to get out of the seat. He made a sucking sound and bellowed, "Vacuum packed!" Amber dug her elbow into him and told him to shut up.

I was only thankful that Jett took Spanish, so he didn't witness this particular humiliation. I wanted to die. But that was nothing new. Daily I faced new humiliations, new tortures, each one killing me a little more than the one before.

It had been six weeks since I'd gotten out of the

hospital. In that time I had gained another eighteen pounds and passed the 200-pound mark.

Eighteen pounds. Three pounds a week. At night I had horrible nightmares: I had turned into a huge, hideous monster, and people were running from me, screaming in fear.

I was totally unrecognizable as my former self. My real self. I was a prisoner in a fat suit.

For three weeks I ate the diet the nutritionist had prescribed for me, and gained three pounds each week. The next week, I ate anything I felt like eating. I gained the exact same amount of weight.

So what was the point?

Not that I ever ate in front of anybody. I never did that. So what if I told people I had a metabolic disorder—if they saw me eating anything other than lettuce, they wouldn't believe me. When you're fat, you're not just fat.

You're sloppy.

Lazy.

A pig.

My father refused to believe we couldn't find a doctor who could control my weight. He had my records sent to Duke and to two famous endocrinologists, one in Michigan, one in San Francisco. The Duke and the Michigan doctors both said the same thing: possible Axell-Crowne. Don't know if it will last forever or be gone tomorrow. The San Francisco doctor said there was no such thing as Axell-Crowne and recommended an inpatient eating disorder facility.

An assistant from a lab at Duke's medical center called and asked if I would join their proposed study. I would have to go to North Carolina for three months and be monitored by video cameras twenty-four hours a day to confirm that I wasn't sneaking any food.

Well, what was the point? I wondered. They didn't have any medication for me. They weren't offering me any hope.

The old pageant winner me would have said yes anyway, so that I might help others in the future.

The new me told the woman to drop dead.

It felt good not to care. Because too often, I still did. I cared what people at school thought. I cared when total strangers insulted me, laughed at me, as if my feelings didn't matter, as if they had a right to punish me for the sin of being fat in their presence.

I knew it was a sin. Everyone made that clear in the way they treated me. My father made it clearest of all. The way he looked at me said everything.

"I'm not going to Opryland," I told Jennie casually.

"But it's going to be so fun!" she protested. "And it won't be the same without you!"

"Thanks," I said. "But Jett and I have other plans."

Her face fell. "Jett isn't coming, either?"

"That's right," Molly told Jennie, coming up behind her. "And you thought this would be your shot at him, huh?"

Jennie threw Molly a nasty look. "You need help, Molly. You are delusional."

"Oh yeah, right," Molly snorted. "Like you aren't totally after Jett. Everyone knows it."

Jennie gave me an earnest look. "I would *never*."

"I know," I lied.

She put her hand on my arm. "I mean, I just think the *world* of Jett! Standing by you after you got so . . . after

118

what happened to you. He's like a *saint* to me, you know?"

"Excuse me while I barf up my sleeve," Molly said.

Jennie narrowed her eyes and backed away from us. "You'd better watch it, Mouth. Lara can't protect you anymore, you know."

"Bye, Jennie, stay sweet!" Molly called, and steered me down the hall.

"You shouldn't have done that," I said. "Now she'll be mad."

"Am I supposed to care?"

"You know what she's like when she hates someone at this school," I reminded her.

"Jennie can't hurt you," Molly said. "Everyone at this school loves you. She can't ruin your rep."

"Molly, wake up." I looked around to make sure no one could overhear us. "Jennie isn't afraid of me anymore. I mean, look at me."

"Your true friends haven't turned on you," Molly insisted as we rounded the corner.

"That would be . . . ?" I asked as I watched Lisa James and Denise Reiser walk by without acknowledging my existence.

"Me and Jett, obviously," Molly said, looking through her books.

Sarah Lodge waved to us from across the hall. "Have a great summer!" she called.

"Plus girls like Sarah," Molly said. "And all the other people who aren't in that stupid little clique that you seem to love so much."

We stopped in front of the auditorium, where the end-of-the-year assembly for the entire school was about

119

to take place. I saw Jett down at the other side of the hall, talking to a pretty, slender senior girl I recognized but didn't know.

"Oh, shoot," Molly said, "I left a library book in precalc. They'll *crucify* me if I don't bring it back. Save me and Andy seats, okay?" She dashed off.

My eyes were glued to Jett and the girl. What was he doing with her? I walked over to the two of them.

"Hi," I said, taking his arm. I put my head on his shoulder and stared daggers at the girl.

"I gotta run," the girl told him. "See you."

"Who was that?" I tried to sound friendly. I failed.

"Suzi Farly," Jett said. "She's a terrific artist—you should see the oil she did for the art show. She's going to Visual Arts in New York this summer."

"Too bad you made plans to stay here with me, huh?" I said, an edge to my voice.

"She's just a friend, Lara."

Just a friend. How many times had I told a jealous boyfriend that one?

I forced myself to let it drop. "You sure you don't mind missing the Opryland trip tonight?" I asked him. "I mean, just because I don't want to go . . ."

"Neither do I," Jett said. "I'll come over, we'll just hang out, maybe barbecue, okay?"

"Sure," I said. My mom had left that morning for Los Angeles to visit her sister, my aunt Deana, and she'd taken Scott with her. Dad was, as always, away on business.

"I'll bring my suit, we can swim," Jett said.

Right. Like I was going to let him see me in a bathing suit. And to think I used to believe he was so sensitive to my feelings.

Danny Fairway, my ex, walked by, his arm around his latest girlfriend, Carrie Ambrose, who had only been at Forest Hills High for a few months.

As they passed, she turned around to look back at me. "You really used to go out with her?" I heard her ask. "I mean, she's as fat as Patty Asher."

Jett pretended he hadn't heard. I knew he had.

"Oh, hey, I forgot to tell Suzi what time I'm picking her up for the art show," Jett said, snapping his fingers.

"Picking her up?" I repeated dumbly.

"I thought we could give her a ride—she doesn't have a car. I'm gonna go catch her—save me a seat in there." He took off down the hall.

In the olden days, before I turned into Blimp Woman, Jett would have asked me if it was okay if we took some other girl with us, especially a cute girl I didn't know, who wasn't one of my friends.

But all that had changed.

The olden days were over.

A few hours later I pulled my car into the Rivergate Mall parking lot. As I walked toward the mall doors my eyes darted around, looking for people I knew. I had chosen Rivergate because it was clear across Nashville—no one I knew *ever* shopped there.

So far, so good.

I had to go shopping. I couldn't last anymore in black stretch pants, oversized sweaters, and T-shirts. For one thing, it was too hot out. For another, I couldn't go anywhere that required other clothes. Because the new me didn't have any real ones that fit.

The old me shopped with my friends. The new me

shopped alone. The old me could shop at a zillion stores, choosing from all the cute clothes out there that all looked so great on me. The new me headed directly for the fat ladies' store: Lane Bryant.

I knew about Lane Bryant, of course. Molly's mom shopped there. And I supposed that was where Patty Asher got her lovely ensembles. But never, ever in a million years did I think *I* would be caught dead in that store, shopping for *myself*.

I slunk past The Limited, The Gap, all my old favorites. The outfits in the window display mocked me. I saw my own fat reflection in the window of the 5–7–9 Shop, superimposed against a slender mannequin in a tiny dress.

"Oh my God, look at that girl!"

I turned around. A group of cute, thin girls my age ran by, laughing together. One of them pointed at me, then said something else that I couldn't hear, and her friends looked back at me and laughed again.

A cute, thin couple walked past me, their hands in the back pockets of each other's jeans.

Lane Bryant. There it was. I walked inside.

"Can I help you?" the young saleswoman asked as I walked into the store. She was very fat, with perfect blond hair and perfect makeup, a pathetic attempt to compensate for her hugeness. She wore a denim jumper over a white T-shirt in a size I could not even imagine existed, it was so big.

"I'm just looking," I said nervously, politely.

"We're having a great sale on denim," she said. "In fact, I just got this outfit." She pointed to herself. "It's cute, huh?"

"Wow," I agreed, like a well-bred pageant-head.

"It would look really cute on you. I'd guess we wear about the same size. You should try it on!"

No, no, no. We couldn't possibly wear the same size. *She* was massive. She was probably some foodaholic who stuffed her face day and night. *I* was a normal person with a disease. We were nothing alike. Nothing.

"What size are you?" she asked pleasantly.

I didn't have a clue.

"About a twenty-two is my guess," she said. "Would you like me to pull this for you in a twenty-two?"

A *twenty-two*? That wasn't possible. Molly's *mother* wore a twenty-two! No. This girl felt so awful about being fat that she wanted me to feel awful, too.

"I'm sure I don't wear a twenty-two," I said coolly. "What's the smallest size you have?"

"A fourteen/sixteen. You aren't a fourteen/sixteen."

"If I need your help I'll call you, okay?" I said sharply.

"Fine," she said smoothly. "My name is Janet, if you need me." She walked away.

I looked through a rack of satin shirts in bright colors, so huge each could house a small nation. Then I looked at dresses. Many of the styles were the same as those in the stores where I usually shopped. The difference was they looked ridiculous in such gigantic proportions.

I grabbed some clothes: a pair of jeans, a white cotton shirt, a long floral dress, all size eighteen. Maybe Janet was right and I wasn't a fourteen. But I couldn't possibly be that much bigger.

I went into the dressing room and pulled on the jeans. I couldn't even get them all the way up my legs.

"Oh, God, Chrissy, I am such a pig," I heard a young voice say from the next dressing room. "I can't zip this."

"Try the dress, then. It's cute," another voice said.

"Maybe it would be cute on you," the first voice said. "I am so disgusting."

I tried on the white shirt. It didn't come close to buttoning.

"Nothing fits," the girl moaned from the next dressing room.

"I thought you were going to Weight Watchers."

"I did, but the third week I gained weight, and I was too ashamed to go back to weigh in. I wish I were dead."

She must be enormous, I thought. I tried on the dress. I couldn't even pull it up over my hips.

"How you doing in there?" Janet called in to me.

Go away. Leave me alone. Drop dead.

"Just fine!" I called out to her.

She had seen me go into the dressing room with my size eighteens. "Just let me know if you need me to get you a larger size!" she sang out.

Shut up. I hate you. Go to hell.

"Okay!"

I used to love helpful salesgirls. "Could you find this for me in a smaller size?" I would ask sweetly. "I can't decide between the pink bikini and the yellow," I would muse. They would tell me how great both of them looked on me. How lucky I was to have such a great figure.

I put my own clothes back on and slunk out of the dressing room at the same time as the two girls in the next dressing room came out.

They were my age, and both were way thinner than I was.

I grabbed a handful of clothes in sizes twenty, twenty-two, and twenty-four. Then I ran back into the dressing room.

I pulled a navy dress with white piping over my head. It was ugly and looked horrible, emphasizing every lump, but it fit. I looked at the tag.

Size twenty-two.

The same size as Molly's mother.

"*L*ara?" Jett called.

"I'm out here," I called back to him.

It was that evening. I had spent hours preparing for my date with Jett. On the way home from the mall I had vowed that I would work extra hard, be extra nice, extra everything, so he wouldn't break up with me. Thank God I still had Jett and Molly. And thank God Jett still loved me enough to stay in Nashville during my senior year so that we could go to New York together.

Thank God I wouldn't be alone.

I had made us a picnic dinner with all Jett's favorites, and it was already laid out on the redwood patio table. I had on one of my new Lane Bryant outfits—pink-and-white cotton drawstring pants with a matching pink-and-white shirt. It was the first time he would see me in something new in months. I had taken extra pains with new makeup I'd purchased, made sure my hair was perfect, and put on a new, sexy perfume. It was the first time I had made a real effort in, oh, about fifty pounds.

"Hi," he said as he came over and kissed my cheek.

Not my lips. But still. He loved me. He *did*.

He looked over at the picnic table. "What's all this?"

"Surprise!" I said gaily. "We're celebrating your graduation." I wrapped my arms around his neck.

"It's not until next week," he reminded me. He didn't put his arms around my waist—or where my waist would have been if I'd still had one.

"I know that," I said. "Consider it an early bonus dinner. I made all your favorite everythings." I leaned into him again.

"That was really sweet of you," he said. But there was something funny about his smile.

He sat on the redwood bench and picked up a celery stalk stuffed with cream cheese. He put it down again.

"So, this summer is going to be great, huh?"

I nodded.

"We'll be able to spend a lot of time together," he promised.

I nodded again. Something wasn't right.

"Hey, I meant to tell you," Jett said, his voice forced. "You know that job I'm starting at the art supply store? The guy called and said it's only for the summer."

"So, you'll find another job in the fall," I said reassuringly. "That shouldn't be too hard."

"Yeah." He brushed some hair off his face and stared at the celery. "I was thinking . . . maybe I should just go to New York this fall. My parents said they'd pay my tuition at Visual Arts. I could get a part-time job, and everything will be all set for us by the time you graduate."

Something turned over in my stomach. "But how could you do that? It's too late to apply to art school for this fall."

He wouldn't look at me. "I already applied."

"You already—"

"A few months ago," he admitted, his voice low.

"You applied to art school *a few months ago* and you didn't even *tell* me?"

"It was just a fallback kind of a thing," Jett said nervously. "I mean, I don't have to go . . ."

"You want to go," I accused him.

"I don't know." He rubbed his face anxiously. "I want to be there, but I want to be here with you, too."

Even though I was dying inside, I forced myself to smile. "Well, I think you should go."

I would do anything, say anything, to keep him.

He looked stunned. "You do?"

"Sure," I lied, a bright smile on my face. "Your art is really important. Why should you wait a year? I'll get there when I get there."

Now he came to me and wrapped his arms around me. "Lara, I was so sure you'd be upset."

"There's nothing to be upset about." I smiled my best pageant smile.

He hugged me. It felt like a hug my grandfather might give me. "You're terrific, Lar."

"Thanks," I said, moving out of his embrace. "So, want to eat?"

"How about if we take a swim? It's still so hot out."

"Oh, no, you go ahead."

"Oh, come on," he coaxed, "it's no fun to swim alone."

"I'm not really in the mood," I said with feigned casualness.

"Hey, sparkling pool, privacy fence, no family . . ." He smiled at me and pulled off his jeans. He had a bathing suit on underneath.

"Come on, Lara, come swimming with me." He pulled me by my hand.

"No, really—"

"Oh, yes, really." He backed me toward the pool, a teasing look in his eyes. He went to lift me. It used to be so easy—I was a feather in his arms. Now he couldn't get me off the ground.

But neither one of us wanted to admit that. So I hopped up a little, hoping to compensate for my weight. To my horror I lost my balance and toppled over into the water. Jett jumped in after me.

I came up sputtering. Jett was laughing.

"It isn't funny!" I yelled, splashing water at him. My new outfit was now transparent, plastered to my rolls of fat like pink-tinted plastic wrap. Mascara ran down my face. My hair was glued to my head, which I knew only emphasized how fat my face was.

"Oh, come on, lighten up!" he told me. "It's funny!"

It would have been funny ninety pounds ago, when I looked cute dripping wet, when I wasn't afraid to be seen without makeup or without my hair fixed perfectly because I felt confident that I looked cute anyway.

It wasn't funny now.

I swam to the shallow end and heaved myself out of the pool, quickly wrapping a huge towel around myself to hide the sight of my disgusting fat. "I'm going in to change."

Jett got out of the pool. "Hey, I'm sorry," he said, water dripping off him. "I didn't realize it would upset you so much."

"Forget it," I snapped.

"It's not important—"

"Yes, it is," I said. "It's really important!" I couldn't help it, tears were coursing down my cheeks, mixing with the tracks of mascara. "I worked so hard so everything would be perfect. I got a new outfit, new perfume, new makeup. And you didn't even notice."

"I'm really sorry, Lara, I—"

"You applied to art school so you could get away from me! You don't want to be with me because I'm disgusting!" I reached out and slapped at him viciously. I knew I was ruining everything, but I couldn't seem to stop myself.

"I don't think you're disgusting," he said. He reached out for me.

"Don't." I moved away from him. "Don't do it when you don't mean it!"

He pushed his wet hair off his face. "Lara, please, I love you."

"No."

"Yes," he insisted. "Please." He held his arms out to me, waiting for me to walk into them.

And I wanted to. So much. I gulped down my tears. "Jett, do you want to make love to me?"

"What?"

"You heard me. Do you want to make love to me?"

He was silent.

"Do you want to draw me naked, then? How about that?"

He just stood there. He couldn't lie to me.

"What about how there are all different kinds of beauty?" I asked him, remembering something he'd said to me. I was barely able to speak because of the tears coursing down my cheeks. "I know you love me. But you aren't *in love* with me anymore. You never kiss me, you don't touch me, not the way you used to. And I miss it so much."

"I never meant to hurt you, Lara," he whispered, tears in his eyes. "And going to New York isn't . . . I'll never leave you."

I took a deep, ragged breath. "You don't have to, Jett. Because I'm leaving you."

And then I did the hardest thing I've ever done in my entire life.

I turned around and walked away from Jett Anston.

Chapter 210

"**Y**ou *what*?" Molly yelped.

"I broke up with Jett."

It was two days later, and Molly had just come over to my house. She'd called many times before, but I'd never answered—I just let the machine pick up. Since Mom and Scott were still in Los Angeles, there were no witnesses to my spiral down into the depths of despair. Until Molly had arrived, all I had done since I'd turned my back on Jett was lie in bed and weep.

And I came to a conclusion: You probably really *can* die from a broken heart.

I'd wanted to call Jett, so many times. But I stopped myself. As much as it hurt, I knew that what I had said to him had been the truth. One part of me said: So what? Wouldn't you rather just be grateful that Jett still loves you, and keep him, than break up with him and be alone?

The other part of me, the part where I still had any self-respect at all, said no. It would all be a big lie. He wanted to leave, he just didn't want to be the one to say it. You did the right thing.

The right thing. Big deal.

Knowing that didn't make me feel any better. The heart is not such a strong muscle. The truth is, I would have gone back to him in a millisecond, would have flown back into his arms. All he needed to do was pick up the phone and call me, tell me that I was wrong, that he loved me as he always had. Even if we both knew that was a lie, I was weak. I wouldn't have cared and I would have been so happy, at least for a little while.

Only he didn't call. Not once. Oh, God, he didn't call.

Mom called from Los Angeles. Molly called four times. I heard their messages on the answering machine.

Jett never called.

Molly finally came over to see what was wrong. She found me huddled in bed in my bathrobe, unwashed, unbrushed, un-anythinged.

She asked me if I was sick. That was when I told her what had happened. Saying it out loud made the pain even worse.

"You're telling me that of the few great guys on this planet, you actually *broke up* with the greatest of the great?" Molly asked. "Has Axell-Crowne destroyed your brain stem?"

"He isn't in love with me anymore, Mol," I said, wiping my red-rimmed eyes with a tissue.

"Of course he loves—"

"Don't you get it?" I cried. "He isn't attracted to me anymore. He was staying with me out of pity!"

"I don't believe that," Molly said firmly.

"Well, it's true." Then I told her that he was going to Visual Arts this fall. "He applied months ago. I wasn't even that fat then. It hurts so much, Molly."

She sat down next to me and opened her arms, and I dived into them. Then I sobbed even harder. We sat there together on my bed, and she rocked me like a baby. When my tears slowed, she plucked a handful of tissues from the nightstand box and handed them to me.

I blew my nose and wiped my eyes. "I hate my life."

Molly didn't say anything.

"Isn't this where you're supposed to tell me how life is worth living, and all that?" I asked.

She drew her knees up to her chin. "Can't," she said. "What happened to you just sucks so hard."

"You're not exactly cheering me up," I said, half laughing through my tears.

"Yeah, I know," Molly agreed. "What can I say? I have a pathologically honest streak. And God, I used to be so jealous of you."

"You were?"

"I desperately wanted to look like you instead of looking like me."

"Past tense," I noted.

"Well, yeah," Molly agreed. "It wasn't that I wanted your life. I just wanted to be me and look like you, you know? I wanted a guy like Jett to fall in love with me . . ."

"Not a guy *like* Jett," I corrected. "Jett."

Molly stared at me. "Okay, you're right. Jett."

"He's free now," I said bitterly.

"Oh yeah, right."

"He is!"

"First of all, Jett would never see me as more than a friend . . ."

"You're wrong," I said bluntly. "He told me so himself."

"He did?" Molly was incredulous. "You actually *discussed* it?"

I nodded. "So go for it, if you want to."

Molly gave me a funny look. "Now I'm positive that Axell-Crowne has short-circuited your brain. Lara, you're my best friend. Whether or not you and Jett are together, you still love him. I would never, ever in a bazillion years go out with Jett. I would never hurt you like that."

Tears leaked from my eyes again. "I don't even deserve you, Mol."

"That's true," she teased. "I am beyond wonderful."

"I mean it." I twisted the tissue between my fingers. "I used to feel so superior because you had fat thighs and big hips . . ."

"Well, I do," Molly said.

"Not compared to me."

"But you have a disease. It isn't your fault!"

I wiped my eyes again. "Mol, when I got fat, were you ever . . . ever glad?"

"Never," she said staunchly.

"Never? Not even for one day?"

Her gaze wavered. "Okay, I'm not such a saint. The day you wore jeans larger than mine, I got a brief thrill of satisfaction."

"I don't blame you," I said.

"But after that I felt bad that I was so low," Molly

continued, "and then I just felt bad that you felt so bad. I mean, I'd wish fat on Jennie Smith. Or Amber Bevin. Or Lisa James . . ."

"I used to think they were my friends," I said sadly.

"Yeah, right," Molly snorted. "Notice how much they hang with you now." She got very involved in picking at the chipped nail polish on her pinky. "I never understood how you could be with those girls."

"You hung out with them, too."

"Please. They tolerated me because of you, and I tolerated them because of you. They treated me like shit." Her eyes met mine. "And you let them."

"What was I supposed to do?" I protested.

"You were supposed to say 'Molly is my best friend, and you can't talk to her like that,' " Molly replied, her voice quavery.

"I did!"

"But you didn't mean it," Molly said. "Not enough to stop them. Sometimes you even laughed with them. 'Molly the Mouth.' What a riot."

I gulped hard. "I didn't mean to—"

"You think I don't have any feelings?"

"Oh, Mol, I'm so sorry."

She shrugged.

"Know what, Mol? I don't miss them. Not at all. It's like . . . like I never saw who they really were. I just hung with them because they were popular and I was *supposed* to hang with them. And I liked being the most popular one of all," I confessed. "Do you hate me?"

"No, you idiot," Molly said. "I love you."

Hearing Molly say that made me cry all over again, which made Molly cry, which finally made both of us laugh. Then she forced me to take a shower, wash my hair, and brush my teeth. And return, for whatever it was worth, to the land of the living.

"*L*ara?"

It was Mom, home from Los Angeles. I was in the living room, playing the piano. That was mostly what I had been doing for the past two days, ever since Molly had come over. Molly had wanted me to stay at her house, but I wanted to be alone. Alone with my piano. I thought I had given it up, but now the only solace I found was losing myself in the music. I had even set up a lesson.

"I'm in the living room," I called back to her.

She came in, looking tired and pale. "Hi, sweetie." She kissed the top of my head. "I called you and called you, but you were never home."

I didn't bother to correct her assessment of the situation.

She looked over the sheet music that I had been practicing. "You're playing again," she said approvingly.

"Yeah, I guess. Where's Scott?"

"He went up to his room." She pinched the skin at the bridge of her nose and then reached into her pocketbook. "I don't think he had a very good time. He was worried about me. Damn, I'm out of cigarettes."

"What's Scott worried about?"

"You've been through so much, Lara, I hate to—"

"Mom, what is it?"

She sighed and pressed her lips together nervously.

"Your father and I . . . we've had some problems lately."

"I'm glad to hear you admit it," I said.

She gave me a sharp look.

"What?" I asked. "You think Scott and I are so stupid that we don't know?"

She was silent for a moment. "We used to have so much fun together. Remember when you and I were in that mother–daughter pageant at the club? For cystic fibrosis? And we wore matching bathing suits, and Dad was one of the judges—"

"That was a long time ago, Mom," I said wearily.

"It seems like yesterday."

"Look, can we cut to the chase here? Are you and Dad getting divorced?"

She looked at me sharply. "Lara! When did you get so cold? You didn't used to be so cold."

"Some things change."

"Well, it isn't sweet," my mother pointed out. "It's especially important now for you to use your pageant training and be sweet . . ."

"Why? Because I'm fat?"

"Frankly, yes," my mother said, fluffing her hair. "Everyone doesn't know you have Axell-Crowne, you know."

"Meaning since they're going to think I'm just a big fat slob, at least they should think I'm a *sweet* big fat slob," I translated.

"You want to twist my words, fine," Mom said, hurt. Even with exhaustion and stress etched on her face she was beautiful. And thin. Two things I would probably never be again.

"Look, I have a piano lesson in a half hour," I told her. "So if you want to tell me whatever it was you were going to tell me—"

"Your father has taken a lot of business trips lately."

To escape from his eyesore of a daughter.

"Yeah, to New York," I said. "So?"

"He hasn't been in New York."

"Where's he been?"

She hesitated. "The Vanderbilt Plaza hotel."

"The Vanderbilt Plaza hotel?" I echoed incredulously. "The one in *Nashville*?"

She nodded.

"He's been right here in Nashville? And he never sees us?"

She nodded again. "He doesn't spend all his time there. He . . . this is very difficult for me—"

"What?" I snapped. "Just say it!"

"He has been spending a great deal of his time at an apartment on the other side of town. At . . . a colleague's."

"Who?"

"Tamara Pines," my mother said painfully.

Tamara Pines? She was the art director at Dad's agency. I had seen her at office Christmas parties for the past four years. She was young—thirty tops—with short, sexy auburn hair, long legs, and the body of someone who lived in the gym.

He doesn't believe in affairs, either. But that didn't stop him from having one.

It was true.

And it was all my fault. For turning into a pig. For letting him down.

"He left us for her?" I asked, my voice low.

"He hasn't left us," my mother said quickly. "Dad's been in a lot of pain—"

"Over me," I said, standing up. "He hates me."

Mom looked shocked. "What are you talking about?"

"Ever since I got fat, he can't stand looking at me."

"Lara, it's not about—"

"He doesn't want to be here anymore because I'm such a disappointment to him. That's why he's with—"

"Lara, I'm his wife, not you!" my mother screamed.

"So act like it!" I yelled.

"What are you talking about?"

My mind was a sea of red-hot rage; the monster burst free and filled the room. "You're always all over him, cooing at him, trying so hard to look so sexy. Do you actually think he likes that? You're disgusting, pathetic—"

That was when my mother slapped me across the face.

Hard.

We both just stood there, shaking.

"It's bad enough competing with her," she said bitterly. "Do I really have to compete with you, too?"

"That's sick," I said.

"He paid more attention to you than he did to me."

"Is that supposed to be *my* fault?"

"You loved it, Lara. You ate it up with a spoon."

"Because he's my father," I said. "My *father*."

"The two of you formed this complete little circle. No one else could even get in."

"Not anymore," I said. I set my jaw hard. "Now *I'm* fat, and *you're* old, and *she's* young and thin. So I guess we both lose."

My mother's face crumpled.

"I'm getting out of here," I said, and walked toward the door.

"Wait," Mom called to me. "Lara, wait."

I stopped, but I didn't turn around.

"Your father has been involved with her for a long time, Lara."

"How long?" I asked. "Three months? Four months? *Five* months?"

"Try three years."

Three years ago. Before I was fat. *Way* before I was fat. Back when I was still his princess. How could he do that? How? I had tried so hard to be perfect, and he still, he still—"

"I found out from a so-called well-meaning friend," Mom said bitterly. "It was months before I confronted him—I was so sure it would just end on its own. But it didn't. Finally, we had it out. He promised me it was over. Only it's never been over."

I sat on the edge of the couch. "You mean all this time . . ."

"All this time," she agreed. She sat down next to me. "My mother always told me, 'Carol, it's a man's nature to cheat. You keep yourself up, hold your head high, and look the other way.' And I did, didn't I?"

I didn't answer her.

"Your father is a very proud man," she went on. "There aren't enough opportunities for him at the agency—he's too creative for them; he's frustrated there. He needed to prove himself, and there was Tamara Pines, ready and willing. If a pretty young woman with enough guts and a great body wants a man badly enough, she can—"

"What about vows? What about love?" I asked dully.

"Men forget," Mom said with exhaustion. "When they feel a certain way, they just . . . damn, I need a cigarette."

"He cheated on you and deserted us and lied to us and you're *defending* him?"

"I love him, Lara."

She loved him.

Love. Now that was a funny word. What did it mean, anyway? I loved Jett, but I couldn't have him, not the way I wanted him. Jett loved me, but he couldn't love me the way he wanted to love me. Dad loved me, but only when I was perfect. Mom loved Dad, but she was so afraid of losing him that she made excuses for the inexcusable.

Love. What a stupid, stupid word. What a joke.

"What's love got to do with anything?" I asked Mom. "Frankly, I'm glad you're divorcing him."

"I'm not divorcing him," Mom said quietly.

"You're not?"

"Before I left for Los Angeles, I gave your father an ultimatum. I told him he had to choose—Tamara or us. Grandpa arranged for your father to get a job offer at a big agency in Detroit. So I told your father that either he accepts the job in Michigan and never sees Tamara again, or . . ."

No, no. It couldn't be true.

"Michigan?" I whispered.

"I told him he had to choose," Mom said again. "We can't stay in Nashville, not with that woman here, not when everyone knows." A tremulous smile came to Mom's lips. "Your father chose us, honey. He chose us."

My heart thudded painfully in my chest. "You're telling me that we're moving to *Michigan*? Because Dad had an *affair*? And you're *embarrassed* about it?"

"It's more than that," Mom said. "That woman is trying to break up my marriage. We all have to get far away from her. And this new agency is supposed to be great. Grandpa will buy us a house, and—"

I stood up. "You understand that I'm not going with you, don't you?"

"Of course you are," Mom said, standing up, too. "I have some wonderful news. Remember the Axell-Crowne specialist in Ann Arbor? I spoke with him about you, and—"

"Don't you get it? My *life* is here. People knew me before I was stuck in this freak show of a body. Everyone here knows this isn't my fault. If I move to Michigan, I'll just be the new fat girl. *Can't you see that?*"

My mother's lower lip quivered slightly. "Lara, I'm sorry. I know it won't be easy. But if I have to choose between something that is going to be difficult for you—"

"Difficult?" I said, getting my face very close to hers. "It's more than *difficult.*"

"Okay, very difficult," Mom amended. "But if I have to choose, I'm keeping our family and my marriage together. I'm sorry."

"Sacrificing your daughter to save your so-called marriage. Well, isn't that ducky," I spat at her.

"It isn't like that, Lara—"

"Oh yes, it is," I said. "It's exactly like that. Exactly."

"Can I come in?"

Scott was at my door.

"What time is it?" I asked. After my fight with Mom, I had gone to my piano lesson and banged the piano so hard that my teacher called it quits after fifteen minutes. Then I'd driven around aimlessly for a while, and finally I

142

had come home and crawled into bed. I'd been there ever since.

"About nine," he said. "I brought you a sandwich." He put the sandwich down on my nightstand. I pulled the blankets farther up over me.

"Mom told you, huh?" He sat on the end of my bed.

"I hate her," I said viciously.

"Why? It's his fault. He's a dirtbag."

"He's not a dirtbag," I said automatically.

"Why are you still defending him? You aren't his perfect little princess anymore."

I couldn't think of an answer.

Scott raised his knees and stretched his ratty Kurt Cobain T-shirt over them. "Remember Dad's office party, two Christmases ago? At the Opryland Hotel? When Dad's secretary got wasted on eggnog and hurled on the president of the company?"

"What about it?"

"I had to go to the john, and I got lost—you know how that place is—all those jungle plants and crap everywhere. So I went the wrong way, and I came over this little bridge, and there was Dad, behind some giant fern. With Tamara Pines. Kissing."

I stared at him.

"I mean, like, *really* kissing," he went on. "His hand was down the front of her shirt. They didn't see me."

"Did you ever tell him you saw him?"

"Nah," Scott said. "I never told anyone. That was the day I totally lost all respect for him."

So *that* was why Scott hated Dad so much. "Maybe if you'd said something, he would have stopped it a long time ago and none of this would be—"

"Yeah, great, blame it on me," Scott said with disgust.

He got off my bed and headed for my door. "Just forget I told you, okay? Just forget I ever—"

"Wait, Scott."

He did.

"I'm sorry, you're right," I said. "It isn't your fault."

Scott turned around and came back over to me.

"What are we going to do?" I asked him.

He shrugged and sat back down on my bed. "Move to Michigan, I guess. It sucks."

I sat up. "They can't make me. I'll move in with Molly for senior year."

"Yeah, that's a good idea," Scott said. "Those guys in Michigan, I mean, they wouldn't know you, so they'd just rag on you and stuff for being . . . you know. God, your life would be, like, this total hell."

"I'm talking to Molly," I said decisively.

"Cool," Scott said. "Although . . . I would kind of, like, miss you."

I leaned over and hugged him. "Thanks."

"Yeah, whatever," Scott mumbled. "Hey, maybe you and Jett could get your own apartment. That'd be rad."

Jett. Just hearing his name was like a surgical cut, swift, sharp, potentially lethal.

"He . . . we . . . broke up."

Scott looked shocked. "But I thought . . . I mean you guys are so . . . You broke up?"

I nodded.

"Oh, man," Scott said, shaking his head from side to side. "He was the first decent guy you ever went out with. Hey, did he dis you for being . . . you know?"

Fat, he meant. I noticed how it was a word with unnatural weight—no pun intended. Kind of like *cancer*. No one likes to say it to you aloud. Sometimes they just don't want to insult you. Or maybe they're afraid that if they say it, they might catch it.

"He didn't dis me," I said.

"I didn't think he would," Scott said. "He's way too cool for that."

I couldn't possibly explain about the difference between love and being in love. About how it is when two people find each other, and everything fits—your minds, your dreams, your bodies. And you want each other so much there's this fire, and it's always there, always. Until, for one person, the flame dims, and one day it goes out completely—you don't even know exactly when it happened—and then it's gone, and you can't pretend it isn't, and you can't ever get it back again.

No, I couldn't possibly explain that.

I smiled at my little brother. "You're going to be a lot cooler than Jett one day," I told him.

"I know one thing for sure," Scott said, brushing his hair out of his eyes.

"What?"

"I'll *definitely* be a lot cooler than Dad."

Chapter 218

illions of girls binge and purge, or swallow hundreds of laxatives, or starve themselves so much that they turn into walking skeletons. Because everyone knows that *anything* is better than being fat. *Anything*.

I vowed to become one of those girls.

Because there was no way on God's green earth that I was moving to Blooming Woods, Michigan, weighing 218 pounds. Axell-Crowne or no Axell-Crowne.

Three weeks before the move date, the final edict came down from my parents. They had thought it over and they had decided that I had to go to Michigan with them. Dad came home so that he and Mom could present the little charade of bonding over "my problem."

They sat on the couch together and told me I couldn't live with Molly's family for senior year. We were a family, and family stayed together—that was the whole point of the move, they said. I would have to face the world eventually at my new "size," they said. Besides, maybe the Axell-Crowne specialist at the University of Michigan's hospital would be able to help me, they said. And anyway, they would be behind me a thousand percent, they said.

What a joke. Almost as big a joke as their marriage.

Well, that was their problem. Fat was mine.

I went to the drugstore and bought a dozen packages of laxatives. That day I ate one small apple and a fat-free yogurt. At dinner I took two mouthfuls of broiled sole, and one of green beans. Both my parents looked at me approvingly. Then I told them I had a little stomachache, and went upstairs to bed.

That was where I swallowed three packages of laxatives. I wasn't sure it was enough. So I chewed another whole package, just to be sure, and lay down on my bed.

It wasn't long before the stomach cramps started. Good. I wanted to feel sick from food, to be empty. I ran into the bathroom and sat on the toilet. My insides were coiled in a knot. I was doubled over, but I didn't care. Everything was coming out of me.

I spent most of the night in there. Even when I finally fell asleep at around two, totally exhausted, the cramps woke me up again, and I stumbled back to the bathroom, again and again, until finally there was nothing left inside me. It wasn't until sunrise that I finally fell asleep.

I felt so sick the whole next day. The cramps wouldn't stop. I didn't care. Molly called and I told her I wasn't feeling well. I spent the day in bed. Dad was supposedly out of town again—who knew where he really was? Between Mom selling her party business and packing up to move, she wasn't paying much attention to me. So no one noticed that all I had that day was some tomato juice and a banana.

That night I took more laxatives.

And spent another night on the toilet. Only the cramps were worse this time, but it didn't matter. It felt good to have the pain in my body be as bad as the pain in my heart.

Then a third day of hardly eating, of ingesting practically nothing but water, a third night of laxatives. I sat doubled over on the toilet, moaning and crying from the pain. All that was left inside me was a fetid liquid that burned as I voided it into the toilet. Every time I tried to make it back to bed the cramps hit me again, so finally I fell asleep sitting on the toilet, my head leaning against the sink. When I woke up in the morning, I was lying on the cold bathroom tile floor, shivering in my own liquid feces. With my sick body weak and vibrating, I cleaned my bathroom and then got into the shower and cleaned myself.

I could barely make it down to the gym to weigh in. Spots danced in front of my eyes. I was short of breath. But if it made me lose weight, I didn't care.

I got on the scale.

It read 218 pounds.

I hadn't lost an ounce.

My body sagged against the wall of the gym and I slid down until I hit the floor. I didn't have the strength to hold myself up. I just sat there, heartsick. Dr. Laverly had warned me that purging by barfing or by laxatives would only make me ill. I hated her for being right.

As I sat there, too worn out to move, I dimly heard the front doorbell. The next thing I knew, Jennie Smith was standing in the doorway of the gym.

"Lara? Are you okay?" she asked, rushing over to me on her skinny legs, clad in faded jeans.

"What are you doing here?" I asked bluntly.

"I heard you were moving and I wanted to say good-bye. Your mom let me in," Jennie said. She knelt down next to me. "Are you okay?"

"I have the flu," I said. "It's very contagious."

She stood up quickly and took a step away from me. "Well, I hope you feel better soon."

I didn't bother to reply. She could care less. And I could care less about her. I had no idea what the real reason was for her showing up at my house.

"How soon are you moving?" she asked.

"A couple of weeks."

"Well, you should come to Bongo Java with us some night before you leave and say good-bye." Bongo Java was the coffeehouse in town where everyone hung out.

"What for?" I asked her wearily.

"Well, because we're all going to miss you," Jennie said as if she really meant it. "Just last night I saw Jett there and he said—"

"You saw Jett?" popped out of my mouth. I hadn't seen him since the night I had broken up with him. But I thought about him all the time. There was a hole in my heart where he used to be.

"Uh-huh," Jennie said, leaning against the handles of the treadmill. "He was there with that girl who sings lead for the Sex Puppets. Remember? From homecoming?"

Now I knew why she had come over. She wanted me to know that Jett was with another girl. Even if she hadn't gotten him, she wanted me to know that I didn't have him anymore, either.

Cramps hit me like a swift punch in the gut. I stumbled to my feet, toward the bathroom.

"I'm sorry you're so sick!" Jennie called. "If there's anything I can do—"

Somehow I found the strength to turn around and face her. "Yeah, there is," I said. "You're a bitch, Jennie. And you can go to hell."

Then I ran into the bathroom and got sick all over again, from both ends at once.

Dear Jett,

Last week Jennie Smith came over and told me she saw you at Bongo Java. And yesterday Molly told me she saw you at the Phish concert, and you told her you're leaving for New York next week.

I can't believe you haven't called me. I can't believe you don't even want to say good-bye. I can't believe that I'll never be in your arms again, or feel the beating of your heart against mine.

Please, just tell me what love is. I mean, I really, really want to know. You said you would love me forever. I guess you meant you'd love me forever unless I got fat. I guess you forgot about that part. If only I could

I stopped writing. Then I balled the letter up and threw it into the trash. What was the point? What was the point of anything? Of living?

Two weeks later, we moved.

My mother and father acted like they were some perky TV sitcom parents from the sixties. No one ever talked about why Dad had been gone for so long. Mom and Dad pretended they were madly in love and the whole family was starting out on a wonderful new adventure.

The hardest thing had been saying good-bye to Molly. That last night, we stayed up talking till dawn. In the morning, when the taxi came to take us to the airport, Molly and I hugged one last time and swore we'd be best friends forever. She stood in our driveway, and I watched her face get smaller and smaller as I left the last remnants of my real life behind forever.

We talked by phone every single night. It was the only thing that kept me going. But it wasn't the same as being with her.

At our new house in Blooming Woods we didn't have a home gym, but my parents put the treadmill and scale up in my bedroom. I counted calories by day and ran by night. It wasn't like I had anywhere to go or anything to do. It wasn't like I wanted to make friends.

I must have been the fittest 218-pound girl in Michigan. But my weight stayed the same.

Dr. Goldner, the Axell-Crowne expert at the University of Michigan, thought it was great that I wasn't gaining anymore. He gave me his own food and exercise plan, said I should come back and see him in two weeks, then patted me on the head like a good little girl.

The night before the first day at Blooming Woods High School, I called Molly. "It's me," I said into the phone. It was late, past midnight. My room was illuminated only by the moonlight coming through the window. There were no beauty queen trophies on the dresser—I had packed them all away when we moved. In my top drawer, where I wouldn't have to look at it, was the photo of me and Jett at homecoming.

"Tomorrow's the big day, huh?" Molly asked.

"*Big* is right. Day one as the fattest girl in the senior class of Blooming Woods High."

I hadn't planned to go to public high school. My parents had felt guilty enough about forcing me to move that they had suggested I go to private school. I'd agreed. So I had started at Cranmoore, the best private school in the area, a week earlier.

My senior class was very small and very rich, and I was the only girl who wore over a size ten. I had spent the entire week walking through the carpeted halls without one person saying so much as hello. The cool girls had looked at me as if I smelled bad. One had actually come up to me and said, "Don't you have any self-respect?" I was too mortified to reply.

I decided to transfer to the public high school—*anything* would be better than Cranmoore. Besides, Blooming Woods High was so big that maybe I could just lose myself in the crowd.

"Hey, cheer up," Molly said. "Maybe someone else will be even fatter than you are."

I had to laugh. "You are really demented."

"Thank you. We start back tomorrow, too."

Back to Forest Hills High, where everyone knew the real me. I felt a lump in my throat. "I wish I was there."

"I wish you were, too."

I wrapped the phone cord around my finger. "What if Blooming Woods is as bad as Cranmoore? What if it's worse?"

"Maybe if you tell everyone you have Axell-Crowne—"

"No one has heard of it; they wouldn't believe me," I said. "And even if they did, no one would care."

"Look, you're a terrific person, Lara. Once people get to know you, they'll like you."

"It's so funny," I said bitterly. "It used to be that people liked me before they knew me, because of how I looked. And now people *dislike* me before they know me, because of how I look."

Molly didn't disagree. I could hear the last crickets outside my open window. The night air was chilly. Outside, things were dying.

"I bet it's not that hard to kill yourself," I said. "With pills."

"Don't say that!"

"It would probably just feel like going to sleep."

"Lar, you're scaring me. Lar?"

"Don't worry," I said. "I wouldn't really do it."

"Are you sure?"

"I'm sure."

"Call me tomorrow and tell me everything, okay?"

"Okay." I hung up. Then I rolled off my bed and gazed at myself in the mirror on my dresser, searching for any remnants of the girl I had been. I supposed that if you looked closely enough at my face, you could still see that I was in there. Somewhere.

Such a shame. She has such a pretty face.

I didn't have any pills. But it couldn't be that hard to get them, could it?

Maybe it really *would* just feel like going to sleep.

"**L**ara, breakfast!" my mother called upstairs to me.

I ignored her and tore off the black shift I had on. It landed on the pile of clothes on my bed. I had tried on every single outfit I had purchased in my new size, size twenty-four.

I hated everything.

I looked awful in everything.

Desperate, I reached for the jeans, white T-shirt, and navy blue vest that had been the first outfit I'd tried. I studied my reflection. Did the vest help hide my huge stomach? I turned back and forth, nervously surveying all angles. Some outfits hid my fat better than others. I obsessed all the time about the magic combination that would make me look somewhat thinner.

It was no use. I looked fat. Enormous. Grotesque.

"Hey, breakfast," Scott announced from the doorway of my new room.

I turned to him. He had on his baggiest jeans and a tie-dyed Grateful Dead T-shirt.

"That's what you're wearing?" I asked him.

It would be Scott's first day of ninth grade, which meant high school. For the first time since grade school, we'd be at the same school.

"Yeah, why?" he asked, looking down at himself.

"What if kids don't dress like that here?"

"Like I care," Scott said. He went downstairs.

I took one last look at myself, decided it was hopeless, and then went down to breakfast. Mom smiled at me. Our new breakfast room had cheery pink-and-white-striped wallpaper.

"Well, Lara, don't you look lovely," Mom said as she put a glass of orange juice in front of me.

"Please," I said, taking a seat.

I stared at the juice. My stomach was a mass of coiled fear. I knew I couldn't possibly squeeze one drop of that juice down my throat.

"Morning, all," Dad called, coming into the kitchen. He dutifully kissed Mom first, then me, then Scott. I figured this was one of those things the therapist Mom and Dad had gone to for a few sessions had told him to do. They didn't go anymore—they claimed everything was fine now and they didn't need to pay someone to solve the problems they had already solved.

"So, today's the big day. Pretty exciting, huh?" Dad asked cheerfully, taking a sip of his coffee.

Scott and I both gave him withering looks.

"Hey, that's not the winning attitude of the Ardeche team!" Dad said. "We never say die, right?"

"You must be on drugs," Scott mumbled, and got up from the table, carrying his English muffin with him.

"I guess we'll go," I said. "I don't want to be late the first day."

"Have a great time, you two," Mom said, kissing us both.

"And remember," Dad added, "it's all in your attitude."

"All right, class, settle down, settle down," the teacher, Mrs. Benson, called. She had written her name on the chalkboard. She was middle-aged, frumpy, with graying dark hair. Her glasses hung from a chain around her neck.

Frankly, I was relieved to have found her at all. The school was huge, and I had gotten lost trying to find my homeroom. In one corridor a boy had puffed his cheeks full of air and waddled behind me. I had pretended I didn't see him.

Once I had finally found my homeroom, I'd slid into one of the few remaining empty seats—actually, a combination chair and desk—and my stomach pushed into the desk part. I sat slightly sideways so that I could breathe.

Everyone seemed to know everyone. They greeted each other with shrieks, laughter, hugs, kisses. Of course, I didn't know anyone. I could feel people looking at me.

"This is, as you know, your homeroom, and I am, as you can see, Mrs. Benson," the teacher said, her tone no-nonsense. She sat on the edge of her desk. "We have some paperwork to get out of the way. When I call your name, please respond."

She perched her glasses on her nose and referred to a long green form. "For some reason I've only got last names and first initials," she said, shaking her head. "Must be some genius in data processing. Okay, people, obviously I know most of you, but please call out your full first name so I can write it into my records. Okay, here we go. M. Abbott?"

"Here," a girl in the back called. "It's Melanie."

Mrs. Benson mumbled, "M. Abbott, Melanie," and wrote it in. "D. Ackerly?"

"Yeah, here," a boy in the seat behind me said. I had noticed him—very cute, blond hair, intense blue eyes. In the past, when I was still my real self, a guy who looked like that would have flirted with me, would have given me that special look that I now knew was reserved for pretty, thin girls. Now he looked right through me as if I didn't exist at all.

"And we all know it's Dave," Mrs. Benson said dryly. I snuck a peek behind me. He grinned.

"L. Ardeche?"

"Here," I said. My voice sounded small and quavery. I cleared it self-consciously. "It's Lara. L-A-R-A."

"L. Ardeche," Mrs. Benson mumbled, and before she could write in *Lara* on her form, it was clear that her pen had stopped working. She scribbled for a second. Nothing.

"Okay, hold on," she told us, and went behind her desk to rummage through her drawer for a new pen.

"L. Ardeche? That's you?" the cute guy behind me, Dave Ackerly, asked eagerly.

So he *had* noticed me! I turned around, and he smiled at me again. Was it possible that I looked sort of cute in my new outfit? Maybe it really *did* flatter me. I nodded and smiled back.

"L. Ardeche—Lardash—Lard-ass!" he crowed triumphantly, leaning his chair back on two legs. "Great name for you, babe: Lard-ass!" He put his hands together like a megaphone. *"Lard-ass!"* he boomed.

"Mainstream," someone sang out in a deep voice from the back of the room.

"That's enough, people," Mrs. Benson called, still rummaging through her desk.

A bunch of people laughed.

I wanted to die. No, I *prayed* to die.

"Okay, we're back in business," Mrs. Benson said, coming around to the front of her desk. She said nothing about what Dave Ackerly had called me. Not that I wanted her to—that would have made it even worse.

After a half hour of first-day extended homeroom, the bell rang for us to go to our first class. Mine was senior AP English, room 211, with a Mr. Downberger. I walked into the hall with everyone else.

"Yo, Lard-ass!" I heard from behind me.

Dave Ackerly. I kept walking.

How could he say something so awful to me? How could I ever, for even one moment, have thought that he might actually have thought I was cute?

Something Molly had said to me years ago came flooding into my head:

You put on a certain outfit, and you go around feeling kind of cute, and then someone says something, and you realize you actually look like a big fat slob and you were the only one stupid enough to think you looked good.

Exactly.

I turned the corner and headed up the staircase, just another face in the crowd, figuring I had left Dave Ackerly behind me. Only the next thing I knew, he was walking right next to me.

"Hi!" he said, his voice really loud. He put his arm around me. I shook him off.

"Hey, you're new, right, Lard-ass?"

"Go to hell," I managed, my heart pounding and my face burning with humiliation.

"What's the problem? I just wanted to welcome a big beauty like you to our school! Wanna go out on a date sometime, Lard-ass?"

I moved away from him and walked faster.

"Come on, Lard-ass!" he yelled after me. "Didn't you ever hear 'the bigger the cushion, the better the pushin'?"

"Shut up, asshole," someone said to him, but I didn't turn around to see who had jumped to my defense.

Instead I ran, my whole fat body jiggling down the hall with every step, until I reached a girls' room. Then I ran inside and locked myself in a stall.

I can't do this, I thought. I'd rather be dead than do this.

I sat in that stall and cried. I felt defeated, worthless. I felt like less than nothing. Just because I was fat. What was I supposed to do, wear a sign that said, "I am a former pageant winner. It is not my fault that I am fat. I have a very rare metabolic disorder called Axell-Crowne Syndrome that many doctors do not believe actually exists. Thank you."?

Nothing else awful happened in any of my other morning classes, and thankfully Dave Ackerly wasn't in any of them. On the other hand, no one was particularly nice to me, either. Just like at Cranmoore, no one introduced themselves or even smiled at me. It was the ultimate irony—I had become both huge and invisible.

At lunch, I got in the food line and chose a fat-free yogurt and an apple. I looked around. Everyone was sitting with their friends. I had no friends. I sat at the end of the only empty table I could find.

"Do you mind if I sit here?"

I looked up. A very thin girl was looking at me. She had a long, pale face, lank brown hair, and a receding chin.

"No, not at all," I said politely. Out of the monster's mouth had come the words of Lara Ardeche, pageant queen.

She sat down with her tray of macaroni and cheese.

"I'm Frannie Jenkins—from calc, this morning?"

"Oh, right." I didn't remember her. "I'm Lara Ardeche."

"You're new," Frannie said, her mouth full. "It's terrible to be new at this school. It's full of snobs. I was new

159

last year." She swallowed her food and took a sip of her milk. "So, how do you like it so far?"

"It's too soon to tell, really," I said, smiling my pageant smile. I could already tell she was someone I would have been nice to but never really been friends with, back in Nashville. I took a delicate spoonful of my yogurt.

"Hi, Frannie," said a short, chubby girl with a bulbous nose, thick lips, frizzy red hair, and a mass of freckles, setting her tray down next to the skinny girl.

"Hi," Frannie said. "This is Kendra Sleezak; this is Lara Ardeche. Kendra was the first person who was nice to me when I moved here—not like the rest of these snobs."

"They can't all be snobs," I said reasonably.

"Ha!" Kendra said. "I've lived in Blooming Woods since I was five. If you aren't thin, gorgeous, and rich, they treat you like a pile of puke."

A fat guy with a ponytail, his jeans so huge that the crotch hung halfway to his knees, sat down next to me. His tray was piled high with two sandwiches, French fries, potato chips, a huge piece of chocolate cake, and a brownie.

"Perry Jameson, Lara Ardeche," Frannie said. "She's new."

"Hi," Perry said. He took a huge bite out of his sandwich.

"Lard-ass, I want you to have my baby!" a voice boomed.

No, no, no. Dave Ackerly.

He had spied me. The next thing I knew, he had his arms wrapped around my neck and was making kissing noises at my cheek.

"Get your hands off me," I said, my voice low.

He obliged and took in the sight of me and Perry sitting next to each other. "I see you and Fairy Perry and the other geekoids found each other. It's so beautiful!"

He pretended to cry copious tears. Nearby, Dave's two friends high-fived each other, laughing.

"Go take your meds, Mainstream," Perry said, biting another monstrous piece out of his sandwich.

"Hey, maybe you'll get lucky this year, Perry!" David said. "Maybe ol' Lard-ass here can be the woman to turn you straight!" He turned and high-fived his buds, and the three of them sauntered out of the cafeteria.

Frannie's and Kendra's faces burned with embarrassment. Perry didn't seem disturbed at all. He was too busy shoveling food into his face.

"Just ignore him," Frannie finally managed. "He's, like, mentally disturbed."

"He used to go to this special school," Kendra explained. "But his dad is this big civil rights lawyer, and he sued to have him mainstreamed."

"My man, Mainstream Dave," Perry said between bites of his second sandwich.

"I heard he used to actually hit people," Frannie said, taking another sip of her milk, "but now he takes all these meds to control his impulses."

"Too bad the meds don't control his mouth," Perry said.

"There's a lot of snobs here, but everyone isn't like him," Frannie added. "I'm really sorry he . . . you know."

"It's okay," I told her.

"Hang in there—you'll meet people you like," Perry said, slurping down his milk shake.

"Yeah, you can hang out with me and Kendra!" Frannie offered.

I tried to smile. But it was hard. The pageant motto was to be nice to everyone, but this was just so horrifying.

I was *surrounded* by losers. They had *gravitated* to me.

Lara Ardeche, former homecoming queen, winner of multiple pageants, the cutest and most popular girl at Forest Hills High, had just been invited to hang out with the geekoids of Blooming Woods High, for one all-too-obvious reason.

They thought I was one of them.

Chapter 218

(continued)

"**L**et's go, girls!" Ms. Perkins, my gung-ho gym teacher, called into the locker room. She blew her whistle. "Let's hustle!"

From my hiding place in a toilet stall I heard the other girls chattering away as they exited into the gym. Finally the locker room was silent and I snuck out of the stall.

For the first two weeks of gym class I had been able to hide under sweats, since my gym uniform was such a large size that it had to be special-ordered. Today it had arrived, and Ms. Perkins had handed it to me like it was a week-old dead carp as a few of my classmates snickered.

I had retreated to the privacy of the toilet stall to put it on: bilious green one-piece shorts and top with an elastic waist, snaps up the front. Size twenty-four.

And it was tight.

I peeked out of the stall. No one was there. I walked over to the full-length mirror beside the lockers.

Oh, God. The material puckered over my breasts and thighs. Every lump, every ounce showed.

Oh, God.

"Ms. Ardeche?" Ms. Perkins called.

I could pretend I was sick. That would work. I could say I had killer cramps—

"Ms. Ardeche?"

Ms. Perkins marched into the locker room and stood over me. "Were you planning to join us this century?"

"I—I . . . ," I stammered. "I don't know if you've seen my records, but I have this disease that made me gain—"

"Ms. Ardeche, you don't have a doctor's note excusing you from gym class. Correct?"

"Correct."

"Then let's hustle!"

I followed her out into the gym. The girls in my class were in two groups, playing three-on-three basketball with each other until one side or the other scored and two new teams stepped onto the court.

"Join that group, Ms. Ardeche."

I walked over to the group nearest me. Allegra Royalton, the Jennie Smith of Blooming Woods High, took one glance at me in my huge green gym suit and shrieked to her friend Bettina Bowers, "Wow, Bettina, look! It's the Jolly Green Giant!"

They laughed together. I knelt down and got very busy tying my left sneaker.

"Jeez, Lard-ass is right," Bettina snickered. "I hope the gym floor holds."

"Ms. Ardeche, you're out there, let's hustle," Ms.

Perkins called to me, throwing me the basketball. I began to dribble it toward the basket.

"Earthquake!" Allegra Royalton yelled. Some of the girls laughed. I kept dribbling, my head down. I would not cry in front of them. Would not.

"Ms. Royalton, a word," Ms. Perkins called to her.

As I worked with my team, trying to score, out of the corner of my eye I saw Ms. Perkins talking with Allegra. Allegra made a face and rolled her eyes.

Someone stole the ball from me. Then the other team scored. I headed off the court.

"I hope you're happy, you fat piece of shit," Allegra spat at me. "Perkins just gave me detention because of you."

I stopped and turned to her. "Why are you saying such terrible things about me? I never did anything to you."

"I have to look at you, don't I?" Allegra said, and then she flounced off.

Finally gym class ended. I scooted into the toilet stall to change in private. Since it was my last class of the day, I could wait until I heard the locker room clear out before I left the stall. Which was exactly what I did.

Frannie Jenkins was waiting for me when I came out.

"Allegra Royalton is a bitch," she told me, pushing some hair behind her ear. "She makes fun of everyone. I hate her so much. I hate all her friends and her whole clique."

I headed for the sink to wash my face.

"She only cares about the perfect people," Frannie went on. "I hate snobs like her. They run this school, it's so unfair. That's why us nobodies have to stick together."

Leave me alone and go whine to someone else, I wanted to

yell at her. *I'm not a nobody. I'm nothing like you and your geekoid friends. Nothing!*

Frannie and I walked toward the main doors of the school. I had nothing to say to her. All I could think was: At least this hellhole called high school is over for another week.

"Hey, what's up?" Perry Jameson asked, falling in next to me. He had on his usual superbaggy jeans and a gigantic long-sleeved T-shirt that read I'M NOT STRESSED OUT, YOU'RE JUST INCREDIBLY ANNOYING. The inner thighs of his jeans swished against each other with every step he took.

"Hi, Perry," Frannie said eagerly. She'd confided in me that she had a crush on him. She thought he had such a handsome face—it was such a shame that he was gay.

"Hey," Perry replied.

"I have to run and meet Kendra," Frannie said. "I'll see you guys. Call me, Lara!" She hurried off.

"Are you two buds?" Perry asked me, surprised.

"No," I admitted. "She kind of whines."

"Tell me about it."

We turned the corner and headed for the doors. Perry pulled a candy bar out of his back pocket and tore it open.

"Want a bite?"

"No, thanks," I said, trying not to show my distaste.

"So, I've been thinking, you really ought to do the piano solo at the winter concert," Perry said, his mouth full of chocolate.

The only extracurricular activity I'd signed up for was a quartet of classical pianists who played with the school orchestra. The teacher, Mr. Webster, had asked me to

166

play a piano solo in a school concert that winter, and I had promptly declined. It was bad enough that I would be playing in public with the quartet—I did not plan to play a solo ever again. No one would be listening; they'd be too busy gawking.

Perry was in the orchestra, too. He played saxophone and he played it well. Unlike Frannie and Kendra, Perry was smart and funny and I actually kind of liked him, although I was grossed out that he never seemed to stop eating. Of course, back in Nashville, I would have been nice to him, but I never would have hung with him. But I wasn't in Nashville anymore.

"I already told you, I'm not playing a solo," I said as we turned the corner.

"Why? You more into blues than classical, I hope?"

"Why do you hope?"

"I live for blues," Perry said. "T–Bone Walker? Gatemouth Brown? Johnny Winter?"

I shook my head.

"They're only everything," Perry said. He took another bite of his candy bar. "I'll make you a tape."

I smiled politely, basically wishing he would just go away so that I wouldn't have to watch him eat.

"Free at last, free at last, thank God Almighty, I'm free at last," Perry sang out as we reached the front door of the school. He popped the last of his candy bar into his mouth and tossed the wrapper into a trash bin.

Kids streamed around us, out into the fall sunshine. Some guy bumped into Perry from behind in his rush to get out the door. "Watch it, Tubs!" he yelled over his shoulder.

"So, have a nice weekend," I said, turning away.

"Wait," Perry said quickly. "Uh . . . there's this club downtown I go to on Sunday afternoons. A lot of great musicians hang out . . . I mean, you're a musician, you might like it."

Was Perry Jameson asking me *out*? How could that be? He was gay. Not that I was even remotely attracted to him, anyway. I mean, he was just so . . . so fat.

"Gee, I'm really busy this weekend," I lied. "Maybe some other time."

"Whoa, it's Fat America!" Dave Ackerly boomed, striding over to us. "It's Fairy Perry the Fatboy and Lard-ass!" He put his arms around our shoulders.

Dave always referred to Perry as Fairy Perry, or Fatboy, or, if he was feeling particularly imaginative, Fairy Perry the Fatboy. This was clearly one of his imaginative days.

"Go take your Ritalin, Mainstream," Perry mumbled, but I could tell he truly was embarrassed.

"You two geekoids could make some bi-i-ig babies, huh?" Dave said gleefully, thrusting his hips forward obscenely. "You ought to give her a tumble. Fatboy! You can't stay a faggot forever!"

Perry's hands clenched into fists, and he turned red with rage. "Get out of my face."

"Oh no, Fatboy and Lard-ass are going to sit on me!" Dave yelled in falsetto horror. "Save me! Save me!" He ran away, laughing, toward the parking lot.

"What an asshole," Perry said, unable to look me in the eye. He slunk off toward the school buses.

Just as I was about to go to my car, I heard a girl's voice from somewhere behind me.

"Is that really your *sister* with the fat guy?" she asked.

I turned around. There, near the doors, stood my

brother with two girls and a guy. They all looked like freshmen and they were all cute.

Scott didn't see me looking at him. Quickly I turned my back so that they wouldn't know I could hear them.

"Yeah, so?" I heard Scott ask belligerently.

"So . . . she's kinda . . . big," the girl said.

"So?" Scott asked again.

"Tell her to go on a diet, man," the boy said.

"She's got a disease that made her gain weight, okay?" Scott said. "She used to win beauty pageants, okay?"

"I am *so* sure," one of the girls said.

"Here, check this out," I heard Scott say.

A beat of silence.

"Wow," one of the girls breathed. "When was this picture taken?"

"Last year," Scott said.

"Last year?" the other girl echoed incredulously.

"She was homecoming queen and everything. I'm tellin' ya, she's got a disease, so don't rag on her."

"Wow," the girl said again, her voice awestruck with horror. "I would just kill myself if that happened to me. I am totally serious."

I walked away and headed for my car. Scott showed up a few minutes later. I was so mad at him I couldn't speak. We drove toward home in silence for a few minutes. Finally I couldn't take it anymore.

"You carry my homecoming photo with you to *school*?"

Silence, as he figured out that I had overheard his conversation. Then he shrugged and stared out the window.

"I thought you thought all that pageant stuff was so stupid," I reminded him.

He shrugged again.

"I thought everyone who's into looks is so superficial, such a hypocrite," I said coldly.

"People say stuff about you," he muttered.

"No shit," I spat at him.

"I'm just trying to defend you—"

"You are not," I snapped, the acid of his betrayal gurgling in my stomach. "You're embarrassed that I'm your sister. Admit it!"

"What, you want them to think you're like that Perry guy—some kind of *pig* or something? It's not your fault that you're fat."

"Did I give you permission to talk about me or to carry my picture around? Did I?"

"Look, I just didn't want them to think that you were . . . you know, like him."

"A fat pig," I filled in as I pulled into the driveway. "So now they can feel sorry for me instead. If they even believe you. So sorry I embarrass you in front of your cool new friends."

I got out of the car, slammed the door behind me, and hurried inside and up to my room.

"Well, isn't this nice, the whole family together," Mom said cheerfully as she scooped some mashed potatoes onto my father's plate. She wore size-six jeans and a tiny, fuzzy pink sweater with too many buttons unbuttoned down the front. As she bent over she looked to see if Dad was checking out her cleavage. He wasn't.

"That's too much, Carol," he protested. "Gotta watch the ol' waistline."

"Oh, honey, you're perfect," Mom said, kissing him.

"So are you, honey," he said dutifully.

It was like watching two terrible actors in some really bad play.

"Well, I'm not perfect," I said, my voice a little too loud as I reached for the potatoes. "Being fat is very freeing. You can eat anything you want." I plopped three heaping spoonfuls of potatoes on my plate.

"If you'd count calories, Lara," my father said, "you might be able to do something about your problem."

Lara. Not princess.

I guessed there weren't any fat princesses.

"Now, honey," Mom chided him. "You know she can't help it. She has a disease." She put the world's tiniest portion of potatoes on her own plate.

"Yeah, poor me," I agreed, putting a big gob of butter on the potatoes.

My father gave me a look of what was supposed to be understanding but was actually thinly veiled disgust. He didn't seem to be able to get his mind around the facts of Axell-Crowne. No matter what anyone said to him, in his heart he still believed that all I needed was discipline: eat less, work out more.

"You'll never know if your Axell-Crowne goes into remission," he said, "if you keep eating like that."

He knew as well as I did that every other week I dropped down to a twelve-hundred-calories-a-day diet and checked my weight, per the instructions of Dr. Goldner. Dad knew that so far there was no change in my weight no matter what I ate or what I did.

And he *still* ragged on me.

I gave him a defiant look and added more butter.

Silence. Chewing.

Then finally, "So, kids, how's school?" Dad asked heartily.

"I hate it," Scott said.

"Me too," I added.

"I want to move back to Nashville," Scott said.

"Me too."

"Well, that's not going to happen," Mom said sharply, shooting me a murderous look. She took a dainty bite of chicken, chewed, swallowed. "How's dinner?" she asked Dad.

"Great," he said.

More silence. We were four strangers sitting there, masticating.

"Molly's coming to visit me for Thanksgiving vacation," I announced. "She called this afternoon."

"That's great!" Mom said. She turned to Dad. "Isn't that great?"

"Great," Dad said.

More chewing.

"Lara's first piano lesson with her new teacher is tomorrow," Mom said brightly. "I hear he's wonderful!"

I had changed my mind and decided I would take private lessons again after all. I was definitely not going to play solos in public, but that wasn't a good enough reason to deprive myself of studying with a qualified teacher. Music was all I had left.

"Terrific," Dad said, nodding his approval. "Remember, Lara, if you can dream it, you can achieve it."

"Geez, did you get that from her pageant résumé?" Scott said.

"Watch your mouth, son," Dad warned him.

Scott stuck out his lower lip and looked down, as if he were trying to literally watch his own mouth. I snorted back a laugh.

Dad pointed at Scott. "I've had just about enough of—"

The phone rang. Before anyone could stop him, Scott was out of his seat to get it. "It's for you," he told me.

"This is family time," Dad said sternly. "Tell them to call back after dinner."

"It's a guy," Scott said.

Jett! It had to be Jett! My heart pounded in my chest. I ignored my parents and ran out of the room.

"Hang up after I answer it!"

I reached the extension in the family room, forced my breathing to slow down, and picked up the phone.

"Hello?"

"Lara?"

"Yes."

"It's Perry. You know. Jameson."

Perry Jameson. Not Jett. The weight of disappointment forced me heavily to the couch.

"Perry," I said dully.

"I, uh, got your number from information," Perry said.

"Uh-huh."

"Can you talk now?" Perry asked.

"We were eating dinner, actually."

"Oh, sorry," he said. "I can say this real fast. The thing is . . . ahm-na-gay."

"What?"

"Yeah, slow down, Per," he told himself. "What I said is, I'm not gay."

"You're—"

"I realized that you might think—I mean, a lot of people at school think . . . but I'm not."

"Oh." I had absolutely no idea what to say. It wasn't like I cared one way or the other.

"It's just . . . last year there was this gay guy at school, a senior, Jack Parton, and we used to hang out," Perry rushed on. "He was one of my best friends and he was real out about being gay and everything, and a lot of kids dissed him. So I guess they just figured I'm gay 'cuz we hung together."

"Uh-huh," I replied.

"I never cared that much, because school is so lame anyway. But . . . well, the thing is, there's never been a girl at school that I liked before. Before now, I mean."

He meant me. He liked me.

"I . . . really have to go, Perry," I said. "Thanks for calling." I hung up.

This was so awful. He had only asked me out because we were both fat. He probably figured I was the only girl at school who wouldn't shoot him down. God.

"Was that a boy from school?" Mom asked eagerly as I came back into the kitchen.

"Yes." I took a sip of lemonade.

"That Perry guy, I bet," Scott said with disgust.

"You know him?" Mom asked. "Is he cute? Was he asking you out, Lara?"

Her neediness on my behalf made my teeth hurt. "I'm not interested," I said, my voice low.

"A boy from your new school just asked you out and you're not *interested*?" Mom was incredulous.

"What, just because I'm fat I'm supposed to go out with anyone who asks me?"

She sighed. "That's not what I meant at all. If you'd just be nice to people, they'd see beyond how you look."

I hated her. I hated her so much.

"Hey, here's an idea," Dad said. "How about if we go shoot some hoops in the driveway?" He pushed his chair back.

"I hate basketball," I said.

"Me too," Scott said.

"Why did I bother to put the basket up, then?" Dad asked.

"Honey, the kids appreciate that you put the basket up, really." Mom hugged Dad from behind. "You look so handsome, Jimbo, I can't resist you." She ruffled his hair.

"You know I hate that," Dad said.

"Okay, grouchy," Mom said playfully.

Dad threw his napkin on the table. "I have to go make a business call," he announced, and left the kitchen.

"He's calling *her*," Scott declared.

"There is no 'her,'" Mom said. "That's a terrible thing to say. That's over."

Scott looked at me. "You think he'd be stupid enough to actually call her from here?"

"Anything's possible in this house," I said.

"It's over," Mom insisted.

"Then why is he treating you like crap again?" Scott asked.

Mom glared at Scott. "You are not the judge and jury of your father, young man. He's just tense because of his new job—"

"When are you going to quit lying for him?" Scott asked, his voice rising. "Do you think we're stupid?"

"He loves me, and he loves you, and—"

"You are so full of it!" Scott yelled, getting up so quickly that he knocked his chair over. "Go ahead. Pretend we're the Brady Bunch. I don't care anymore." He stormed out.

Mom and I silently cleared the table, since Friday was the new housekeeper's day off.

"He is not calling her," she insisted as she swiped at the counter with a sponge.

"If you're worried about it, why don't you just ask him? Better yet, pick up the phone."

She lit a cigarette and inhaled deeply. Her hands were shaking. "Everything is fine."

I loaded the dishes into the dishwasher and turned it on. Mom smoked furiously, eyeing the phone that hung on the wall.

"Just pick it up!"

She didn't move.

"Fine, *I'll* pick it up." I reached for the phone.

"Stop it! Don't you dare."

I put my hand down.

"This is between your father and me," Mom said. "It has nothing to do with you."

"How can you say that? I'm stuck here in Michigan and my life is ruined because of it!" I whirled around and snatched up the phone.

There was a dial tone.

Dad walked into the kitchen. He eyed the receiver in my hand. "I have to go back to the office for a while."

"Why?" Mom asked.

"Conference," he said, pulling on his jacket. "I won't be long."

"Want me to come?" Mom called to him. "I could use the fresh air!"

Dad didn't answer. He was already gone.

Chapter 218

(continued)

"**H**ello!" I called out as I entered the City Center Rehearsal Studios. The outer office was empty. I was already fifteen minutes late for my first piano lesson with Dr. Alex Paxton, the teacher Dr. Carson in Nashville had recommended. I had gotten lost in downtown Detroit, and then I hadn't been able to find a parking space.

I heard loud music coming from an interior room, so I walked down the corridor to a glass door marked STU-DIO ONE. Studio One featured a beautiful black grand piano. Seated at the piano was a huge woman with wild, dark, curly hair, wearing black jeans and a fitted white T-shirt. A roll of fat on her back bulged under the line of her bra. Her upper arms jiggled as her fingers flew across the keyboard, playing something modern and jazzy.

When she finally finished, I knocked on the door and opened it.

She turned around. She looked to be in her late twenties. If she hadn't been so fat, she would have been pretty, I realized. She had huge blue eyes, high cheekbones, and full lips. But she *was* fat. Really fat.

"Hi, excuse me," I said. "I'm looking for Dr. Paxton?"

"Car accident," she said. "Are you Lara Ardeche?"

"He had a car accident?"

"Two days ago," she said, coming over to me. Her bust was massive; her T-shirt clung to the rolls on her stomach and midriff.

She should wear something looser-fitting so that her fat doesn't show quite so much, I thought.

"Someone rammed him at a stop sign," she continued.

"Is he okay?"

"He's got whiplash, but he'll be all right. You are Lara, right?"

"Right. I was supposed to start—"

"Didn't you get my message? I called on Thursday and talked to your brother."

"He didn't tell me. So, I guess I have to wait to—"

"I'm taking Dr. Paxton's students," she said. "That was the message I left. I'm Suzanne Silver, Dr. Paxton's assistant. Call me Suzanne." She put out her hand and we shook.

"What was that piece you were playing?" I asked her.

"Did you like it? I wrote it."

"Very nice," I lied. "Listen, maybe I should just wait until he's better."

"I really am qualified to teach, you know," Suzanne said, smiling. "Promise."

"Well, I only play classical—"

"Oh yeah, I've heard of that." She sat back down at the piano and flawlessly played a short passage from a very difficult Chopin waltz. Then she turned to me.

"I wasn't doubting you."

"Oh yes you were," she said, laughing. "But that's cool. You don't know me. So, how about if you play for me now?"

"All right." She got up, and I sat down at the piano. I closed my eyes and blocked out everything. Then I played Mozart's Sonata in B flat major. The music went through me, filled me up, until I *was* the music and I wasn't fat anymore. I was flying, released, free.

"Wow," Suzanne said softly.

I opened my eyes.

"That's a good 'wow,'" she explained, leaning against the piano. "Oh, I'm getting that feeling—"

"What feeling?"

"Goose bumps," she said. "Down my spine. When someone walks in here with the real thing, I get this feeling. You're really good. Dr. Paxton told me you're a senior, and he said—" She stopped herself.

"What?" I asked.

"It doesn't matter. Where are you going to college?"

"I don't know yet," I replied.

"You're going to be a piano performance major, though, aren't you?"

"No."

"But why not?"

"I don't perform solo," I said tersely.

"Oh, come on!" Suzanne exclaimed. "You just did!"

"Look, I don't want to talk about it, okay? I'm just here for lessons."

"Is it a stage-fright thing? Because I know ways to—"

"I said I don't want to talk about it," I repeated. "If you don't want to teach me because I don't want to concertize, just say so."

She stared at me a moment, then shrugged. "Let's check out your sight-reading."

She put sheet music on the piano for a mazurka, which I played, and then we worked on two other pieces I had already learned.

"I know the perfect music for you," Suzanne said. "I have to unearth it from the files. Be right back."

I turned back to the piano and idly played a minuet I had learned as a kid. In fact, I had played it when I had won Miss Tiny Tennessee. Mom and Dad had been so proud when they called my name. And Dad had lifted me up in his arms and kissed me and said, "That's my perfect little princess," and then—

"Hey, where's Suzanne?"

I turned around. A truly gorgeous guy was standing there—medium height, dark blond hair, dark eyes, and a cleft in his chin.

"She went to find some music for me," I explained.

"Good luck, her filing system stinks," he said good-naturedly. "You a new student?"

I nodded.

"Jazz?" he asked.

"Classical."

"Too bad," the guy said.

"Found it," Suzanne said as she rushed back in, brandishing the sheet music. "I really think you'll—"

"Hi, remember me?" the guy said, grinning at her.

She smiled back. "I do seem to remember you, but I'm busy now, so I'll remember you better later, okay?" She turned to me. "Did you two meet?"

"I'm Lara Ardeche," I said.

"Tristan McCoy," the guy said. He turned back to Suzanne. "I'll meet you at the Captain's when you're done, okay?"

"Okay," Suzanne said.

"Nice to meet you," he called to me as he left.

"That guy is gorgeous," I blurted out as I watched him walk through the outer office.

"Yeah," Suzanne agreed. She put the new sheet music up on the piano. "Okay, this is Ravel's *Sonatine,* and—"

"Are you good friends?"

"You could say that," Suzanne agreed. "He's an incredible musician. Guitar." She tapped her finger on the sheet music. "Okay, from the top."

The next hour passed in a blur of concentration. It felt good to be challenged again, to think about something other than my horrible life.

"Wow, time flies and all that," Suzanne said, looking at her watch. "So, are you going to study with me? I'm a slave driver, I'll tell you that up front. I'll kick your butt. But if you work hard, I'll also be your biggest fan."

"It's a deal," I decided. "And I love the Ravel."

"You really should think about two lessons a week, you know," Suzanne said. "If you want to make big progress before college—"

"I don't even know if I'm going to be a music major."

"Uh-huh." She gathered up some of the music. "So, I understand you just moved here . . ."

"From Tennessee," I filled in.

"Right. How do you like Michigan?"

I hate it.

"Fine."

"Really? Isn't it hard for you to be at a new school for your senior year?"

Of course it's hard, you fat idiot.

I bit my tongue. Monster-me was going into rage mode for no good reason. I fought back the beast.

"It's fine," I forced myself to say.

She cocked her head at me. "Yeah? What high school are you going to?"

"Blooming Woods."

"No kidding?" she asked, laughing. "That's where I went. I graduated ten years ago, and I still have the scars to prove it." She tapped her temple.

"It's okay." I got my purse from the chair.

"Well, it must have changed, then." She shook some curls out of her eyes. "I don't mean that I didn't have friends, because I did. But certain kids just loved to make fun of me."

I stared at her coolly. I knew what she was saying in fat-people code: I got teased, you get teased.

How pathetic. We had nothing in common. She probably ate all the time like Perry Jameson and deserved her fatness, whereas I was a prisoner in a body I hadn't earned.

"It's not a problem for me," I said flatly.

"Oh, well, good. It was torture for me. I'll never forget this girl Diane Levy. She made my life a living hell. Every day, when I walked into school, she'd yell out as loud as she could, 'Hey, it's Two-Ton Silver!' I wanted to sink through the floor and die, you know?"

She looked at me expectantly, waiting for me to share some personal story about similar humiliations I had suffered. So we could bond over our fatness. The rage welled up in me again.

183

"Thanks for the lesson," I said stiffly. "I'll see you next week." I turned toward the door.

"Wait a sec," she called to me. "Do you like jazz?"

"It's okay."

"Why don't you come over to Captain Bizarro's with me? I'm meeting Tristan and a bunch of our friends for lunch, and then we'll all play something or other."

I had absolutely no reason to say yes. I didn't really like her. On the other hand, I had nowhere to go but home, where Mom was so depressed and stressed out over Dad that all she did was chain-smoke, walk on the StairMaster, and obsess about her upcoming facelift, often simultaneously.

"What's Captain Bizarro's?" I asked.

Suzanne laughed. "It's sort of indescribable," she said. "So I guess you'll just have to see for yourself."

Captain Bizarro's was kind of rundown looking, on a side street near the campus of Wayne State University, in a neighborhood where you wouldn't want to be alone at night.

Inside, the empty room was filled with tables covered with white butcher paper, and the chairs were red vinyl, peeling at the corners. Billie Holiday blared from the jukebox, singing "Strange Fruit." I recognized it from an album my grandmother played sometimes.

"Hey, Mamacita!" a tall, skinny, brown-skinned man with a straggly beard called as we entered the restaurant. His skin was leathery; his voice was hoarse. He wore a white apron tied around his waist, faded jeans, and a green army camouflage jacket, and had a red bandanna tied hippie-style around his forehead. He hurried over to Suzanne and wrapped his arms around her in a bear hug.

"Captain, this is a new friend of mine, Lara Ardeche. And this is Captain Bizarro."

"Welcome to my humble abode," the man said, bowing from the waist. "Your beauty does me honor."

Was that supposed to be some kind of a joke? I didn't smile.

"Lara plays keyboards," Suzanne said.

Keyboards. I had never heard it put that way before.

"Everyone is downstairs already," Captain Bizarro said. "You're late!" He wagged a finger at her.

"My teaching went overtime," Suzanne explained.

"You want the usual?"

"Sure," Suzanne said.

"You like raw clams?" she asked me.

"Raw?" I repeated, aghast.

"Food of the gods," Captain Bizarro said, kissing his fingertips. "I also do fried that'll melt in your mouth." He kissed Suzanne's hand and took off toward the kitchen.

"So, why is he called Captain Bizarro?"

"It's a long story," she said as we walked down the stairs. "I'll tell you some other time."

Jazz grew louder as we descended, and we entered a room with a small stage at the rear. At the moment four guys were playing, with Suzanne's gorgeous friend Tristan on electric guitar. A fat older woman with caramel-colored skin and almond-shaped eyes, her graying hair in a long braid, stood at a microphone, snapping her fingers and swaying to the music. She had a flower in her hair.

185

Tristan took a guitar solo.

"Yeah!" an Asian guy called from a long table near the stage. "Play, Tristan!"

There wasn't much of a crowd: four people, including a young girl and guy who looked about my age. She was petite and slender. He was very cute, with short brown hair. He wore sunglasses, even though the room was dark. In the words of Molly—*très* affected. He bopped his head to the music. I sat down next to him, but he was too cool to even acknowledge my existence.

"Hey, gimme some sugar, sweet lady," an old black man told Suzanne.

She leaned over to kiss his cheek. "Hi, Asa."

She didn't bother to introduce me to anyone, so I turned my attention to the stage. I didn't listen to jazz much—only at my grandparents' house, really.

Tristan finished his solo, and everyone at the table applauded and whistled. The woman at the mike began to sing in a smoky voice. When the song was finished, everyone applauded again.

"I'll tell you what, that child can play the guitar," the old black man said, slapping his knee.

"Get your booty up here, girl!" the woman at the mike beckoned to Suzanne.

Suzanne bounded up to the stage, as did the Asian man and the old black guy. That left me with the young girl and the cute guy in the sunglasses. She whispered something in the guy's ear, gave me a cool look, and left the table.

My eyes slid back to the cute guy next to me. I smiled at him. He continued to ignore me.

"Hot food, make way, hot food," Captain Bizarro called, and he placed two huge platters in the center of the table—one with fried clams, one with raw clams in their shells, both surrounded by lemon slices. "Go ahead," he urged me. "Dig in."

"Try a raw one," the cute guy sitting next to me said.

"You can't nibble at it, neither," Captain Bizarro said. "You got to drop that whole sucker down your throat!"

The idea of swallowing a raw clam was beyond vile. "Well, I . . ."

"Go on," Captain Bizarro said.

Gingerly I lifted a raw clam to my mouth. I closed my eyes and slurped it down, trying hard not to gag.

"There's more where that came from," Captain Bizarro assured me as he blew me a kiss and headed back upstairs.

I picked up the nearest glass—someone else's half-full glass of ginger ale—and downed it quickly, trying to wash away the hideous taste.

"Hey, you just drank my soda!" the guy next to me said.

"I'll buy you another one," I said, humiliated.

"I have a feeling you've never eaten a raw clam before." He smiled a superior little smile.

"I'm just not hungry," I said frostily.

That terrible feeling of impotent rage came over me again. A year ago this guy would absolutely have flirted with me. He would have taken off his stupid sunglasses so that we could make eye contact, and then his eyes would have gotten that certain look in them, full of desire. But now I never, ever saw that look. And I missed it. I missed it so much.

He nodded his head along to the music as Suzanne took a solo at the piano.

"So, what do you play?" he asked.

"How do you know I play anything?"

"Suzanne brought you here, that's why," he said, still bopping to the music. "My name's Devon, by the way."

"Lara."

"You meet everyone yet?" he asked.

"I met Tristan at my piano lesson."

"Great guy," Devon said. "My guitar teacher. I wish Suzanne would just give it up and marry him already."

"They're a *couple*?" I asked incredulously.

"You didn't know that?"

"But he's so . . . and she's so . . ."

"So what?"

I raised my eyebrows. What I meant was obvious. He was gorgeous. She was huge. I really didn't need to say it out loud.

When I didn't answer him, Devon turned back to the music. The fat older woman in front of the microphone moaned lyrics about a guy who did her wrong. She swayed her large hips and sang with half-closed eyes. She looked ridiculous.

The girl came back to the table. "I gotta book—my mother just had a hissy fit over the phone," she told Devon, rolling her eyes. "You coming to the party next week?"

"Yeah," Devon said. "You?"

"If my mother lets me live." She leaned over and kissed him on the cheek, eyeing me coolly again. "See ya."

"Nice meeting you, too," I murmured after her sarcastically.

Devon laughed. "Don't mind Crystal. We used to be a couple. She still gets jealous if there's another girl around me."

188

Yeah, like he'd really be interested in me.

"Why did you break up with her?"

He shrugged. "She's just not cute enough," he replied.

I stared at him. What an asshole.

"That was a joke," he finally said.

"Well, it wasn't funny," I snapped.

He threw his head back and laughed. Everyone on stage finished playing their song. The black man took over at the piano; everyone else came back to the table.

"You two met, I take it?" Suzanne asked us as she reached for a raw clam and sucked it into her mouth.

"Hey, Suze, I just told Lara here that I broke up with Crystal 'cuz she isn't cute enough, so now she's pissed off at me!" Devon said, his voice full of glee.

Everyone at the table laughed, and I could feel my face flushing with anger and humiliation. "I don't see what's so funny," I said, jutting out my chin.

"It is funny, though," Suzanne said, grinning.

I pushed my chair back and stood up, pulling my T-shirt away from my stomach. If Devon thought Crystal wasn't cute enough, I could only imagine what he thought of porky me.

"Thanks for inviting me," I told Suzanne. "I'll see you—"

"Wait, wait, hold on," Suzanne said, biting her lip to keep from laughing. "You don't understand."

"I understand just fine."

"No you don't," Devon said. He grinned in my direction and waved his hand in front of his face. "See, I have no idea *what* Crystal looks like. I'm blind."

Chapter 218

(CONTINUED)

I stood there with my mouth hanging open while everyone laughed.

"Well, how was I supposed to know?" I protested. "And how did you know I drank your ginger ale?"

"I'm blind, not stupid," Devon said. "I heard you."

"Oh." I sat back down.

"Want another raw clam?" he asked devilishly.

"No, thanks," I said.

Still laughing, Suzanne and everyone but Devon went up onstage again and began playing a Cole Porter song. I studied his face. He was so handsome.

"Were you born blind?" I asked him.

He leaned forward. "It happened when I was fifteen."

Fifteen! That's awful, I thought.

"Do you mind if I ask—how it happened?"

"It's not a pretty tale," he began solemnly. "My mom told me that if I masturbated too much I'd go blind, but I said I'd just do it until I needed glasses, and—"

"You, you . . . God!" I sputtered.

"I'm sorry, I'm sorry," he said, trying to speak through his own gales of laughter. "So, here's the answer to all your burning questions. Yeah, I was born blind. Yeah, my other senses really are more acute. And no, I have no idea what you look like. So why don't you tell me? Better yet, let me see."

He reached over with one hand and touched my face. Very gently, he began to trace it with his fingertips—I closed my eyes as they lingered over my cheeks, neck, chin, lips.

"Nice," he said. "Soft skin."

I opened my eyes. "Thanks."

His gorgeous face was very close to mine, his voice low. "You smell like lemons."

"That might be the clams," I said.

He chuckled. "Good one."

Low, sexy music came from the stage. The air felt charged with something electric. Devon couldn't see that I was fat. So he was flirting with me.

"Where do you go to school?" I asked Devon.

"Wayne State," he said. "Freshman music major. You?"

"Still in high school," I admitted. "A senior."

"Comin' through, comin' through, hot stuff," Captain Bizarro said, flying across the room with two new trays of food. He set them down on the table and pointed at Devon.

"Hey! You coming to my birthday party next week?"

"But of course," Devon said.

"You gotta date?" Captain Bizarro asked, raising his eyebrows.

"Nah, man," Devon said.

"Me neither," Captain Bizarro said. "Ain't life a bitch?" He cocked his head slightly. "What?" he asked, though no one had said anything. "Don't bother me *now,* for crying out loud!" Then he hurried toward the stairs.

"He's a very strange man," I commented. "Why is he called Captain Bizarro?"

"It's like this," Devon said. "He's this brilliant guy—a chef, musician, just incredible. Only he got shot up in Vietnam and they put this plate in his head, and sometimes it makes him weird. Like, he'll hear voices talking to him, and he talks back. Last summer some bikers thought he was being a smartass, so they just about beat him to death."

"That's terrible!"

"I know," Devon said. "So now one of us always tries to be here, to keep him safe. Next Saturday is his forty-ninth birthday. We're closing early to give him a party. There'll be a lot of jazz. I think you'd have a blast."

He's going to invite me, I realized.

My God, life was so ironic. In the last forty-eight hours, I'd been asked out by a fat guy and was about to be asked out by a blind guy. If I'd even wanted to go out with the fat guy, everyone would say he had only asked me out because he knew a fat girl wouldn't turn him down. And if I went out with the blind guy, everyone would snicker that he didn't know he was out with a fat chick.

I didn't need that kind of humiliation in my life.

"Listen, Devon—"

"Listen, Lara—" he began at the same moment.

"Go ahead," he said.

"I just wanted to say that you're a really nice guy," I said earnestly. "And while I'd really like to go to the party with—"

"Oh! You're gonna come?"

"Well, I mean, if I'm invited, but—"

"Cool," he said, nodding. "You can come with me and my friends, if you want."

So he *wasn't* asking me out, he was being nice.

Was it because he'd felt my puffy face when he'd touched me? No, because he'd said "nice" when he'd touched me, and he'd meant it. I knew he'd meant it.

Which meant that he wouldn't have asked the old me out, either.

Huh. But then I had this thought: The old me would never have been sitting with a blind guy in some dump in downtown Detroit, listening to a fat lady sing.

Never.

"And here's what's so weird," I told Molly through the portable phone as I padded over to my door and closed it, trying to shut out the Grateful Dead blasting from Scott's room. "Suzanne is really fat and Tristan is about the best-looking guy I ever saw."

It was that evening. Dinner had been a silent, sordid little affair. While Scott and I ate, Mom chain-smoked and stared into space. No one mentioned Dad, who basically had been a no-show for days.

As soon as I could, I'd escaped to my room.

"Tristan's a chubby chaser," Molly said.

"What's that?" I lay down on my bed, my feet propped up on the wall.

"Guys who get turned on by fat girls. It's like a fetish."

"But Tristan doesn't seem weird."

"Neither do half the people in my mom's practice," Molly said. "They look as normal as you or me. But one guy—he's an accountant—he can only have sex if he's wearing his dead mother's panties."

"You made that up," I insisted, laughing.

"True," Molly admitted, "but the chubby-chaser thing is for real. I saw it on *Sally Jessy Raphaël*. There's this guy who wrote a book about how much he loves fat girls. Talk about living in a parallel universe!"

"So, wait, you mean that if Suzanne lost a lot of weight, Tristan wouldn't want her anymore?"

"It's a big, bizarre world out there," Molly said.

I thought a moment. "It would be kind of cool, though, wouldn't it? If fine guys thought you were gorgeous and perfect just like you are, instead of in *spite* of how you are?"

"Yeah," Molly agreed. "Except the only guys who think that way are like, these *deviants*."

There was a knock on my door. "Hold on a sec, Mol," I said, and pulled my mouth from the phone. "I'm on the phone!"

The door opened. It was Dad. I hadn't seen him in at least a week.

"Mol? My dad's here, I'll call you back." I hung up.

"Hi," Dad said, coming into my room.

"Hi."

He sat on the chair at my dresser, looking perfect, as usual. "How's school?"

"You haven't been home for a week, so you thought you'd pop in for a few minutes to ask me how school is?"

"School is important."

"Thanks for the insight."

He smiled a wan smile. "I know I haven't been here for you lately. I'm sorry, princess."

Princess. It had been such a long time.

"Are you going to tell me what's going on?" I asked.

Dad looked down at his hands dangling between his legs; then he looked back at me. "Life can get pretty problematic when you're a grown-up, Lara—"

Ping, as he hit a nerve.

"As opposed to my life," I said, "which has been so problem free."

He ignored my remark. A weird thought flitted through my brain: Had he really ever seen me at all?

"I've always believed in doing the right thing," he said, looking at the wall above me. "But sometimes a person's heart doesn't listen to what's right."

"You're seeing *her* again, you mean." And then the truth dawned on me. "You never stopped seeing her! That's the truth, isn't it?"

"I meant to. I wasn't lying when I said I'd stop—you have to believe that. But I love her."

"And you don't love Mom."

"I *do* love Mom," Dad said earnestly. "I'm just—I'm not *in* love with her anymore."

Ping, as he hit another nerve. Just like Jett and me: If a woman gets fat or old, there's no happily-ever-after.

"How could you do this to us?" I said bitterly.

"What about me?" he asked, finally looking at me. "Don't I deserve happiness? God, I've played by the book my whole life. What about me?"

195

I looked at him, and something strange happened. My whole life, I had seen him as a knight in shining armor, my perfect daddy. But now the knight was gone. In his place was this spoiled brat who really only cared about himself. Mom, Scott, me—we were just a reflection of how wonderful he was.

I stood up. "So, you're divorcing Mom. Fine. Have a good life with Tamara. Bye."

Dad stood up, too. "We're not getting divorced."

This was like an instant replay of the conversation I'd had with Mom back in Nashville before we moved.

"Sit down, princess," Dad said. He sat. I did, too.

"I don't plan to explain this to Scott—he's not mature enough to understand—but I think you will. Divorce is . . . messy. And expensive. And then there's you kids to think of. Your mother has very generously agreed to let me have my own life and keep our marriage together."

My head was pounding. "What does that mean?"

"Our marriage will stay together; we'll have an arrangement."

I was stunned. "You mean you get to have them *both*?"

"It's a very loving thing for both women to do—"

I stood up again. "Loving? You call that *loving*?"

"Lara, I didn't have to tell you about this, but I thought you were old enough to understand—"

"You—You make me sick. You make me want to throw up!"

"Lara—"

I pushed past him, went downstairs, and found Mom in the family room looking through an old photo album, smoking.

"Throw him out!" I demanded.

She just gazed at me.

"Don't you have any pride? How can you let him do this to you?"

"He told you," she said dully.

"What is wrong with you?" I demanded shrilly.

Mom closed the photo album slowly and looked up at me. "I'm forty-one years old, Lara, that's what's wrong. You think I could ever attract a man like your father again? Well, think again, honey. My mother was right: A woman keeps herself together, keeps looking the other way, and keeps her man."

From behind me I heard my father clear his throat. I turned around.

"I never meant to hurt either of you," he said from the doorway. "I love you both very much. And we'll still be a family." His eyes beseeched mine. "You're still my princess, you know."

I walked over to him and looked him in the eye. "We are not a family. You're a cheater and a liar, and you disgust me. And don't you ever, *ever* call me your princess again."

And then I walked out the door.

Chapter 218

(continued)

Dear Jett,

Remember Hilton Head, on the beach? I think I fell in love with you that first night we were together. I just felt so filled up with loving you. And now there is just this big hole inside me, where my heart used to be. I'm the same person inside, so what I really want to know is, how could you stop loving me?

No. Way too needy. I crumpled up the letter and started again.

Hey, Jett,

So, what's been going on? Things are really great for me here in Michigan, and

The bell rang for the end of homeroom, and I stuck both letters inside my notebook. Who was I kidding, anyway? I wasn't going to send Jett any of the dozens of letters I had written to him. What was the point? It was painfully obvious that he'd forgotten all about me.

I got up and headed for the hallway. Fortunately for me, Mainstream Dave wasn't in homeroom that day, so I had a brief reprieve from his insults.

HOMECOMING IS COMING! TICKETS NOW ON SALE IN THE STUDENT CENTER. SUPPORT OUR COUGARS!!

Overnight, the homecoming committee had filled the halls with signs and banners. Everyone seemed to be talking about it—who was going with who, who would be queen, whether the Cougars would keep their homecoming football winning streak.

Homecoming. Had it really been just a year ago? I had been so happy then. I was thin. My family was still together. I was thin. I lived in Nashville with all my friends. I was thin. I was the queen. I was thin.

I had Jett.

I was thin.

VOTE FOR HOMECOMING QUEEN! CAST YOUR VOTE AT THE STUDENT CENTER BY FRIDAY. Then, scrawled on the banner were the names of the cutest, most popular girls in my class: Christy-Lynn Lakewood, Allegra Royalton, Samantha Levine, Jane Neissan.

Jane Neissan was in my bio class and played third violin in the orchestra. She had shoulder-length auburn hair, green eyes, and a slender, graceful figure. Kind of like mine used to be, before I got robbed of my real life. And she was actually nice. We had shared a frog for dissection and she hadn't treated me like a leper.

"Hey! Hey, Lara!"

It was Allegra Royalton, of all people, hurrying over to me with another girl in tow.

A girl I recognized.

She was very pretty, with long brown hair and dimples. Her name was Willow Larken, and she and I had been in many regional pageants together. I knew she lived in Michigan, but what was she doing here at Blooming Woods High?

"This is Willow," Allegra told me. "She's been out with mono. She says she knows this really gorgeous girl from Tennessee who was in pageants with her, and this girl's name is also Lara Ardeche."

Allegra turned to Willow. "See, I *told* you it was a different girl."

Willow stared at me. Her eyes got huge.

"Lara?" she asked uncertainly.

There was no place to run, no place to hide.

"Hi, Willow," I said.

"What *happened* to you?" Willow asked me.

"Wait—wait—wait," Allegra sputtered. "You can't be serious, Willow. You're telling me she's the *same girl*?"

"I have a metabolic disorder," I told Willow. "It made me gain weight."

Willow put her hand on my arm in the sweetest, kindest pageant-winner way possible. "You poor thing!" she cried.

"Time out," Allegra said. "Are you telling me this fat tub was a *beauty queen*?"

"Is there anything I can do for you?" Willow asked, her eyes full of pity.

"Why do you hang out with her?" I blurted out.

"What?" Willow asked, taken aback.

"Her," I said, cocking my chin at Allegra. "She's such an ugly person."

"Now that is funny, coming from an ugly pig like you!" Allegra jeered.

"Oh, she doesn't really mean anything by it," Willow said mildly. "Just ignore her. Well, nice to see you, Lara. And if there's anything I can do . . ."

Right. Sure. Super.

I could feel them watching me as I headed down the hall: Pity. Disdain. Disgust.

I tried not to care. About Willow, or Allegra, or homecoming, or the zillion little soul-crushing insults that came my way every day. I had other things on my mind.

Like my mother, who now totally obsessed about her looks during every hour that she was awake. Some doctor had given her a prescription for sleeping pills, which conked her out early and kept her asleep until noon. After that, she worked out like a demon, chain-smoked, and consulted with new plastic surgeons about the facelift she was certain she absolutely had to have, which my grandfather would pay for. I asked her why she needed to consult still more surgeons when she'd already seen seven. She said she was looking for one who would promise to make her look twenty-five again.

And then she laughed in a way that wasn't funny.

Like my father, who called daily from Tamara's apartment in Nashville, leaving messages for me and Scott.

He'd actually been hired back at his old advertising agency. Of course I had clued Scott in on the truth about what was going on with our parents. He wasn't surprised. Dad's messages on the answering machine said how much he wanted to talk to Scott and me, how much he loved us, how he'd be home to see us soon.

It made me laugh in a way that wasn't funny.

"Hiya," Perry said, running a little to catch up with me in the hall. "What's shakin'?" He chewed on the last remnants of a muffin, peeling back the paper to get the crumbs.

"Not much." I dodged Kyler Trustus and his friends, who were ogling a copy of last season's swimsuit issue of *Sports Illustrated,* and stopped at my locker to get out some books I needed.

Allegra and Willow walked up to Kyler and his friends, and Allegra snatched the magazine out of Kyler's hands. Then she leaned over and told them something, and then they all looked over at me.

"No way!" I heard Kyler say. "That must have been a really *big* beauty contest!"

They all cracked up. Willow told them to stop, but she was smiling when she said it.

"Hey, Lard-ass belly-bumped me, I can't sto-o-o-p!" Dave Ackerly yelled as he ran by, careening into a locker on one side of the hall, then pretending to bounce off and careen into a locker on the other side.

Jane Neissan walked by and gave me a friendly wave. She looked very cute in a short suede jumper over a long-sleeved white T-shirt. She looked thin.

"How's it going?"

"Oh, fine," I said, closing my locker.

"Did you study for the bio quiz?"

"Two hours," I replied, rolling my eyes.

"I've got frog diagrams dancing in my head," she said ruefully, and walked on by.

"She's kinda nice," Perry said.

"Yeah." We headed down the hall.

"I have a theory," he said. "God doles out one decent human who is also popular to each high school. This is to partially make up for all the other popular people, who are essentially a human wasteland."

"There's nothing wrong with being popular," I said as we turned the corner.

"Confucius say: 'To be popular with all is to be special to none.'"

"Confucius didn't say that."

"No, but he would have if he'd thought of it." Perry handed me a cassette tape. "Here."

I looked at it blankly.

"Johnny Winter. I told you I'd make you a tape. He's out of control."

"Oh, thanks." I slipped it into my purse.

CHRISTY–LYNN SHOULD SURELY WIN! VOTE CHRISTY–LYNN OUR HOMECOMING QUEEN!

"Whoa," Perry said, wincing at the banner that hung over our heads. "I think the mental giants who created that banner meant to rhyme *Lynn, win,* and *queen.*"

"You mean *quin,*" I said.

He laughed. "Yeah. Homecoming is major lame, huh?"

"I think it's fun." We headed up the stairs.

"Yeah? You think?" He puffed up the stairs and threw the muffin paper into the trash can. "I guess it could be, ya know, if you went with the right person." He gave me a pointed look. There was a lopsided grin on his handsome face. Funny, it was the first time I had really realized that his face truly *was* handsome.

But that didn't mean I was attracted to him, or that I wanted him to ask me out.

"Excuse me, I need to use the girls' room," I told him, and ducked in the door of the john. It was the first thing I could think of to get away from him. I was sure he had been about to invite me to homecoming. What a frightening thought. I didn't want to hurt his feelings, but I didn't want to go out with him, either.

I brushed my hair and studied my reflection in the mirror, concentrating on myself from the neck up. A toilet flushed.

"Hi again."

I turned around. It was Jane Neissan.

"Hi," I said.

Jane washed her hands. "I saw you talking with Perry Jameson."

"Uh-huh."

"He's nice," she said.

"He's okay."

"Did he invite you to homecoming?" Jane asked.

"We're not *dating*!" I said, aghast. "He's so . . . I mean, we're just friends."

She pulled out some paper towels and dried her hands. "I hope you don't take this the wrong way, Lara," she began slowly, "but . . . well, I've been wanting to talk to you. You really have a very pretty face, you know? And I know it must be hard for you. I mean, some people in this school can be really cruel."

I stood there, rooted to the spot, mute.

"In junior high," she continued, "I weighed, like,

fifteen pounds more than I do now, and I found this great diet to take the weight off, and it worked."

My face burned with rage and humiliation. "You want to give me your *diet?*"

"I don't want to offend you," she said quickly. "I just know what it's like to want to lose weight, and—"

"You don't know anything," I said in carefully measured tones. "You look at me and think you know, but you don't."

"Listen, just forget I said anything—"

"No," I replied, "you listen. A year ago, at my old school, I was homecoming queen. *Queen!* I was thinner than you are. Then I got this disease called Axell-Crowne Syndrome, and it made me gain all this weight. You think I'm just this fat girl that you pity—"

"I didn't mean it like that—"

"Yes, yes, you did," I said earnestly. "I know you did, because I was once exactly like you."

She gave me a kind look. "If it makes it easier to say it's because of some disease—"

"It is!" I cried. Two girls came barreling through the door of the bathroom, laughing about something, but I ignored them. "I'm telling you the truth."

"Okay, sure," Jane said. She checked her reflection in the mirror. It was perfect. She turned back to me. "Well, if you ever change your mind or anything . . ." She smiled at me again, then walked out of the bathroom.

All I could do was stand there. She didn't believe me. Neither did Allegra and Willow, probably. They all thought I was a big fat liar. And even if they did believe me, it wouldn't make any difference.

I mean, fat is fat.

"All your test results look fine, Lara," Dr. Goldner told me over the phone.

Every month he gave me the exact same news.

All the tests looked fine. No change.

"Are you staying on your food plan?" he asked.

I plucked at a stray thread on my bedspread. "Most of the time."

"Well, try to stick to it. And the aerobics plan, too. The best way for us to know if you go into remission is for you to follow this plan."

I sighed. I had heard this same thing from him each time I'd seen him. I said good-bye and hung up the phone.

Remission. It seemed too much to hope for. Thin again. I would destroy Allegra Royalton. I would demolish Dave Ackerly. Jett would come groveling back to me on his knees, but I wouldn't even take him back because—

I caught my fat reflection in the mirror on my dresser. Who was I kidding?

I grabbed my car keys. I had a piano lesson. There was zero point in dreaming dreams that would never come true.

"More flowing into the *fortissimo,*" Suzanne said, leaning toward me. She cupped her hands as if she were playing the keys of the piano and sang a line of my sonata. "And then dum-dum-de-*dum!*—like a volcano at the end there, but with control, right? Okay, try it again."

I closed my eyes, willing myself to block out the world except for the music, and played the last move-

ment of the sonata again. It was my third lesson with
Suzanne. She talked about music like it had color,
weight, passion. She got so excited, and her excitement was infectious.

"Yes, that's it!" Suzanne cried, jumping up and applauding when I finished playing. "Didn't it feel great?"

"Yeah, it did, actually," I said, "but I'm curious.
You're so passionate about music, but you love jazz. And
jazz is so cold."

"Nah, I just need to turn you on to the good stuff."
She glanced at her watch. "I've got an hour before my
next student. You want to get some dinner?"

"I'd have to call home . . ."

"So call." She indicated the phone on the desk in the
office outside the studio.

I left a message on the answering machine. It didn't
matter, since we never ate dinner as a family anymore,
anyway. That little charade was history. Scott grabbed
food and ate in his room. My mother didn't seem to eat
at all.

"You like Italian?" Suzanne asked.

"Sure."

"Good. We'll go next door to Antonio's. It's great."

The restaurant was small, with red-and-white-
checked tablecloths and a blackboard listing the daily spe-
cials.

"It doesn't look like much, but the food is amazing,"
Suzanne said. As she studied the blackboard I studied
her.

She had on shocking-pink denim overalls over a white
lace T-shirt, and a faded denim jacket. Her hair was up
on her head in a cute, messy ponytail. One of her little
dangling earrings was a bass clef, the other one a treble.

207

Why would someone so fat wear shocking pink? I wondered.

"You know what you want?" She looked over at me and caught me staring.

I blushed. "Oh, I'm not that hungry."

"Well, I'm starved, and I hate to eat alone, so order something."

A young waitress with spiky black hair came to the table, depositing a basket of fresh, hot rolls. The smell was fantastic. "Hey, Suze," she said. "Wazzup?"

"This is a new student of mine, Lara Ardeche. Lara, this is Carolyn Tucci. Her mom owns this place."

"How ya doin'?" Carolyn asked.

"Fine."

"So, what'll it be, ladies? The lasagna is to die for today, by the by. Mom says to push it."

"Sold," Suzanne said. "And a green salad with blue cheese dressing, and tea." She looked over at me.

"Oh, a small salad, no dressing," I said. "And water."

"Uh-huh," Carolyn said. "What else?"

"That's it."

Carolyn looked at me like I was crazy. "Be back in a jiff." She hurried off.

Suzanne reached for a roll. "Are you on a diet or something?"

"I told you, I'm just not very hungry."

"That still doesn't answer my question." She buttered the roll and took a bite.

"Obviously I don't need to be force-fed, okay?" I eyed her buttered roll pointedly.

"Oh, that look is supposed to tell me you don't think I should be eating this, right?" She took another bite.

"Well, now that you mention it . . ."

Suzanne smiled at me. "People are so funny, you know?" she mused. "Did you ever hear this one? Groucho Marx said he would never join a club that allowed someone like him to be a member, something like that."

"Meaning what, that because I'm conscious of my weight I hate myself or something?"

She took another bite of her roll. "Do you?"

"What?"

"Hate yourself."

"No."

"But you hate that you're fat."

"So? Don't you?"

"No," Suzanne said. "I used to. I just tell myself I missed my era. This thin obsession is a very modern American thing. I mean, I heard Mae West weighed like two hundred pounds."

"That's disgusting," I said.

"Why?" Suzanne asked. "Just because *they* say it's so doesn't make it so."

"Who are 'they'?"

"The billion-dollar diet industry," she said. "Every year the standard of beauty gets more unattainable, and every year they make more money."

"So that's why you shouldn't diet?" I asked dubiously. "Because someone might make *money* off of you?"

"Diets are self-abusive and they don't work."

"If you combine a low-calorie diet with exercise—"

"I do exercise," Suzanne said. "I take a dance class three times a week."

"Look, no offense, but it sounds to me like you're just looking for an excuse so you can give up on your weight."

Carolyn brought Suzanne's tea and my water.

"When I was a kid," Suzanne said, stirring sugar into her tea, "I was already chubby. What can I tell you? I come from a family with chubby genes, and we all love to eat. Not that I ate more than other kids, because I didn't. But I got fat, and they stayed thin."

Like Molly and me, I thought.

"I remember in sixth grade, we all got weighed and measured in the gym by the school nurse," Suzanne continued. "The nurse would call out each kid's weight to her assistant, who sat at a little table writing everything down. So she's calling out each kid's name and weight—'eighty pounds, seventy pounds, ninety pounds'—and then she gets to me." She made her hands into a megaphone. " 'Suzanne Silver! One hundred fifty-eight pounds!' Everyone laughed. I thought I was going to die."

"No, you *wanted* to die," I corrected her.

She nodded. "I guess you know how it feels, then. After that, I went on a diet. I didn't eat anything but lettuce for a week. My parents were crazed, begging me to eat, but I refused to give in. I remember I felt so virtuous, and it felt so good."

She paused. "So then I went to this coffee shop with my older cousin, Lorraine. She went off with some guy and left me sitting alone, sipping this fat-free hot chocolate. So, this guy is sitting at the next table, and he's having real hot chocolate—you know, with a pile of whipped cream on top—and he's got these two huge chocolate chip cookies. So he eats one, and he gets up and leaves, and the other cookie is just sitting there."

She sipped her tea, a slight smile on her lips.

"Anyway, I stared at that cookie for what felt like forever. I was so hungry. And he had just left it there.

And my cousin had deserted me. So finally I couldn't stand it anymore. I reached over, picked up the cookie, and took a huge bite. And just at that moment the guy came back to the table with another cup of hot chocolate."

"That's horrible!" I clapped my hand over my mouth.

Suzanne laughed. "It's funny to me now, kind of. But it felt like the end of the world at the time."

"What did you do?"

"I ran out crying. And I gave up on my diet. I've been on a zillion of them since then. You name it, I've been on it. I always lose weight for a while. And then—same old story—I gain it all back, and more, as soon as I eat anything more than what you're eating now, because I have totally trashed my metabolism! I used to be so ashamed. I just *hated* myself for being fat. I thought I deserved to die, I was so disgusting. But then, finally, one day after I'd binged and purged and cried until I thought I would die from dehydration, I just said: No more diets. That's it."

Carolyn set two green salads on the table, mine plain, Suzanne's covered in creamy, fattening blue cheese dressing.

"That's it? You just gave up?"

She picked up her fork. "It's more like I changed my attitude. I decided I don't have to believe the world when it tells me I'm not okay." She dug her fork into her salad.

I fiddled with the earring in my left ear. "Look, I know you assume we have a lot in common, but we really don't. A year ago I weighed one hundred eighteen pounds. I never had a weight problem in my life. Then I got this disease. It's called Axell-Crowne Syndrome. It's very rare, and it makes you gain a lot of weight no matter what you do or what you eat. And there's no cure."

"I had heard something," Suzanne said.

I was surprised. "From who?"

"Your piano teacher in Nashville told Dr. Paxton that you'd gained a lot of weight in a really short period of time, and you were talking about giving up piano. But I didn't know you had a disease . . ."

"Well, now you do. So if you want to rationalize why *you're* fat, go ahead. But it doesn't apply to me."

Suzanne tapped her chin with a finger. "Not that it's the same, mind you, but you know who you remind me of? A doctor who gets AIDS from a needle stick, who feels superior to a person who gets AIDS from sex." She took another sip of her tea. "But, hey, they both still have AIDS, right?"

She was so irritating.

"No matter what you say, it doesn't change the reality of being fat," I said. "People laugh at you, you can't wear cute clothes, guys don't ask you out—"

"Guys ask me out."

Carolyn set Suzanne's huge, steaming plate of lasagna in front of her, and Suzanne picked up her fork and dug in.

"Tristan, you mean," I said. "You are so lucky that he's attracted to . . . well, you know what I mean."

"I do," she agreed. "It's insulting, but I do."

"Devon says Tristan asked you to marry him."

"He did." She looked down at her plate a moment, and then her voice changed. "I love Tristan. And Tristan loves me. But I don't know if I can ever marry him. The thing is, he hates that I'm fat."

She smiled, but the smile never reached her eyes.

"If I married him, I'd always feel judged and found

212

wanting, insecure, diminished, constantly scared of losing him . . ."

"Which is worse than not having him at all," I finished.

"So you know," she said, her eyes meeting mine.

I nodded and forked a dry lettuce leaf, then put my fork down. "If you ask a thin girl with no talent or brains if she'd rather be her or you, she'll pick her. Skinny girls who chain-smoke four packs of cigarettes a day would rather get lung cancer than get fat. Being fat is the worst thing in the world. Everyone knows it. So no matter what you say, the world wins. And we lose."

She didn't bother to contradict me. She just picked up her fork and ate her lasagna. Which meant I had won the argument, in a certain way. But all it made me feel was really, really sad.

Chapter 218

(The End)

"You're the best pianist in the quartet, you know. That Mozart really rocks," Perry said, brushing his hair out of his eyes.

I laughed. "I never heard Mozart described quite that way before."

"Hey, he was a major rebel. Beethoven too—totally out there. If they lived today, they'd be dating supermodels and trashing hotel rooms."

It was the next evening, and I was giving Perry a ride home after orchestra rehearsal. For once he wasn't eating anything.

"It's the third house on the right," he told me, and I turned the car into his driveway. It was a two-story colonial with a wide front porch in need of paint, very homey looking, lights shining from every window. A colorful flag that read WELCOME hung over the porch.

"Thanks for the ride," he said.

"Sure."

I waited for him to get out of the car. Instead he turned to me. "Hey, um, so, some friends of mine are having a party Saturday night. I . . . uh . . . thought you might like to go."

"Oh, gee, I'd love to, but I already have plans," I said quickly. It made it somewhat easier to say this, since it was true. I was going to Captain Bizarro's birthday party with Devon and his friends.

"Oh, yeah, okay. I guess I didn't give you very much notice. Maybe another time."

"Sure," I lied.

"See ya." He heaved his huge body out of my car.

My house was dark when I pulled into the driveway. The grounds were immaculate, the lawn perfectly trimmed.

"Hello?" I called out. I wandered into our black-and-white family room and set my schoolbooks down on the black marble coffee table. "Anyone home?"

It was so quiet. I went upstairs, past my room and Scott's, and poked my head into my parents'—now basically my mom's—room. She was sitting on the bed, smoking. The only light in the room was a small Tensor lamp trained on the family photo album she had open in her lap.

"Hi," I said. "I didn't think anyone was home."

"These photos are so wonderful," she said, not looking up at me.

"Where's Scott?"

She took a puff on her cigarette. "Come look at these, Lara."

I sat down next to her on the bed. The album was

open to the photo of her and Dad at her homecoming dance, when she had been crowned queen. He looked impossibly handsome, impossibly young, and his arm was snaked proprietarily around her tiny waist. She wore a pink satin dress and a tiara. Her arms were full of roses.

"You were so beautiful, Mom," I said.

"I was, wasn't I," she agreed. "And you know what's funny? I thought I was fat."

"No!" I exclaimed. "How could you? You were so thin. You've always been thin!"

"But I never *felt* thin," she said. "Or pretty. Not really. So I never got to appreciate it." She turned to another page in the book. "Oh, look: Scott's tenth birthday party. Remember how we took a family trip to Hawaii? Look, here we are on the beach. We were all so happy. Everything was so perfect!"

It was Mom, Dad, Scott, and me on the beach in Hawaii. We looked like an advertisement for America.

God, I was so thin then, I thought, staring longingly at the photo.

"God, I was so young then," my mom said. She put her hand to her cheek.

I looked at her gaunt face in the harsh light of the gooseneck lamp, and for the first time I saw lines, shadows, the stark signs of aging. For the tiniest moment, mean gladness filled my heart. But then it was gone, and I realized how much weight she had lost, how sick she looked.

"Want me to make you some dinner, Mom?" I offered.

Puff, puff on the cigarette, her eyes still on the photo. "I'm not hungry."

"You really need to eat something, Mom."

"I'll get something later," she said vaguely.

"Where's Scott?"

"At a friend's, I think."

Fine, I thought. Sit here and obsess about what used to be, when you were pretty and young and life was perfect. Abdicate all maternal responsibility. Scott and I don't really need parents anymore, anyway.

I left her there and went back downstairs, where I pulled some cheese and an apple from the refrigerator and went into the family room to do my homework. My bio teacher had given us twenty pages to read on arachnids—also known as spiders—and we had to do a cute little spider diagram.

I had read all the pages and was halfway through my spider diagram when I heard the front door slam. Scott walked noisily into the kitchen, which I could see from where I sat, opened the refrigerator, and took a long drink out of the milk carton.

"Did you eat?"

"At Gordon's, but it sucked." This was his new friend, Gordon Pinzer, who lived down the street. Gordon claimed to know someone who knew someone who was actually related to Kurt Cobain, which was how Gordon had acquired the signed photo of Kurt that hung over his bed. The week before, Scott had asked why Gordon's handwriting matched Kurt Cobain's handwriting on the poster, and they'd had a big fight. Evidently they had made up.

"Do you have to drink from the carton?" I asked.

He didn't answer, just drank some more, then left the empty milk carton on the counter. Then he rummaged in the fridge for food, found some cold chicken our housekeeper had broiled the day before, and stuck a drumstick in his mouth.

"You could wash your hands, at least," I said as he came into the family room gobbling the chicken. Watching him eat made me hungry. I went to the fridge and got out a piece of chicken, too.

"You don't need that," Scott said, his mouth full of chicken.

"Who are you, the food police?"

"I'm just saying—"

"Well, just don't," I snapped, wounded. "I didn't even eat dinner."

"Yeah, I'll bet," he muttered under his breath.

"Okay, class, let's review," I said in a singsong voice. "*Someone* gained weight because she has a disease, not because of how much she eats, and that someone would be . . . ? Anyone? Scott?"

"Well, you could fight it or something," Scott said. He threw his chicken bone at the wastebasket, missed, and left the chicken bone lying there on the rug.

"What's your problem tonight?" I asked.

He threw himself on the couch. "I'm sick of kids saying stuff about you."

"Like what? No—don't tell me, I know what."

"It's just . . . I hate it here," Scott said. "I don't even like Gordon—he's an idiot. And when people say stuff about you . . ." He shrugged. "It was just a lot easier when you were thin."

"Well, I'm so sorry if my *disease* has made you *suffer* in any way," I said sarcastically.

"Forget it," Scott said, getting up. "I knew you wouldn't understand. Where's Mom?"

"Up in her room reliving her glory days."

"I should just run away," he said.

"Don't say that!"

"I should just hitch back to Nashville. Mom wouldn't even notice I'm gone, I'll bet."

"She would too. And I would."

"Yeah, sure." He picked up his skateboard and headed for the stairs.

Gee, didn't *I* have a happy home. Lah-dee-da. I picked up my pencil to finish the spider diagram and decided to click on the TV for company while I worked.

"There's word this week of a health breakthrough that might change the lives of millions of people," came Barbara Walters's voice. "It's a hormone that researchers claim drastically and rapidly eliminates fat. Just imagine if this hormone proves successful in humans!"

My head rotated toward the TV. It was a special Tuesday-night edition of *20/20*.

"As you saw in a very revealing story that John Stossel brought you awhile back, coming of age is hard enough, but for overweight kids, it is particularly painful."

"No kidding," I muttered.

The screen filled with a chubby young girl and her mother at the mall, clothes shopping. "I wish I could shrink," said the little girl. "I'd rather be Thumbelina."

"Kids call her names," John Stossel's voice-over said, "such as Shamu the Whale."

"It gets my heart broken," the little girl on the screen said.

"Now, in this age of enlightenment where kids are taught not to make fun of disabilities or differences, are kids still mean about someone being a little overweight? Well, listen to what happened when I offered these five-year-olds some choices. Who would they pick as a friend?"

Now the screen filled with a group of little kids. John Stossel sat with them. "Would you rather have as a friend a stupid kid or a fat kid?"

"A stupid kid," piped up one little boy.

"I hate fat kids," said another.

"Well, which would you rather be," Stossel asked them, "ugly or fat?"

"Ugly!" the kids all yelled.

"Okay," John Stossel said, "if you had to live your life without one arm or be fat, which would you pick?"

"One arm!" the kids yelled again.

I clicked off the TV. Five-year-olds would rather have one arm than be me. Even Scott, Mr. Looks-Are-So-Superficial, hated me for being fat.

And *I* hated me for being fat.

A solitary tear tracked down one of my cheeks. I felt as if I were starring in someone else's life, and her life sucked.

I closed my books and trudged up to my room, dropped my clothes in a heap, and went into my bathroom to take a shower. I don't know what possessed me to get on the scale. It wasn't my workout week. After my first visit to Dr. Goldner I'd set my home scale to match the one in his office. But it never changed. So I only weighed myself every other week so that I could report to my mother and Dr. Goldner. Who wanted to look at 218 pounds on the scale any more often than was absolutely necessary?

213 pounds, the scale read.

My heart thudded in my chest. It couldn't be true.

I got off the scale and got back on.

213.

I repeated this three times, but the scale showed the same thing.

213 pounds.

I had lost five pounds.

With trembling hands I threw a T-shirt over my head and ran down the hall to my mom's room. The door was closed. I knocked. No answer. I knocked again. Nothing.

Fine. Some mother. She had probably taken her little pills and nodded off to dreamland, where she could pretend she was still young and life was still a ducky little bed of roses.

I ran back into my room and quickly punched a familiar long-distance number into my telephone.

"Hello?"

"Molly? Oh, my God!"

"Lara? Are you okay?"

"Mol, I . . . . I lost five pounds!"

"No!"

"Yes! I just weighed myself! I lost five pounds! It's true!"

She screamed into the phone, and I screamed back.

"I'm so happy for you, I am sitting here totally dying of happiness," Molly said.

"Me too. I can't even believe it. Wait, I have to weigh myself again. Hold on." I dropped the phone and ran back into my bathroom, and got on the scale. 213.

"It's true!" I cried into the phone. "It's really true!"

"So, this means it's all over, right? You're just going to lose it all now, right?" she asked eagerly.

"I don't know," I said truthfully. "Dr. Goldner says there are now seventeen documented Axell-Crowne

221

cases, and four of them have lost all the weight they gained, so maybe."

"That's what's going to happen to you," Molly insisted.

"I'll call him tomorrow," I decided. "You don't think this is some, just, I don't know, natural fluctuation in my weight or something?"

"No, no, the curse is broken; ding, dong, the wicked fat witch is dead!"

"I'm afraid to get my hopes up," I admitted, even though my hopes were already up, through the ceiling, the sky, the stratosphere.

"So, listen, promise you'll call me tomorrow after you talk to your doctor, okay?"

"I will. Oh, Mol, I'm so happy!"

"Me too," she said, and then we both hung up.

I had to tell someone else, but who? I pulled on some sweats, padded down to Scott's room, and knocked on the door. No answer. Then I heard noises downstairs. Scott was foraging for more food. Food. Who cared about food? If I could only lose weight and get my old life back, I would never eat again!

I stood outside Mom's door and knocked again. Maybe she wasn't that soundly asleep after all. I opened the door just a little and peeked in.

She was lying half on and half off the bed, a spilled glass of something next to a full ashtray, her bottle of sleeping pills on the rug near her lifeless-looking hand.

"Mom!" I ran over and shook her. Her eyes were closed. She was limp and cold. And so pale.

"Mom!" I screamed again. I looked at the pill bottle. Empty.

"Hey," Scott said from the doorway, "someone named Suzanne is at the door and she says—"

Then he saw Mom.

"Call nine-one-one!" I yelled, cradling my mother's head in my arms.

"What happened?" he asked in a tiny voice. "Is she—"

"Just shut up and call nine-one-one!"

Scott picked up the phone and dialed. I tried to get Mom to sit up.

"It's my mom, she took all these pills, I don't know if she's alive!" he cried into the phone. "Two-four-two-six Blooming Terrace Lane. Hurry! I don't know what kind." He turned to me. "What kind of pills?"

"Look over there!" I ordered.

Scott picked up the empty vial. "Valium," he said into the phone. "No, I don't know how many. No, I don't know if she was drinking—why are you talking to me, why aren't you doing something?"

"Give me the damn phone," I demanded, still holding my mother. Her head flopped against me; her mouth hung open.

He handed me the phone. "Stop asking questions and get my mother an ambulance!" I screamed at the operator.

"Calm down, miss, we're doing everything we can. An ambulance is on the way. Does your mother have a pulse? Is she breathing?"

I grabbed my mother's wrist and tried to find a pulse. "No!" I shouted wildly. "There's nothing! There's—"

And then I felt something. Faint, but there. And she was breathing. Barely, but breathing.

"Wait, yes! I feel her pulse."

"Good. Do you know how many Valiums your mother took?"

"No!"

"Do you know if she was drinking alcohol when she took the pills?"

"No, no, I don't know anything! We just came in the room and found her—"

"Is your mother conscious at this time?"

"No!" I cried. "Please, please do something—"

"Try to stay calm, okay?" the operator said. "Do you see any signs that she's been drinking, or any other pill vials around?"

I picked the glass up from the rug. I sniffed it. It smelled like wine. I told the operator.

"Do you know how much wine your mother consumed?"

"I just told you, I don't know anything!" I was hysterical. "When will the ambulance get here?"

"They're on their way, miss. Your mother needs for you to stay calm now, okay? Help is on the way."

"What should I be doing?" I asked wildly.

"Just wait calmly," the operator said.

I screamed in frustration, threw the phone across the room, and cradled my mother in my arms.

"Mommy," Scott whimpered, kneeling down next to me and taking Mom's limp hand in his. "Mommy."

"You can't die," I said, sobbing hard. "Please, please, I'll do anything, but you can't die!"

"Lara?"

I looked up. Suzanne Silver was standing in the doorway. But that didn't make any sense. Suzanne was my piano teacher. What was she doing in the doorway of my mother's room while my mother lay in my arms dying?

"An ambulance is coming," I sobbed. "She took pills."

"What kind?" Suzanne asked, striding across the room toward us.

"Valium," I said.

"Good news," Suzanne said. "She won't die unless she drank with it."

"You're not a doctor." I held my mother close.

"There's wine spilled on the carpet, from that glass," Scott said through his tears.

Suzanne looked at Mom, then at me. "Put her in my car. We'll take her to the emergency room," she ordered.

"But they said—"

"Do you want to wait for the ambulance or do you want to do something?" she asked pointedly.

Together the three of us carried my mother down the stairs and out to Suzanne's car. Mom felt very heavy.

"Don't die, don't die, don't die," I kept chanting to her as Suzanne zoomed through every light, her headlights on bright, one hand constantly on her horn.

Scott sat in front, his body twisted around in the seat so that he could see us, tears streaming down his face. His eyes met mine. I knew that the terror I saw there was mirrored in my own.

And I prayed.

Chapter 213

Scott, Suzanne, and I sat silently in the hospital waiting room. Every part of my body hurt. Nothing seemed real. Scott kept crying. It was Suzanne who'd suggested that we call my father—it hadn't even occurred to me. I told her he mostly lived in Nashville and gave her Tamara Pines's phone number, which I had memorized in spite of myself.

After an hour that felt like forever, a harried-looking African American doctor came out to talk with us. Scott and I held hands.

"I'm Dr. Kellogg," he said. "Your mother is going to be fine."

"Oh, thank you, thank you!" I cried.

Scott just nodded, too overcome to speak.

"As it turned out, she didn't take all that much Valium or drink all that much wine," Dr. Kellogg said, "just

226

enough to make her pass out. We didn't know that until we pumped her stomach. There wasn't much in there—it doesn't look as if your mother has been eating lately."

"No, she hasn't," I said.

"Can we see her?" Scott asked.

"Only for a little while," Dr. Kellogg cautioned. "She's feeling pretty punky right about now. Just be gentle with her, okay?"

He led us down the hall to a room and opened the door. "Five minutes."

She looked so tiny, lying there in that bed. Tiny. And old. Her eyes were closed.

"Mommy?" Scott whispered.

Her eyes opened. She smiled, sort of.

Scott ran to the bed and put his head down on her shoulder, sobbing.

"Shhh," she whispered, stroking his hair. "It's okay."

"You almost died," he managed between his muffled sobs. "Is that what you wanted? Did you want to die?"

"I just wanted to sleep," she said, her voice raspy.

"You mean you weren't trying to kill yourself?" I asked her. My voice sounded sharper and more accusing than I had intended.

"I just wanted to sleep," she repeated. "I wanted to wake up and find out it was all a bad dream and your father loved me again." She turned her head away from us.

It was everything I could do not to run to the bed and beat my angry fists into her. But you're our mother, I wanted to scream. You're supposed to take care of us, we're not supposed to have to take care of you! How could you? How *could* you?

But I didn't say any of that.

227

I just left her there with Scott and walked out of the room.

When I got back to the waiting area, Dr. Kellogg told me he wanted to keep Mom overnight for observation, but she could probably be released the next day. She had convinced him that it was an accident, that she had not tried to kill herself. If it had been a suicide attempt, he'd have admitted her to the psychiatric ward, he explained.

Funny, I thought. Since it *wasn't* a suicide attempt, she could be terminally depressed on an outpatient basis.

I thanked him and numbly lowered my oversized body into one of the ugly orange plastic chairs. I overflowed at the sides.

"Hi."

I looked up. It was Suzanne. She sat next to me. She overflowed, too.

"How's your mom?"

"She takes a lickin' and keeps on tickin'," I muttered bitterly. I leaned my head back against the wall and closed my eyes. I felt a zillion years old. "She didn't take that much. She says she wasn't trying to kill herself, she just wanted to sleep. She can probably come home tomorrow."

"That's good," Suzanne said.

I opened my eyes and looked at her. "How did you know that you can't die from an overdose of Valium?"

"Practice," she admitted.

"You mean you—"

She nodded.

I reached for her hand. "Thank you. For helping me. I mean it."

"You're welcome."

"What were you doing at my house, anyway?"

She gave a short, sharp laugh. "My parents live practically around the corner from you. I was at their house and I found the sheet music for this great old jazz tune I used to play, and I thought, Lara would love this. So I decided to drop it off. After your brother let me in, I heard all the screaming from upstairs, and, well, I'm just nosy enough to want to see what was wrong."

"I'm glad you did," I said. I gulped hard. "I don't know why you're so nice to me. I haven't been very nice to you."

"I guess because, regardless of what you told me the other day, you still remind me of me."

It was so strange. For some reason I wasn't insulted. I didn't feel like I should protest yet again that we were nothing alike, that she was this out-of-control fat person, whereas I was a thin person stuck in a fat person's body through no fault of my own.

No, I didn't feel that way at all. I put my head on her shoulder.

Just then Scott came trudging down the hallway toward us, his sneakers untied, his eyes red. He wiped his nose on the sleeve of his sweatshirt, like a little boy. I got up and wrapped my arms around him.

Suzanne took us home, and though I told her she didn't have to stay, she refused to leave us alone and said she'd stay until my father arrived.

When he finally did, near dawn, Suzanne left. Dad tried to hug me but I moved away. He had already been to the hospital, he told me, and had spoken with Dr. Kellogg. Mom had refused to see him.

As the sun came up, I sat in the family room, numb.

Dad came and sat next to me. "Do you want to talk about it?"

"No."

"Look, princess—"

"I told you never to call me that," I snapped.

"Lara," he corrected himself. "You're blaming me for this, aren't you?"

A reply hardly seemed necessary.

"No matter what you think," Dad said, "this is not my fault."

"No? Then whose fault is it?"

He sighed. "Your mother has to be responsible for her own life."

"Even if you're the one who ruined it."

He sighed again. "I'm not perfect, prin—Lara."

"Funny, you always tried to tell us you were."

He smiled a sad little smile. "People are complicated, honey. It hasn't been easy for me—"

"This isn't about you," I said with disgust.

He sighed and ran his hand through his hair. "I just thought you were mature enough to understand—"

"You know what, Dad?" I said, getting up from the couch. "I don't *feel* like trying to understand. I'm your daughter, not your shrink."

"This isn't like you, honey . . ."

"Here's a real news flash for you, Daddy," I said. "You don't have any idea what I'm like. I'm only beginning to figure it out myself."

"Mom?"

She was sitting on the hospital bed, facing the window, dressed in the jeans and sweatshirt I had brought over for her. Her face was pale, and so thin. She wore no makeup, and for once she wasn't smoking. She smiled at me.

"Well, that was an adventure none of us needed, huh?" she whispered.

"Does your throat hurt from the stomach pump tube?"

"Like crazy."

"So, you can go home?"

She nodded. "Is your father there?"

"Yeah," I said. "I told him to leave, that Scott and I could take care of you. But he gave the housekeeper the day off."

"Can't have the hired help know that the Ardeche family is less than perfect," she croaked.

"Do you want me to call and tell him to leave before we get back?" I asked her.

"No. I need to talk to him."

"I don't want to talk to him at all. Ever. Neither does Scott."

"He's still your father," she said.

I didn't say anything.

She smiled sadly. "My life wasn't supposed to end up like this. I was supposed to marry your father and stay thin and beautiful, he was supposed to stay madly in love with me forever, and we were supposed to live happily ever after. I wish I knew where I went wrong."

I went over to the bed and sat down next to her. "You and Dad always made me think that if we just tried hard enough, if we were just perfect enough, we could control everything. But it isn't true, is it, Mom? I mean, sometimes stuff just happens. And there's nothing you can do about it."

I struggled to find the right words. It was so hard.

"Last night when I got home, I couldn't sleep," I went on. "All these tapes just kept playing in my head. It was like watching a movie of my whole life, right up until now. I could even stop this tape in my mind, you know? If I wanted to take a really good look at something?"

I reached for my mother's hand. There were tears in her eyes.

"And I did look, Mom. I looked at the time when I was little and I heard you and Daddy fighting, the time I heard him hit you."

"Lara—"

"I looked at all the other fights, too," I went on, "when you and Daddy yelled at each other and called each other horrible names, and then at all the mornings afterward when I thought I was crazy because you both pretended it had never happened."

"I didn't mean for—"

"Even though you were young and thin and perfect looking, you weren't happy. You and Dad always fought, and you always lied to us about it. You were always afraid that you weren't good enough for him, or that he'd leave you."

"And he left anyway," she whispered.

"Yeah, he did," I agreed. I gulped hard. "I used to think that if I was just perfect enough, everything would be great. But it wasn't. And I used to think that everything in my life was so perfect when I was thin. Only it wasn't. I mean—don't get me wrong—I'd give almost anything to be thin again, but being thin didn't fix my life."

"It didn't fix mine, either," she rasped.

Tears were streaming down my face. "The happy, perfect Ardeche family has always been one happy, perfect lie, Mom. And I'm not going to lie anymore."

Two big tears slid down her cheeks. "I'm sorry," she sobbed. "I'm sorry I've let you and Scott down, Lara."

I put my arms around her. "It's okay, Mom," I said.

But even *that* was one last lie, because nothing was really okay at all, and she really *had* let me and Scott down.

But at the moment, it was the best I could do.

Chapter 211

I stepped onto the scale. It read 211. I couldn't believe it. It seemed too good to be true. I got on and off the scale again. And again. Same weight.

It was Saturday evening, a few days after my mom had come home from the hospital, and with everything that had happened, I hadn't called Dr. Goldner until that morning. So I had called him at home—he was excited, I could tell. He told me it was possible that I was going to lose all the weight I had gained, but it was also possible that it was just a fluctuation, which everyone had. Then he moved my next appointment up to the following week so that he could check me out himself.

I had resisted the urge to get on the scale again all day, but now, straight out of the shower, as my wet hair dripped on the scale, there it was, staring at me.

I hopped on, not daring to hope for anything.

I had lost two more pounds.

I went to look at myself in the mirror on my dresser. Was it my imagination, or did my stomach stick out a tiny bit less? I rolled my shoulders forward. Couldn't I almost see my collarbones again?

I reached into my drawer, got out some underwear, and put it on. My bra was a little looser. I felt full of hope and scared to hope, both at the same time.

Please, God, I prayed, please let it all be over. Please let me be thin again. I'll do anything if only—

And then I stopped, midprayer. The last time I had prayed this way was when I was afraid that my mother would die. And I'd prayed to God that I'd do anything that time, too, if only my mother would live.

How could being thin be as important to me as my mother's life? How could it?

I'd rather lose an arm than be fat, the five-year-olds had said.

I only hoped they wouldn't rather lose their mothers.

Knock, knock on my door.

"Just a sec." I pulled on my robe and opened the door.

It was Mom, cigarette in hand. She had already had two sessions with a psychiatrist. She looked a little better. Though she was still chain-smoking, she was eating again. Not much, but something.

"Your dad just called from Nashville," she said. "He wants you to call him."

My father had left that morning. I had refused to hug him good-bye. Scott wouldn't even see him—he'd spent the night at Gordon's house.

"Too bad," I replied.

"He's still your—"

"Do me a favor, Mom. Save it."

She changed the subject. "What are you wearing to the party?"

Tonight was Captain Bizarro's birthday bash. I had told her I would stay home with her, but she had insisted that I go.

"Are you sure I should go?" I asked her again. "I don't mind not—"

"I want you to go," Mom said. "Really. You've finally made some friends here. I want you to have fun."

I went to my closet and took out a dress I had purchased months ago but never worn. It was pale pink with a scoop neckline and a lacy skirt that fell just above my knees. I had fallen in love with the dress and had bought it without even trying it on. It had reminded me so much of what I used to wear, who I used to be.

But then, once I got the dress home, I knew it was ridiculous. I mean, someone as fat as me did not need to wear pale pink or draw attention to herself with delicate, feminine lace.

"That's beautiful," my mother said.

"I don't know . . ." I held the dress up to myself and studied my reflection in the mirror.

"Black would be more slenderizing," my mother said.

I would *definitely* wear the pink dress.

Mom took a deep drag on her cigarette. "I wanted you to know . . . before your father left I told him I was going to see a lawyer."

"I guess that means you're not jumping through hoops for him anymore."

She exhaled some smoke. "There's nothing wrong with trying to make your guy happy, Lara."

"Please." I snorted derisively.

Her hand shook a little as she raised her cigarette to her lips again and inhaled. "Maybe you've just never really been in love, so you don't know how I feel. I still love him, and I still hope that he'll come back to me."

"Why would you want him?"

She thought a moment. "I've been with him since I was fifteen years old. I guess . . . I don't know who I am without him."

I looked her in the eye. "Find out."

"Maybe I'll try to, someday." She came over to me, kissed my forehead, and left.

Right. She wouldn't leave him if he moved Tamara Pines into the guest room. I hated him for what he was doing to her. But I hated her even more for letting him do it.

But I loved them, too. That was the crazy thing— how I could hate them and love them at the same time.

I dried my hair, put on some makeup and some perfume, then lifted the pink dress over my head and let it fall around my body.

I looked in the mirror.

And I looked . . . oh, could it really be possible?

I looked pretty.

But how could I look pretty? I still weighed more than 200 pounds! I was mammoth, huge, enormous, and yet . . . as I looked at my reflection in the mirror I saw a pretty girl staring back at me. Round, to be sure. Too round. But still.

"Lara? Someone named Devon is downstairs at the front door waiting for you," my mother said, sticking her head in the door. "He's so cute!"

"I know," I said, looking around for my purse.

"You didn't tell me your date was so cute! How did you do it?" she asked eagerly.

Irritation crept up the back of my neck, my positive experience with the mirror instantly forgotten. She was so sure a cute guy couldn't possibly like me. After all, I was *fat*.

"Easy, Mom," I said bluntly. "He's blind."

"He . . . he can't be," she sputtered. "He's standing in the front hall all by himself. How did he get there?"

We went downstairs. There was Devon, wearing his dark glasses, standing alone just inside the front door.

"Hi," I said.

"Hi," he said. "You look great."

"How would you know? You're blind."

"True, but my mother raised me to be a gentleman."

I laughed.

"But how did you get here?" Mom asked.

"My bud drove."

I peered out the window at our driveway, which was lit by bright spotlights. Sure enough, there was a car, and someone was sitting in the driver's seat.

"To answer your next question, Mrs. Ardeche, my friend walked me to your door," Devon added.

I walked over to Mom. "Are you sure this is okay with you? Because I could stay—"

"Stop worrying," Mom told me. "I'll be fine."

I got my jacket, and Devon and I walked out to the car, his hand resting on my elbow. I got in the front seat, Devon in the back. Devon's friend, Mike Terry, was cute. He had eyes the color of spring grass.

"So you're Lara," he said as he drove the car into the street. "I've heard a lot about you. Keyboards, right?"

"Right," I replied.

"I play bass," Mike said. He gave me a quick smile. "That's a pretty dress."

I was stunned. Mike Terry was cute. He was neither fat nor blind. And he was treating me like I was a cute girl. How could that be?

He popped a cassette into the cassette player and some great music—kind of rock and blues at the same time—blared through the excellent sound system.

"Wow, that's great, who is it?" I asked.

"The Allman Brothers Band," Mike said. "They rock, huh?"

That reminded me, I had never played the tape Perry had given me. Maybe I should have. And speaking of Perry, we were driving down his block. Then Mike turned his car into Perry's—

"Wait a minute," I said, confused. "What are we doing at Perry Jameson's house?"

"You know him?" Mike asked. He honked his horn.

"We go to school together."

Perry came out quickly, carrying his saxophone in its case. When he saw me his jaw fell open, but then he recovered and got in the backseat.

"Hi," I said.

"Hi," he said.

So much for small talk. We didn't say another word to each other the rest of the way. Mike and I talked in the front seat, and every time I looked back at Perry, he was talking to Devon or scowling at me. We stopped in Southfield to pick up Crystal and headed for Captain Bizarro's.

The party was already in full swing by the time we arrived. There must have been a hundred people of every race, age, size, and shape crammed into that downstairs room. There were some really cute guys like Mike and Devon, some very cute girls, a bunch of alternative types, and some adults who looked like they could have been my parents' friends. There was also a woman in a wheelchair, blowing bubbles from a small plastic bottle while a chubby little boy toddled after the bubbles.

On the small dance floor in the center of the room some people were dancing—some hot-looking college-age couples, two girls who had Mohawks, and a middle-aged guy with a grass hula skirt over his jeans who danced around throwing confetti on everyone.

For some reason this thought flew into my mind: Jennie Smith would be so *incensed* that someone had let the geeks come in with the cool people.

That made me laugh.

Suzanne was onstage, playing something jazzy on the piano. Tristan was on electric guitar. The same older brown-skinned woman I had heard last time I'd been there was at the microphone, snapping her fingers and egging Suzanne on as she played her solo.

"That's Cleo," Perry told me over the music, indicating the woman at the mike. "She's the best."

Cleo's red high heels matched the flowers on her dress, which flowed around her oversized curves. Her long hair had been braided into tiny plaits, each fastened with multicolored beads.

"You go, girl!" Cleo called to Suzanne.

"*Compadres, compadres,* you honor me!" Captain Bizarro called out when he saw us. He was wearing a KISS ME, IT'S MY BIRTHDAY T-shirt under his old army jacket. He held out his arms and embraced each of us, kissing us on both cheeks.

"Happy birthday!" I yelled to him over the music.

He bowed at the waist and kissed my hand. "You are a vision of loveliness," he said solemnly. He straightened up. "Hey! I shucked lots of raw clams for you!" He hurried off to see to his other guests.

Devon and Crystal went off to dance. Mike went up onstage and joined in on stand-up bass.

Which left me standing there with Perry. He pulled a candy bar from the pocket of his jeans.

Only Perry Jameson would bring his own candy bar to a birthday party.

"So . . . this is pretty funny, huh?" Perry said, unwrapping his chocolate. "That you told me you were busy tonight?"

"Well, I was," I said. "I didn't lie."

"How do you know these people?" Perry asked, munching away.

"Suzanne is my piano teacher."

He took another bite. "For real? I thought I was the only one crazy enough to come downtown for lessons."

"She's great," I said. "She's worth it."

"See that guy in the hula skirt? He's my sax teacher."

"Why is he wearing a hula skirt?"

"Why not?" Perry finished off his candy bar and stuffed his hands in the pockets of his jeans. "So . . . you look really nice. Great, I mean. Beautiful, actually."

"Thanks."

The musicians onstage brought their song to a close, and everyone applauded, whooped, and hollered their approval.

"Hey, Perry!" Tristan called down from the stage. "Come on up here!"

Perry shrugged at me and went to pick up his saxophone; then he went up onstage. Asa replaced Suzanne at the piano. He counted the musicians off, and they began to play a beautiful, bittersweet ballad. Perry played with his eyes closed, the music pouring from his sax. I knew that feeling, when you *became* the music.

"Is he hot or what?" Crystal said, gazing up at Perry.

"Perry?" I asked incredulously.

She nodded and sighed. "He keeps telling me he only sees me as a friend."

"Perry's so—"

"Talented," she finished. "I know."

"Dance?"

It was Devon.

"Do I have to lead?" I asked archly.

"Hey, I get points for every couple we mow down," he explained.

He reached for me, and I panicked. As soon as he put his arms around me, he would know how fat I was.

I moved stiffly toward him, barely letting him touch me. We swayed to the music—or rather he did, while I held every fiber of my body at red alert.

"You seem kind of tense," he said.

"Oh, no," I lied. "I'm not tense."

His hand moved to the small of my back, or in my case, the *large* of my back. Now he could feel every lump, every roll of fat that was me.

"Hey, I just learned something about you," he said.

Great. I was about to be rejected by the blind.

"What?" I managed.

"How fine you feel." He held me even closer. "Tense, maybe, but fine." He nuzzled his face into my hair.

242

I looked up at the stage. Perry was staring at me. He kept playing the sax, but he didn't take his eyes off me.

He looked angry.

No, not angry. Jealous.

Devon and Perry.

Terrific. I was the pinup girl for fat guys and blind guys.

The song finished, and a new group of musicians went up to the stage. Devon went off somewhere with Mike, and I decided to go call my mother, just to make sure she was okay. I found a pay phone near the bathrooms.

"Mom?"

"Hi, honey. Is everything okay?"

The loud party made it difficult to hear. I put my finger in my left ear. "Yeah, everything is fine. I just wanted to make sure you're all right."

"I'm fine," Mom said. "Scott and I are playing Monopoly."

"Scott hates Monopoly. He thinks it's a capitalist tool."

"I think he's humoring me," Mom said. "You don't have to worry about me."

"Okay," I said. "Remember to eat something."

"Lara?"

"What?"

"I'm glad you're having fun again," she said.

"Thanks, Mom."

I hung up and went back to the party. Suzanne and Cleo were sitting together at a small round table, talking and laughing. I walked over to them.

"Join us," Suzanne said.

I sat down.

"I don't know if the two of you ever officially met. Cleo, Lara Ardeche. Lara, Cleo. Cleo is probably the smartest woman I know. The only thing she lacks is a last name."

"Correction." Cleo grinned. "I've had many last names, my dear, I just don't choose to use any of them." She fanned herself with an advertising flyer that had been lying on the table. "I hear you play some tasty keyboards."

"Only classical," I said.

"Well, you need to broaden your horizons," Cleo said, daintily pressing a napkin against her sweaty cleavage. "Get Suzanne here to teach you some jazz!"

"I don't think I'm going to be able to stop her."

"I need to find myself a drink," Cleo said, getting up. "Can I get you anything?"

We said no, and Cleo worked her way through the crowd toward the bar in the back of the room.

"How's your mom?" Suzanne asked.

"Better. I would have stayed home with her but she really wanted me to come tonight—"

"Hey, you don't need to feel guilty," Suzanne said. "I'm glad you're here."

We listened to the music for a few moments. Perry took a hot solo.

"Perry's cooking," Suzanne commented.

"I know him from school," I told her. "He keeps asking me out."

"You're not interested?"

"Everyone would think we were going out because we're both fat," I said.

"Forget what other people think," Suzanne said. "It's

such a colossal waste of time. The question is, do you want to go out with him?"

I hesitated. "I'm not exactly attracted to him."

"Would you be attracted to him if he was thinner?"

I thought about that a moment. "I think so," I admitted. "God, that's so terrible! I get mad because people are superficial and then I'm . . ."

She shrugged at me and smiled.

From across the room we could see Cleo talking with Captain Bizarro. He said something and she threw her head back and laughed, her tiny beaded braids dancing around her head.

"She is something else," Suzanne marveled. "She's fifty-eight years old, and she's been singing jazz since she was fourteen. She's half black and half Asian. Growing up, black kids dissed her for looking Asian, Asian kids dissed her for looking black, and everyone dissed her for being fat."

We looked across the room at Cleo as she worked her way through the crowd.

"But they were blind," Suzanne said. "She's beautiful."

I watched Cleo as she gracefully walked toward us. And it was so weird, because I really *did* think she was, kind of, in her own way, beautiful.

"It's hot as a pistol in here, isn't it?" Cleo said when she reached the table. She held a perspiring can of soda against her forehead.

"Come dance?" Tristan asked Suzanne, holding out his hand. She accepted and they went to the dance floor. He took her into his arms.

Cleo watched Tristan and Suzanne dancing. "Now, that man is fine as wine," she said. "Husband number three was that fine. He was walking bad news, my dear, but he was fine."

She looked over at Perry, onstage. "Perry can't take his eyes off you," she told me.

"We're just friends."

"A boy that pretty and talented? My dear, you ought to be on that child like white on rice."

"But he's kind of overweight."

Cleo just looked at me.

"I know I am, too," I said in a rush. "I mean, in my case it's—well, I used to be thin. And I'd lose weight if I could. But Perry doesn't even try."

Cleo took another sip of her Coke. "I want to tell you about husband number three, the fine one. He was always after me to lose weight. He'd told me I was fat and ugly so many times that when I looked in the mirror, I saw fat and ugly looking back."

"So what happened?"

"I woke up one day and I said to myself, 'Cleo, that man is not good enough to shine your red high-heeled pumps.' And I got rid of him."

"Just like that?" I asked dubiously.

"Just like that," Cleo said, snapping her fingers. "I threw him out, threw a party, and invited all the other tasty men I knew. And now when I look in the mirror, instead of fat and ugly, my dear, I see fat and fine."

"But you'd be thin if you could be."

"Wrong, my dear," she told me with a smile. "You're young, Lara, and silly things like size seem so important to you. But I'm old. And I've learned to look at the size of someone's heart, and not the size of someone's waist-line."

I shrugged. "You can be thin and still be a good person, you know. My heart didn't get any bigger when I got fat."

She raised her eyebrows at me. "Didn't it? Well, that's a shame, then."

"Would you like to dance?"

It was Perry, standing at our table. I hadn't even noticed that he had come off the stage.

"Okay," I said, and I started to get up.

"I didn't mean you," Perry said. "I meant Cleo."

Cleo laughed. "You are a lying dog, Perry Jameson. You know you want to dance with this girl."

"I don't think she wants to dance with me," Perry said.

Before I could answer, someone turned off the lights. Suzanne came into the room carrying a huge birthday cake, ablaze with candles.

We all sang "Happy Birthday." Suzanne set the birthday cake down, and Captain Bizarro blew out all the candles. Everyone applauded.

"Hey, Captain, did you make a wish?" Mike called out to him from the stage.

"Didn't need to," Captain Bizarro said. He threw his arms wide. "I love you all, my *compadres*! Now, let's kick up the jams and scarf this cake!"

Everyone began to laugh and talk, Suzanne cut the cake, and the musicians onstage began to play something upbeat and snappy.

"That's my cue!" Cleo said, and hurried to join them.

" 'It's very clear, our love is here to stay,' " she sang, snapping her fingers and swaying her outsized hips to the music. Her large arms reached out and beckoned to the crowd—old and young, fine and plain, high-style, no-style, and every color of the rainbow—and her voice dipped and swooped into the mike in front of her.

"Hey, Perry, wanna dance?"

It was Crystal. She gave him a very nervous smile.

"Go," I told him.

"I guess this means you aren't having wild fantasies about me," he said sadly.

"I'm sorry."

Perry smiled at me. "Hey, who knows? Maybe you'll change your mind one day." He reached out and took Crystal's hand, and they went to the dance floor. And as I sat there alone, listening to the music, watching Perry and Crystal dance, watching the party swirl around me, I realized something. No, *two* somethings.

I wasn't really by myself at all.

And for the first time in a long, long, *long* time, I was happy.

Chapter 210

"**P**eople, listen up!" Mr. Webster, our school orchestra conductor, called out, tapping his baton on his music stand. "I have an announcement to make."

It was the following Friday, and we were onstage in the high-school auditorium, finishing up orchestra rehearsal. I was sitting with the other three pianists in our piano quartet. The pianos were arranged to form a box so that we could hear each other when we played.

Kyler Trustus was tickling Jane Neissan's hair with the end of his trombone, but Mr. Webster shot him a look and he stopped.

"Thank you, Mr. Trustus," Mr. Webster said dryly. "Concerning the winter concert, I want to announce one change in the program. We will have a soloist. Lara Ardeche will be playing Schubert's Impromptus."

I could feel people looking at me. From the saxophone section Perry gave me a thumbs-up.

"All right," Mr. Webster said, "let's take the Smetana one more time. And violas, please try to stay with us . . ."

We played the Smetana, and then the rehearsal was over. I was putting my sheet music into my backpack when Perry came over to me.

"What made you change your mind?" he asked me.

I shrugged. "Temporary insanity, probably."

He grinned at me. "I like that in a woman."

"Hey, Lara, congrats on the solo," Jane Neissan said as she walked by with Kyler Trustus. "I think you just elevated our concert by about a hundred percent."

"You're gonna be great," Kyler added.

"Thanks," I replied.

"Have a fun weekend," Jane said, and she and Kyler walked out the door.

"You ready to go?" I asked Perry. I assumed I was giving him a ride home, per usual.

He blushed. "Uh, actually, Crystal's picking me up. She's probably waiting for me, so . . ."

I smiled at him. "So, go."

"Ready to turn out the lights, Lara?" Mr. Webster asked me. We were the only two left in the auditorium.

"Would you mind if I stay and practice my solo?"

"Not at all," Mr. Webster said. "I have some papers to grade in my office. Just let me know when you're done."

I walked to the edge of the stage and looked out at the empty seats. In just two weeks those seats would be filled with hundreds of people, and I would be right up here again, playing a piano solo.

And I would still be really, really fat.

I'd lost another pound. One measly pound. Dr. Goldner still wasn't certain whether or not my Axell-Crowne was going into remission. My tests revealed nothing. But even if—please God—I was going to lose a lot of weight, there was only so much I could lose before the concert.

I had been so sure I would never play solo again in public, as long as I was fat. But that afternoon I had found myself walking up to Mr. Webster, and I'd heard myself tell him that, if he still wanted me to, I would play a solo in the winter concert.

It was like *Invasion of the Body Snatchers*.

So, now I was committed. I half closed my eyes, blurring my vision, imagining the seats full of people. You can do this, I told myself. You are a musician.

Allegra Royalton's face came into my mind. She was in the audience, jeering at me, yelling out some ugly insult that made everyone laugh, and—

No. Forget Allegra Royalton. Pretend Suzanne is out there, I told myself.

I stood a little taller and bowed to my imaginary audience. Then I walked over to the piano, sat down, and began to play.

I closed my eyes. The music washed over me, through me, and I could hear Suzanne saying, "passion, with control," and the music swelled under my dancing fingers, filling me up, until the final chords, *fortissimo*, thrilling, and then the silence that is also music.

Now everyone would be applauding, perhaps cheering. Or maybe they would yell, "Bravo!" I stood up to bow again to my imaginary audience, and that was when I heard the sound coming from the back of the auditorium: one person clapping.

I looked up.

Standing there, in the back of the auditorium, a huge grin on her face, was Molly.

"Molly!" I screamed. I ran down the steps from the stage and she ran toward me, and we threw our arms around each other.

"I guess you're surprised," she said, laughing and crying at the same time.

"I can't believe you're really here!" I cried. I pulled away to make sure it was really her. It was. I hugged her again. "I've missed you so much!"

"Me too," she said fervently. "You look wonderful!"

"I do?"

"Yeah!" she said.

"How did you find me?"

"Your mom gave me directions," Molly said.

"But why didn't you tell me you were—"

"I didn't even know until the night before last," she explained. "Right after you called me and told me what your doctor said, in fact. My parents were ready to give birth—they were like, no, you are not driving from Tennessee to Michigan, no, you can't miss school, it's stupid and irresponsible, and like that. Finally I told them you were deeply depressed and needed me desperately. They love that girl-power thing—it's so p.c.—so they finally gave in. I waved *adiós*, jumped in the car, and we've been on the road ever since."

"*We've?*" I echoed. "As in you and—"

"Me," said a deep voice from behind Molly.

I looked up.

And standing there, like some dream, like a wish I had wished a thousand times to come true only I knew it never could, was Jett Anston.

"He came by my house Wednesday night and asked me if I was up for a road trip to come visit you," Molly explained.

I couldn't move.

"Hey, I've got a brilliant idea," Molly said. "Why don't I go check out Jett's car? Yep. That's what I'll do. Cool. So, that's where you'll find me."

She slipped out of the auditorium. Jett walked over to me. His eyes searched mine.

The next thing I knew, his long, skinny arms were around me, and I was crying so hard.

"I'm sorry," I sobbed, "I'm sorry, I don't know why I'm—"

"It's okay," he said, but his voice sounded funny, muffled, and that was when I realized that he was crying, too.

"Excuse me, Lara?"

It was Mr. Webster, up on the stage.

I wiped my eyes and walked down the aisle. "Some friends from Nashville just surprised me."

"Go have fun," he said, smiling down at me. He handed me my backpack and my coat. "I'll close up."

We walked out the back doors of the auditorium, and I turned to Jett, to make sure he was really there. "I'm not dreaming this, am I?"

"Not unless we're having the same dream," he told me.

Then he put his arm around my shoulders, and we walked to the car, where Molly was waiting.

Jett pulled his car up in front of my house. It was already dark out, but the bright floodlights lit up our driveway. I twisted around to the backseat so that I could see Molly. "Mol, you should come with—"

"Wrong," she said. "You guys need some time to be

alone. And if I don't study for the chem test I missed, I'm flunking out of high school. Just don't leave me here for more than two hours, or your mom will probably force me to exercise with her."

"We won't be gone long," I promised her.

Jett pulled out of the driveway. "Where to?"

"I don't know."

"Me neither." He gave me a quick, uncertain look.

"If you turn right at the light and then keep driving, you'll end up at a small pond," I suggested.

He made the turn. "We gonna swim or ice-skate?" he asked me, turning the heat on in the car. "It's freezing here."

"We're going to talk," I said quietly.

The paved road turned into a dirt road, and finally we came to the pond, where Perry, Devon, Mike, Crystal, and I had held a crazy winter picnic last Sunday. I'd been home, wearing sloppy sweats and doing my homework, when they had come over and kidnapped me. We went to the pond, ate Chinese take-out, and huddled against the cold while Perry serenaded us, and the woodland creatures, on his sax.

Jett turned off the ignition. Moonlight illuminated the car.

"I can't believe you're really here," I whispered.

"Me neither."

"So . . . you live in New York now?"

"Yeah."

"I guess it's great, huh?"

"Some of it," he said. "It can get lonely. And my apartment is this little dive in the East Village. My mom did a cool thing for me, though. You know that sculpture, *Things I Cannot Change*? She gave it to me, for my apartment."

"Don't you worry it'll get stolen?"

"Yeah," he said. "So does she. But she did it anyway. I mean, it's insured through the roof. But it's priceless, you know? She said she wanted me to have it more than she was scared that it would get ripped off."

"That's nice."

Silence.

"How's Visual Arts?" I asked.

"It's great," he said. "To be with so many artists is just so . . . Nashville seems like this dream that never really happened."

"Oh."

"Except for you." He turned to me. "I missed you."

"You did?"

He nodded.

"In New York, with all those really cool, artistic, *thin* girls?" I asked pointedly.

He didn't answer.

"You never even called me."

He looked out at the lake. "God, Lar, I'm so much less cool than I thought I was," he said. "I'm a joke. You gained weight and I couldn't deal with it, only I didn't want to admit it, not even to myself . . ."

"Well, maybe that's just one of those 'Things I Cannot Change,' huh?" I asked bitterly.

I could see tears glistening in his eyes. "Maybe it's one of the things I *can* change," he said quietly. "When I got to New York I told myself, 'She dumped you, you didn't dump her.' So I started seeing all these other girls. Only I just kept thinking about you, missing you, and feeling like a fool because I let you go."

How many times had I dreamed this moment? How many times had I wished that Jett would come back to me? I had fantasized diving into his arms, his apologies, his passionate kisses. And now the moment was actually, really here, so wonderful, so perfect—

Only it wasn't perfect. And I couldn't pretend that it was. One part of me wanted to kiss him, and another part of me wanted to pound him. Why couldn't he be the perfect guy I wanted him to be? What was I supposed to do if he *didn't* change? And if he didn't, how could I possibly live through his breaking my heart again?

I took his hand. "My parents broke up," I told him.

"I'm sorry," he said.

"I'm not. She still wants him back. My mother's been jumping through hoops for my father for years. She's so afraid she's not good enough just the way she is." I hesitated a moment. "I won't jump through hoops for you."

"I'd never ask you to—"

"And I *am* good enough just the way I am—even if you don't think so," I said, and I tried with all my might to believe it.

Jett was silent.

Then I looked down at my small fat hand in his large skinny one.

"I love you," I said. "But . . . I can live without you."

He nodded, and I saw the sadness in his eyes. "I love you, too."

"It might not be enough," I told him.

He put his hand on my cheek. "Can we try?"

"I don't know," I said, and a tear fell from my cheek

onto his hand. "Either way, it's really risky. And either way, it really hurts."

I laid my head against his chest, and, wrapped in his arms, I once again listened to the steady beating of his tender heart.

I was half asleep in Jett's arms. We were back home now, in the family room. I had no idea what time it was, but I knew it was late.

"I should go see Molly," I finally whispered.

"Your mom said if you didn't kick me out, it was cool for me to stay in the guest room," Jett said.

"Down that hallway." I cocked my head toward the kitchen.

We got up, and he put his arms around me again and kissed me. "Will you visit me in New York?"

"Yes."

"I'm really glad I came."

"Me too."

I crept up the stairs. Molly was fast asleep, sprawled across one of my twin beds, her chemistry book open, her clothes still on.

"Mol?" I said, shaking her lightly.

"Huh? What?" She opened her eyes and squinted at me. "Did you and Jett kiss and make up?"

"We kissed," I said. I quickly got undressed, pulled on a big T-shirt, and crawled into the other bed.

"He still loves you, Lar," Molly said sleepily. "He told me so."

"I still love him, too," I admitted.

"God, it's all, like, so perfect!" Molly said with a sigh.

"No, it's not," I said.

"You mean you're not getting back together?" she asked, incredulous.

"I don't know," I said.

"Even though you love him so much?"

"Yeah."

"Wow. That's way too complex for me." She got up and pulled off her jeans, then stumbled back into bed and under the covers. And for a moment she looked just like she had at thirteen, when she'd lain in my twin bed and confessed how much it had hurt when Tommy Baigley had said she looked pregnant in her new babydoll dress.

And I realized something: Molly had always been way more honest with me than I had ever been with her. I had *pretended* to be honest, but really I had always been putting on a front—Lara Ardeche, Pageant Queen, with her happy, perfect family and her happy, perfect life.

I hadn't really let her in at all.

But then, I hadn't let myself in, either.

"My parents broke up," I told her. "My dad's been having an affair for years."

"No!" Molly exclaimed, rising up on one elbow. "Your perfect father?"

"He's not perfect," I said. "He's not even close. Neither is my mother. And neither am I."

Molly sighed. "I told you, you're going to lose all your weight—"

"I didn't just mean my weight," I said. I put my hands under my cheek and looked at her.

"So, what did you mean, then?"

I struggled to explain. "I always let you think my life was so wonderful. Before, I mean. But it wasn't. I was a big fake." I thought a moment. "Being thin and popular and winning all those pageants—who was that girl? It's not like it made me happy. Not really."

"Okay, the pageant thing was always lame," Molly allowed. "But wouldn't you give, like, *anything* to be thin again?"

"I'd give a lot," I admitted. "But not *anything*."

She looked at me in the dark. "You really *are* changing, Lar."

"Yeah, I guess I am."

"Well, don't change too much," Molly said with a yawn, " 'cuz I love you just the way you are." She snuggled her head against the pillow. "Remember that summer I went away to camp and we signed our letters to each other, 'Love You Till Mount Ever Rests'?" She yawned. "God, I am so beat. When I close my eyes, I see huge trucks passing us on the highway. If I snore loud, just throw a pillow at me or something."

I stared up at the ceiling. "There's so much I want to tell you, Molly. About my family, and all the lies we told everyone. And I finally made some friends here. I want you and Jett to meet them, and—"

She was already snoring.

I smiled at her in the dark. "Love You Till Mount Ever Rests, Mol," I whispered.

I turned over and closed my eyes. And I, too, saw a highway that stretched into a future I couldn't know. Some of that future I could control, and some of it I couldn't. And some days it would be all right, and some days it wouldn't.

That was just the way it was.

I'm not telling you everything was fine, or that I knew what would happen with Jett, or that I didn't still long to be thin, because I did. So much.

But it wasn't *everything* anymore.

And so, though the bedsprings creaked from my weight as I rolled over, I had a happy–sad–cool–hot–classical–jazz–angry–peaceful–thin-girl–fat-girl smile on my lips.

I wasn't perfect. But I was okay.

About the Author

Cherie Bennett often writes on teen themes. Her play *Anne Frank & Me* ran off-Broadway to a stellar review in *The New York Times,* and her play *Cyra and Rocky* was a winner at the Kennedy Center's national youth theater festival, "New Visions/New Voices." Her teen advice column, *Hey, Cherie!,* is nationally syndicated by Copley News Service, and she has written many novels for young adults, including the award-winning *Did You Hear About Amber?* She and her husband, writer and producer Jeff Gottesfeld, live in Nashville and Los Angeles. Cherie Bennett can be contacted at P.O. Box 150326, Nashville, TN 37215, or by e-mail at authorchik@aol.com.